For Margaret, my dear wife

Past But Very Present

By

Note for Librarians: A cataloguing record for this book is available from Library and Archives Canada at www.collectionscanada.ca/amicus/index-e.html
ISBN 1-4251-1474-1

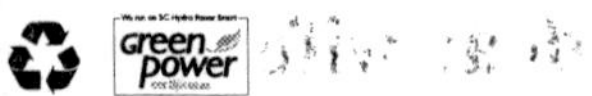

Printed in Victoria, BC, Canada. Printed on paper with minimum 30% recycled fibre. Trafford's print shop runs on "green energy" from solar, wind and other environmentally-friendly power sources.

TRAFFORD
PUBLISHING™
Offices in Canada, USA, Ireland and UK

Book sales for North America and international:
Trafford Publishing, 6E–2333 Government St.,
Victoria, BC V8T 4P4 CANADA
phone 250 383 6864 (toll-free 1 888 232 4444)
fax 250 383 6804; email to orders@trafford.com
Book sales in Europe:
Trafford Publishing (UK) Limited, 9 Park End Street, 2nd Floor
Oxford, UK OX1 1HH UNITED KINGDOM
phone +44 (0)1865 722 113 (local rate 0845 230 9601)
facsimile +44 (0)1865 722 868; info.uk@trafford.com
Order online at:
trafford.com/06-3233

10 9 8 7 6 5 4 3 2

Author's Note

The prologue that follows is, in part, a work of fiction. But in content it is unlike stories that are described as fiction. The difference here is that the prologue tells a true story of my grandfather's adventure in France, in the winter of 1942. All the information is correct, although joined together by a web of fiction. However, it must surely be close to what actually happened.

Charles Burton
Grandson of Flying Officer Henry Burton

PROLOGUE
November 1942

It was a dreary, late November afternoon at RAF Honiley, a night-fighter airfield near Coventry, and Flying Officer Henry Burton looked sourly at the row of four night-fighter Beaufighters. Each was equipped with AI, as interception radar was then called. There were many aircraft of this type, but these were a surprising oddity. Instead of RAF roundels, they carried the stars of the US Air Force.

Henry should in fact have had nothing to do with these strange machines as he was a Navigator/Radar Operator on 96 Squadron RAF which was based in his own location at Honiley, but now he had been detailed to help with the delivery of one of the four Beaufighters to a surprising destination. His pilot, Captain James Peters of the US Air Force, whom he had met only a few hours ago, smiled at him. "Cheer up, old son," he said, "just think what the good old US of A is doing for you…tonight we'll have dinner in the English Riviera, and tomorrow morning we'll have breakfast in southern sunshine and, with any luck, we'll have several days there to enjoy it. That must be better than the Scotch mist you were looking forward to on your leave!"

But Henry was not consoled, as the day had gone badly for him ever since just after breakfast, when he was packing his bags to go off on a week's leave, only to be told that the CO wanted to see him. The Wing Commander had in fact been apologetic. "Look, Henry, I'm sorry to involve you in this, but the navigator, who was crewed with Captain Peters, one of the American pilots who have come here to take these Beaus to Gibraltar, has gone down with, of all things, mumps, and I've got no alternative but to ask you to take his place. It's irregular of course for you to fly with him, but it is an emergency. I'm sorry about your leave, but you should get back to England within a few days as, since the Yanks are now in North Africa, there is a regular shuttle of aircraft between England and Gib."

As Henry went back to his quarters to unpack his bags, and to repack what might be needed, he remembered the good times he had had at Honiley over several recent weeks, when two US Air Force squadrons, to provide night fighter defence in North Africa, were being refitted with Beaufighters to replace their Black Widows, one of the few really bad aircraft the Yanks had produced. The Americans, and RAF experts like Henry, who helped them make the transfer, had become good friends, and the American food and drink had been most welcome. Sadly, however, after they had reached North Africa, the American squadrons had, for some reason, chosen to park their Beaufighters on an airfield near Algiers in two neat parallel lines and had been shot up by a pair of German fighters. The necessary replacements had now to be flown to Gibraltar, where they would be picked up by other American crews. But Henry's reverie was broken by his pilot. "Come on, Henry, stop dreaming about that lovely French wife of yours, and let's get the show on the road. She'll still be there, ready and waiting for you, when you get back to Scotland in a few days' time."

The first leg of the journey was a short one, a flight of only an hour, to Predannack in Cornwall, the most south westerly aerodrome in England, where the aircraft could be tanked up to the brim, to 'overload' level, giving a range of 1,500 miles. Then, while this was being done, James and Henry, and the other three crews, could have dinner and a spot of kip before setting off again. The timing of their take-off was crucial, the aim being to make a direct flight over the sea to the northwest corner of Spain, then first follow its coast, followed by the Portuguese one, in darkness, before turning east to arrive at Gibraltar at first light. Three of the four Beaufighters did get off at midnight, which would time their arrival after the 1300-mile flight at around six or seven in the morning, but the one for James and Henry had what was called a 'mag-drop' (a magneto fault) in the port engine, and it took until nearly 1.00am to rectify it. The Station Commander did suggest that they should defer their departure for a day, but James would have none of it, and said to Henry, "Look, if you are game, I think we'll first skirt the coast of France, then cut across Spain, going straight down…they have no night fighters to worry us…and as for overflying Spain, if anybody sees us, well, it's a Yank aircraft, nothing to do with the RAF!

"Anyway, we'll strike the sea again just to the west of Seville, and we can then arrive…all innocent…from the sea, when we get to Gib. Perhaps this is the time to make a confession, and I can tell you that I am bloody glad that we'll be on our own tonight! You see, I have had a phobia all my life. I'm terrified of water; and I can't bear the thought of having to take to that damn rubber dinghy if anything goes wrong, particularly as I can't swim. The way I suggest, we'll never be far away from a coast, and I'll feel a lot happier, knowing that if anything goes wrong we can get to dry land. So, Henry, how about it?"

What could he say? Captain James Peters was one of the most famous American fighter pilots, having won a number of decorations, including a DFC, during a time when he had flown in the RAF before America came into the war. But before he could reply, James continued. "There is also a plus for us. As that route is shorter, by the best part of two hundred miles as compared to the track the others are taking, going all round the various countries, we should get to Gib not long after them. He paused for a moment, then, "Come on! Cross your fingers, chum, let's go!"

But Henry wasn't a canny Scot for nothing. "But look, James, flying down near the coast of France is like trailing a scent in a drag hunt…Jerry must have some night fighters of his own in France, and all we want to do is to get this kite to Gib in one piece and with no heroics on the way."

But James would not be convinced, and he pointed out that since his suggested route was so much shorter they could save further time by flying faster. "Just remember," he said, "that by taking the long way round, the others must fly at their most economical cruising speed, only about two-twenty miles per hour, but we can push it up to maybe as much as two-fifty. That's way below our top speed, and wouldn't it be funny if we got there first!"

So, take off they did, each wearing a headset so that they could talk to each other – this was necessary in a Beaufighter as the pilot was up front and the navigator was amid-ships with his radar set. Henry felt it was a stupid track to take, and he soon had another thing to worry about as there must have been a flock of birds, perhaps migratory, in a hedge at the end of the runway, and they rose in a cloud in front of the aircraft. Bird strikes are, of course, a hazard, and the usual course is for the aircraft concerned to return to base for careful checking, but James would have none of that nonsense. "Everything is okay, nothing to worry about, just look forward to soaking up the sunshine in a few hours' time!"

Well, for a couple of hours all did go well, but then Henry heard a sudden change in the engine noise, and while the port engine which had caused a problem earlier still sounded normal, the starboard one was certainly running rough. "You've heard that?" said James, "Well, we do seem to have a problem, just in the last few minutes the oil pressure has dropped, and my bet is that one of these bloody birds damaged an oil pipe, and any moment now that engine is going to have no oil, and give up the ghost."

He was quite right. Just a just a few minutes after he spoken there was a crash and the engine came to a shuddering halt. It only took a moment for James to feather the propeller in order to reduce the drag. "Well," he continued, "that's that, we can, or rather I hope we can, soldier on with just the one engine, but we are going to be bloody late, and it will mean crossing at least several hundred miles of Spain in daylight, so I can see that I am going to have some very awkward questions to answer once we get there."

But it wasn't long after that when things resolved themselves. "Damn it!" he said, "I was optimistic then, I should have said "*if* we get there". Now the bloody port engine seems to be losing power."

For a while, they flew on, flying much slower, and with the remaining engine straining to keep them airborne. Then James had to speak again: "If it's any consolation to you, Henry, I owe you an apology. No way is this kite going to make it to Gib, and it is too far for us to go back…where are we exactly?"

Henry had been doing his sums carefully. "We've just passed Bordeaux on the port side," he said, "and we are only about twenty miles offshore. If you are thinking about a landfall in Spain, that is a little over one hundred miles from here, but remember that the Pyrenees are then ahead of us and the ground rises quite steeply from the Spanish coast, so I think that about five thousand feet is a minimum."

"Damn it," said James, "but I'm afraid that the Spanish mountains make things impossible…we are only making about one-seventy mph now so we'll never make it, all we can do now is to turn east to strike the French coast, and bale out when we are over land as far south as we can get. It's been a hell of an unlucky flight, but at least I picked the right chap to come with me…someone mentioned that you speak good French."

They chatted for a while, making what preparations they could and, although there was a moon, it was behind clouds. Henry was able to pick up the coast on his AI set and he confirmed when they had overflown it, just one minute before the remaining engine suddenly gave up the unequal battle and died. There was no time to waste, as a Beaufighter without power has the flying ability of a brick, and so they both opened their escape hatches, which were quite separate in a Beaufighter, with the pilot sitting up front, and the navigator aft of the main plane. Henry waited for the order to come from James. It wasn't long in coming. "Good luck, Henry, GO!"

The peace and quiet was wonderful for Henry after all the mechanical disaster noises, and the moon chose that moment to come out from behind the clouds. He was able, therefore, to see that he was dropping towards quite a large lake but, by judicious tugging on his parachute lines, he managed to get down on dry land, not far from the water's edge. He looked round to see if there was any sign of James but, to his horror, he saw in the faint light a parachute descending about a half a mile away, right in the centre of the lake. Obviously, James had been delayed by something so had dropped a little later. There was nothing, but nothing, that Henry could do, and the moon chose that very moment to go behind a cloud again. There wasn't a vestige of sound, and nothing now that he could see. For a while, he just sat on the ground and tried to come to terms with things. Obviously, James just had to be dead…he'd said that he couldn't swim, and now he was weighted down with full flying kit, and about a half mile away in the water.

What a misfortune, he thought, *for James to take every precaution to stay within reach of land, only to drown in a lake, and could he have helped in any way?* But then common sense surfaced...he couldn't possibly have done anything, so now, self preservation was the order of the day. From the position of the moon, he knew where south was, so with the feeling that the nearer he got to Spain the better, he set off in that direction. Eventually, he struck a minor road, and set off down it, hoping to find a village with some helpful people. His good fortune, as James had said, was that his French was not just good but perfect, as his mother was French and had made sure that he grew up bilingual. Not only that, but just before the war he had married a lovely French girl who came from his mother's home village, near Nice, so he'd had plenty of 'pillow talk' to keep him fluent. And some of that had paid a dividend, as his wife, Marie, was expecting their first child early in January. It was maybe about two hours later, just as the sun was showing its first light, when he came to a small village and, just before it, an isolated house with a dilapidated old truck parked beside it.

Why not? thought Henry, *Got to start somewhere.* He went up and knocked at the door. Obviously, the man who answered his knock had already been up, as the door opened almost at once, and he saw an elderly man frowning at him, with no signs of welcome. Henry gave him no time to make enquiries, before explaining who he was, and at once the man gave him a beaming smile. "Entre´, entre´, Monsieur... vite, vite!" And he was hustled into a lived-in room, which doubled as the kitchen and everything else. At once, the man introduced himself as M. Emile Jeanfils, and he listened with interest as Henry, with a large glass of brandy in his hand, told his story to him. At the end, he smiled at Henry. "That is bad luck about your pilot, but as for you...you are in luck, as from time to time I have helped with an escape line to Spain for allied soldiers, usually air crew, so I can put you in touch with contacts in an organisation near Bayonne."

"But for now," he went on, "let's have some breakfast, and after that you can spend the day catching up on your sleep. I am an odd job man, and I must stay on my normal routine so as not to show any irregularities. I'll be free to go to Bayonne tomorrow evening, and make enquiries on your behalf. But now…eat!" So Henry was left on his own for much of the day, and the thought kept nagging at him that surely there might have been something he could have done to rescue James, but then he came to terms with the fact that he couldn't have done anything, and he realised again how lucky he himself had been. When M. Jeanfils came home he brought a problem of his own with him, and he explained that he had met a regular client of his, who had asked him to do an urgent job for him the next day. "He is a funny old man," he said, "he lives in the only large house in the district, all on his own, with just an elderly couple to help him, and they live in a cottage adjoining the big house. But now, if you please, they are going to be away for a few days, as the old woman has to go into hospital in Bayonne for some kind of minor operation. So, there he will be, on his own, in that big house with about a dozen bedrooms. I think it was because he'll be on his own that he asked me to do this job tomorrow, which involves repairing some of the plumbing to the kitchen quarters at the back of the house. Some of the work will call for appliances such as washing machines being moved, and it occurs to me that the safest place for you in the meantime is to be working with me. If anyone sees you, I'll call you Henri, and explain that you are the son of a cousin of mine in Bordeaux who has come down for a visit. It only means putting off my trip to Bayonne for a day, and I'll go there with you the day after tomorrow. What I shall do there is to contact a friend of mine who runs a motor haulage company, and I'm sure he will be able to get you to Spain."

They talked that evening about the war, and what things had been like in Britain and in France over that period, and Jeanfils was particularly interested in learning all he could about the Free French, especially about General de Gaulle who, he said, was a non-person in French newspapers. "I can tell you," he went on, "that there was much bitterness in France after the withdrawal of your soldiers through Dunkerque, but now it is understood, and we realise that it was only because you stood up to these bloody Huns that we have a hope of freedom again. It is wonderful that you and the Americans, with the help of the Free French, are now clearing them out of North Africa, and roll on the time when France is free again."

They were about to go to bed when Henry realised that he would need to write a report of the affair when – not if, but when – he got back home, so he asked the name of the lake where they had dropped. "It is the E´tang de Laguibe," M. Jeanfils said, "it was unfortunate that you came over the coast just there, as there are quite a few lakes, right along this coast."

Come next morning, Henry got himself dressed in working clothes, which was no problem as he was more or less the size of the Frenchman. They drove in his old truck to what Henry saw was a small chateau, set in quite extensive park lands and surrounded by woodlands, both of which were in obvious need of considerable care and attention. M. Jeanfils smiled at Henry. "It's a shame, isn't it? The old man's only son was killed in a car crash some years ago and his married daughter now lives in Avignon so, with nobody with him, he has just lost heart. He had an exclusive jeweller's shop in Biarritz before the war, but some time after the death of his son, he sold it to one of his competitors, and has been more or less a recluse since then. Local legend has it that he is extremely rich, and I very much wonder what he has got locked away in the house. Certainly there is a huge safe in his study."

He drove the truck round to the back of the house, parking it in a big garage and Henry saw a rather elderly man come out of the back door of the house to greet them. After Jeanfils had introduced Henry – as Henri, his cousin's son – to the owner, a M. Martins, there was a discussion about what was to be done, and then Martins left them to get on with it, but not before asking them to join him for a drink before their midday meal. When they were on the second of these drinks, the old man smiled at Henry. "You can trust me absolutely, so please don't pretend any longer to be a relation of M. Jeanfils. That accent of yours is basically Parisian, but is not quite true, and my bet is that you are English!"

"You are too clever, M. Martins," Henry laughed, "but while it is true that I am not French, equally I am certainly not English!"

"Not English? Surely you aren't American?"

"No, Monsieur, I come from a country which for many years was the ally of France against the hated English!"

M. Jeanfils was making nothing of this exchange, but Mr Martins laughed. "Welcome to France, Scotsman, let's have another drink together, but it would be foolish to drink to the perdition of the English, as we both need them…for the moment at least!"

By then they had become quite a cheerful party and for a while M. Martins joined them in their work; it was after three o'clock and with the job nearing completion when they heard the sound of a car driving up to the front of the house. "I wonder who that can be?" said M. Martins. "You boys carry on here, I'll go and see to it."

There was a murmur of voices for a while, but then, a few minutes later, there was an angry shout from M. Martins.

"That's outrageous, surely a German officer doesn't stoop to stealing!" Then, a reply in heavily accented French:

"Just think of it as a small price to pay for being looked after so well by we kind Germans… Get on with it and open that safe. If you don't, I'll shoot you and will have no hesitation in doing so."

There was the sound of a blow, and the German went on, "There now, that is just a small sample of what you can expect if you don't do exactly as I say."

M. Jeanfils whispered to Henry, "I can recognise that bastard's voice, he is Major Hassell, the commander of the Germans in this area, so obviously he is here to steal whatever treasures Martins has. But there is a second man there, I wonder who he is?"

He didn't have long to wait for an answer, as M. Martins shouted, "Pierre, I am ashamed of you, how can you stoop so low as to collaborate with scum like this?"

There was then the sound of a further blow, and the Major snarled, "Keep your opinions to yourself old man, just open this bloody safe…if you don't, I'll shoot you here and now. I've no time to waste – do it!"

M. Jeanfils turned to Henry. "These bastards…are you game for a little war? There is a backroom we can get to without their seeing us, and I know that Martins keeps a shotgun there." Henry didn't answer, but just stretched out his hand to Jeanfils, and nodded. They ran round the corner of the house and in through a side entrance, which led to a corridor of store rooms, and into the one where Jeanfils expected to find the gun and the cartridges. But he was out of luck. "Damn it," he said, "he sometimes takes it up to his bedroom, I'll bet that is where it is…stay here, I can get up there without them seeing me."

He was back in just a few minutes with the gun, but while he was away Henry listened to the conversation with increasing anger. Obviously, they had now opened the safe, and the Major and Pierre were examining its contents, and were delighted with what they had found. Anyway, now all was haste, and Henry was relieved to see how confidently Jeanfils handled the gun, obviously as a countryman. He was no stranger to weapons of this type, and as he lovingly stroked it he whispered, "I daren't do anything but try to kill the bastard immediately. I've only got two cartridges before having to reload, and as his gun is probably an automatic, so I'm going to give him no chance at all, just go in and fire."

"But look," Henry said, "surely if you do that you will be in terrible trouble here, and there is the second man, this young Pierre…what do we do about him?"

"What we do," said Jeanfils, "is to scare the living daylights out of him. He is a young lad, about seventeen, and I have wondered about him for a while. But as for me, I shall be in no danger, as this affair has decided me to get the hell out of France…so I'm coming with you to Spain and then to England!"

But just as he said that they heard the Major say, "Thank you, M. Martins, you have collected very well, and I can congratulate you on your collection, but now your usefulness to us is over…"

"My God !" said Jeanfils, "they are going to kill him…"

They heard an agonised shout from M. Martins of "NO!", followed by a gunshot.

"The bastard!" Jeanfils exclaimed. "Come on, Henri!

But then they heard an odd sound, it was from young Pierre laughing as he said, "That was good, mon cher, I am loving this, as the old bastard caught me stealing apples once, and he took a cane to my backside."

But he was interrupted by the Major, who spoke in laboured French, but in a soft, caressing voice. "I'm glad you are pleased, Liebchen, "we talked of this, and agreed that he had to go, and just think of all these happy years we'll have together. This lot, along with what we've collected already, will certainly pay for them!"

"Let's disappoint them!" said Jeanfils. "The door at the end of this corridor takes us into the hall and, if we are quiet, we'll be able to surprise them...the study door is the second one on the left, I'll go first, and you keep out of the way till the shooting is over...the sooner I deal with the Major, the happier I shall be."

They went quietly and, when they were just outside the study door, they heard the Major say, "Pierre bring in that case from the car so that we can pack up all these treasures."

So then, with Pierre now about to come into the hall, Jeanfils could not delay, so he burst into the room and fired both barrels at the German. He was devastatingly wounded, but not mortally, and Henry saw him trying to raise his gun to fire at Jeanfils, but he managed to jump forward and tear it from his hand, and one shot to his head put an end to him. The young Frenchman, Pierre, looked in horror at the carnage, and looked as though he was going to have hysterics, but Jeanfils slapped his face. "Pierre, you are a greedy young fool...I've heard stories that you were too friendly with the Germans, but I would never have imagined that you were this friendly. And to take pleasure in the death of this fine, elderly man is almost unbelievable...you disgust me. Go and sit over there till Henri and I decide what to do with you."

Then he turned and took me over to the other end of the room, out of earshot of Pierre. "I haven't the heart to kill this young bugger, so we'll just need to frighten him into keeping silent while we two get away, and we daren't complicate things by telling him that you are an escaping airman. Also, we must keep this treasure they found in old Martins' safe, and hope to come back after the war and restore it to his daughter. Yes, that is our first job, to ensure that these treasures get to Martins' daughter. After this nonsense, they certainly aren't safe here, so we'd better bury them somewhere. But let's deal with this young fool Pierre first."

Henry looked over and saw him sitting in the chair, a picture of despair, a slim young man with his rather long blonde hair falling across his face. Then he looked down at what had been the Major, and saw him stocky, powerfully muscled, and with a swarthy complexion. *What a bloody pair!* he thought. As he contemplated them, Jeanfils went over and said to Pierre, "You have been an idiot, and I should kill you, but I haven't the heart to do so...I know your parents and they are decent folk. Your only hope of survival is to get off home now, and never ever mention what happened here today. Henri and I are leaving now, and as for this lot we are going to bury it and, after these bloody Germans are chased away, we'll be back to give everything to Martins' daughter."

He nodded eagerly. "Thank you, M. Jeanfils, I promise I'll say nothing. Can I go now?"

Jeanfils nodded, but Henry had been looking at the amazing pile of jewels and other valuables and an idea came to him. "Wait a minute, Pierre," he said, "just have a look at this lovely gold bowl, pick it up, it is solid English gold, there is the London hallmark, isn't it beautiful?" Pierre did pick it up, and they could see by the way he handled it that he loved beautiful things. But he was given no time to enjoy it, and Henry snatched it back from him, saying, "That will do very well! You see, if ever we suspect that you have given us away, we have only to say to the authorities, 'Dig up the treasures, and you will find Pierre's fingerprints on the golden bowl'...and that will put you right in the frame. Now you can go, but remember that we hold your life in our hands!"

"You're a clever chap, Henry," said Jeanfils as they watched Pierre running across and into a stretch of woodland. "That really will seal his mouth shut, so let's beat it ourselves. I know just where we can bury this stuff...and it is a place which we'll be able to find again!"

"Just a minute," said Henry, "let's try to muddy the waters a little." And he carefully wiped the shotgun to remove the fingerprints of Jeanfils, and then put it into the dead hands of M. Martins. Then, for good measure, he cleaned his own from the revolver before putting it into the dead German's hand.

"That should puzzle them. I'll bet they will have a hard job trying to work out how just the two of them could have killed each other. Now, let's shut the safe door, and lock it again, and throw away the key. That can be just another puzzle for them. Now look, the Jerry mentioned a case in their car, let's get it and pack this stuff into it." So they were soon able to pack away – in the leather case which they found – the many little bags, which were stuffed with jewellery and with jewels. These included diamonds, sapphires, emeralds, and various other stones, and also, of course, the gold bowl.

"Good lad, that's everything," said Jeanfils, "I could almost wish that I could be here to see what explanations they come up with...but now let's get the hell out of here!"

They drove a few miles in the direction of Bayonne, till Jeanfils stopped the truck beside a little wood and took Henry to the edge of it where he pointed to a huge boulder, and said, "I've always been curious about this, so we'll bury the case near it." Henry chose a position in the wood, thirty paces due south of the stone and, as there were spades in the truck and the ground was soft, it didn't take them long to dig a deep hole, put the case at the bottom, and then cover it with soil and a further covering of branches to make it quite undetectable.

As they finished, Jeanfils looked at his watch. "It's only four o'clock, with all that has happened I had thought it must be later. Anyway, I'll now have to go back to my house to collect some money and my passport. I have my identity papers on me, but we are going abroad, so the more papers I have the better. You should be okay when you get to Spain, as you will have your RAF papers. If we hurry, we'll be able to do all this and still get to Bayonne before the curfew."

It sounded a bit risky to Henry. All he wanted to do was to get away from the area as soon as possible, but in the event there were no problems. Jeanfils collected his cash and passport, and Henry got a few of his things, but stayed in the workman's clothes, to remain an assistant to Jeanfils. But all went well, and it was dark, getting on for about six o'clock as Jeanfils drove the truck up a back street in Bayonne and then turned in to the entrance of a company named *Jacques Juvenal – CHARRIER.*

"Jacques is an old friend of mine," said Jeanfils, "and has a motor haulage business, sending many vehicles to Spain, and some even as far as Portugal, with loads of fine claret from Bordeaux."

As they were getting out of the car, a man came out, before running over and embracing Jeanfils. "Hello, my friend, this is a pleasant surprise."

When things were explained to him Jacques smiled at Henry, saying, "You have a good fairy watching over you, you see that truck of mine over there with all the cases of wine…well, I am leaving in about an hour for Lisbon and I can take you right on to Portugal where, unlike the Spanish, they like the British!"

Everything was arranged with what Henry felt was ridiculous ease, and soon he was packed into a little nest, which was arranged in the middle of the load of cases while Jeanfils took the part of a spare driver. They were about thirty miles from the Spanish frontier, so Henry had only to lie most uncomfortably in his little cell for about an hour and a half, before he heard the sounds and the bustle of the post at the border. Then, after a few anxious minutes, the truck started again and soon he heard the sounds of Spanish being spoken. They didn't want any confrontation with the border police, so the truck drove on for a further half hour or so till the driver, Jeanfils' friend Jacques, pulled off the road and released Henry, saying, "Welcome to Spain…your troubles now are over!"

CHAPTER ONE

The present day

The small chapel at the crematorium in Paisley was full to overflowing; as well it might be following the sudden death of such a popular local man as John Burton. But, with every seat taken, and a crowd standing at the rear, the family pew at the front held only two people, an old lady, my grandmother, and me, Charles Burton. The row of empty seats was worrying me. *Should we have asked the people to join us?* I considered. But then my thoughts ran on: *No, I don't think so, damn it, this service is for my father, Granny's son, who has died, so we should be on our own.*

For a while, I just sat and let the minister's platitudes wash over me, but then I turned and glanced at Marie, my beloved grandmother, and I felt – as I so often did – how lucky I was to have her. She had become the only mother I had ever known, as my real mother had died when giving birth to me. But then my thoughts took a different track. *What a tenuous line we Burtons have had in these last fifty or more years, here is my father dying so unexpectedly from a heart attack, my mother dying so young and my grandfather,*

Henry, being killed in the RAF early in 1943, just a matter of days after Dad was born.

But I couldn't pursue these thoughts, as the minister reached the end of his address, and the service moved on to its climax with the coffin descending slowly out of sight. The only good thing about that day was the sun was shining, so Marie and I could stand outside to face the ordeal. Meanwhile, our friends filed past to offer their condolences and, as the procession went on and on, I was glad that we had come to the decision not to have any post-funeral assembly of drinks and tea and small eats, which we had both felt was barbaric. It wasn't as though we had relatives coming from any distance to attend the funeral, as our only near relative was a great-aunt of mine – a sister of my grandfather – who lived locally, but who was now bedridden. She was, however, still very alert mentally, so it was to her house, in Kilmacolm, a village some twelve miles away, that we went for lunch. It was a tradition that when we had a meal with Great-Aunt Agnes, we ate in her bedroom, so her housekeeper set up not only a table, but a sort of mini-bar. This arrangement enabled us to help ourselves to drinks, and it was when I was handing her a second glass of sherry that she turned to Granny. "Marie, do you think that Charles will be any more successful than dear John was in solving our old mystery?"

That was not the kind of remark I had expected to hear on such a day, so I pricked up my ears and said, "Come on Great-Aunty…what old mystery?"

But Granny was displeased. "Agnes, why bring this up today, of all days? It's bad enough having lost my son, without going back to the old days when I lost my husband."

"Rubbish, Marie, today is just the time to look back to these far off, and mostly happy days, when we were young, and if perchance young Charles can do better than we've done so far, well I'm sure that your Henry would have been pleased."

There was a pause before Granny replied, "All right, Agnes, we'll talk about it...but let's have lunch first!"

I was amused by this remark, as it exhibited a well-known trait of hers. "That's right, Granny," I said, "you've lived in Britain for some sixty years, but you still have a French woman's desire not to mix serious conversation with anything as important as eating!"

"Quite right!" she said, and for the first time that day there was a sparkle in her eyes. "We French have a clear idea of what is important in this life, and it was certainly no Frenchman who invented fast food."

So with that, we were drinking coffee after lunch when Granny looked up at me. "Well, Charles, from what Agnes said, you may be thinking that you are about to hear something exciting. Well, it might have been at one time, but it is now only a tiny bit of wartime history, and I'm afraid it can't be of any importance after all these years." She paused for a moment to take a sip of coffee, then went on. "As you know, my dear husband, your grandfather Henry, was in the RAF and you will have heard the story about the Beaufighter in which he was flying to Gibraltar developed engine trouble; how he and his pilot bailed out in the south of France, not a great many miles from the Spanish border. What is fact is that the pilot died when he descended by parachute into the middle of a large lake, but Henry and a Frenchman – a M. Jeanfils, who aided his escape – did get back to England, first through Spain, and then after being stuck in Portugal for several weeks. So, although Henry landed in France in the last days of November – on the 30th I think it was – they didn't get back to Britain till the 10th of January. But two most unfortunate things then happened almost immediately after that; the first, only two days after they got back, was that M.

Jeanfils forgot that the traffic here is on the other side of the road, and stepped off a pavement in London right in front of a bus. That was about January 12th, and I had gone into hospital for the birth of your father a few days before then and the second misfortune occurred soon afterwards..."

She stopped and smiled at me. "No, the misfortune wasn't the birth of your dear father, it was that I got septicaemia, and was very ill for several weeks. Now Henry did, of course, get leave following his return, but it was only for three weeks, and he must have thought that – in hospital as I was – I wasn't well enough for him to tell me the dark side of his time in France. Of course, he never lived to tell to tell the tale as he was killed in a flying accident on the very day that he rejoined his squadron. But before that, he did say something to Agnes." Granny glanced in her direction. "Come along, dear, it is your turn now to speak to Charles!"

Great-Aunt Agnes sat up straight in bed, obviously glad to be the centre of attention, and said, "Come closer, dear, I get tired when I have to speak loudly, Marie knows it all, but you don't...which I find surprising. You see, back in those days, septicaemia was a much more serious illness than now –there were no antibiotics – and for a while we despaired of Marie's life, so nothing much interested your father in those weeks of his leave except the health of his beloved wife, and of course his very healthy young son. During this time, I couldn't see him often as I was very busy on civilian war work, but I did see him twice as we sat in the hospital waiting room, and on the second time he spoke of the brave Frenchman, Emile Jeanfils, who helped him escape. He told me that on the very day they began their escape, they happened to be in the large house of an elderly man where M. Jeanfils was doing some repair work. It was when they had almost finished their work for the day and were sitting in the kitchen out of the way, that a German major drove up, accompanied by a young Frenchman, and they demanded that the old man open his safe. Apparently, the old man had been a jeweller in Biarritz and had a big safe in his living room. I can remember your father's words exactly even after all these years:

"It was like a nightmare, here was this defenceless old man, and these two bastards forced him to open the safe and then, after he had done so, the Major shot him like a dog, for no reason at all, except to conceal their crime. But my friend Jeanfils knew where there was a shotgun in the house, and he managed to shoot the Major and, I'm glad today, I did my bit by getting hold of the Major's revolver and finishing him off. What we found was an incredible pile of jewellery and jewels, worth God alone knows how many thousand pounds. Jeanfils decided to spare the life of the young Frenchman, but before we left he put the fear of God into him not to tell anything about us."

He had just said that when the nurse came in to say that we could go into see Marie. I pressed him then to go on, but we had no time, and this is all he said:

"No time for the details now, but we buried the treasure where I can find it again and I'll give it to the old man's daughter after the war. It is the least I can do by way of saying thank you to my poor friend Jeanfils who hasn't lived to get back to France again."

I still pursued my questions, however, and said, "But what about the young Frenchman?"

"Oh, we put the fear of God into him…but now we really must go in to see Marie."

I was then already late for an appointment, so I could only stay with her for a few minutes before I had to hurry away, so I said, "Look, Henry, when we next meet you must tell me more about this. And again I can remember his exact words."

"It's a long story, Agnes, but I promise that I'll tell you when we have more time...and I'll write it down too ...and that's all I can tell you."

"Come, on Great-Aunt," I said, "you can't stop there!"

"But stop there I must, because I never saw him again. He was killed less than a week later, and nobody has found any writings of his. Now, I knew your grandfather well, and, of course, Marie knew him even better, so were both aware of his habit of writing down important things, but sadly he didn't do so in this case."

She stopped again, and it was Granny who took up the tale. "You see, Charles, I was really very ill in hospital and dear Henry obviously didn't want to worry me, so he made light of his time in France, and mentioned nothing of the episode with the German. After his death, of course, we had to go through all his papers, and the Air Force did their bit by sending on all his belongings, but nothing turned up. Anyway, there was still the war going on, and I had to come to terms with the loss of my beloved husband, and learn to bring up my dear son John – your father – and that seemed far more important than a crime in faraway France – even though it was, and still is, my own country. I did think of paying a visit to that part of France, near the Spanish border, a few times after the war, but maybe you don't know that for many of these years, we were tightly controlled as to the amount of money we could take out of the country, and for me it was far more important to spend my allowance in going to see my parents who, as you will remember, lived down near Nice. It wasn't till your father got to, I think, about eighteen, when Agnes and I told him what little we knew of the story. The only solid fact we had was the name Emile Jeanfils, but we didn't know the name of the village where he lived, or the name of the old man who was killed, or even the name of the friend of Jeanfils, who had the haulage business and who had driven them to Lisbon. So once again, we decided not to bother, and to let sleeping dogs lie. Your dear father did not have a very large bump of curiosity, and while Agnes and I might have gone with him to France – even although nearly twenty years had then gone by – he was not very interested, so that was that!"

"I can tell you one thing though, Charles, that your father and I did discuss the matter again, only a few weeks ago, and he was then of a mind to tell you about it, and to go off, the pair of you, to see if anything could be found. I think he had suddenly developed a conscience about that buried treasure, and the unfortunate girl who should have got it after the war." She stopped there and reached over to take my hand. "My dear Charles, I can't tell you how much it means both to me and to Agnes to have you, a strong young man, to carry on the family, and maybe you will be able to do what we have failed to do for nearly sixty years, and find out the truth about this old affair. But for today that is enough. All I want now is to go home, put my feet up, and have a nice nap and a rest till supper time. You must make allowances for me, I'm now over eighty you know!"

The next few days were a busy time for all of us. My father, John Burton, had been a successful lawyer in Glasgow and there were many arrangements to be made with his firm, regarding his interests and what monies were due to him. These arrangements also concerned me as although I was a very junior member in the same firm, I now moved up an important step of the seniority ladder. But this wasn't just because of my father's death, as the senior partner told me that my promotion had already been agreed before his death, and he wished me every success with my career in the firm. Fortunately, there were no money problems, as my father had made very good arrangements for Marie, his mother, and for me, so there were no concerns on that score to worry us.

There were, however, a mass of my father's papers to go through and deal with, so it took a lot of my time over the next fortnight to do what had to be done, but in none of these papers was there any mention of the events in France. It was about three weeks later that I got an idea of a possible new approach and, after dinner, I had an idea. "Look, Granny," I said, "something has just occurred to me. When Granddad got back from France, he must have written a report to the Air Force about what happened in France after that ill-fated flight...and if so it will probably still be filed away somewhere. I'd like to write to the Air Historical Department of the Ministry of Defence and ask them to look it up. Is that OK by you?"

"You're a clever boy," she said, "of course I agree, and I can hardly wait to see what they turn up...we should have thought of doing this these many, many years ago."

Well, that was the first week in May, and it was three weeks later before the reply came in, and we got a copy of that report by my grandfather, dated 14th January 1943. It was short, and very formal, as official correspondence had to be in these days, and addressed to his Commanding Officer.

Sir,

I have the honour to explain hereunder the details of my successful escape from France. The facts regarding the engine trouble which occurred with my Beaufighter, and the unfortunate death of my pilot, Captain Peters, have been dealt with in a separate report to the US authorities.

I landed by parachute in the early hours of November 30th. near the á´tang de Laguibe in southern France and was fortunate to find a small village where I contacted a M. Emile Jeanfils who had been involved on a few occasions with escaping aircrews.

Before making my escape I became involved in a strange affair as I went with M. Jeanfils to work with him on a job he was doing in a large house in his village – he took me with him in the guise of a cousin of his – and while we were working in the kitchen a German officer Major Hassell drove up with a young Frenchman, and demanded that the house owner open a large safe. Eventually he did so, and they found an incredible collection of jewels and other valuables. At this point, the German shot the house owner, and it was obvious that the two of them, who seemed to be very good friends, intended to steal the treasures, and the old man's death must have been to hide the crime.

Fortunately, Jeanfils knew where the old man kept a shotgun, and he shot the German, and I finished him off with a shot from his own gun.

Jeanfils then did what he felt was necessary to ensure the silence of the young Frenchman, and as we felt it would not be safe to leave this treasure in jewels to be found by the Germans, we buried it nearby with the intention of returning it to the old man's daughter after the war. With the sad death of Mr Jeanfils, this is a duty which I shall perform as soon as it becomes possible.

That same night, 2nd December, we drove in a truck belonging to Jeanfils to see a friend of his, M. Jacques Juvenal, who operates a motor haulage company in Bayonne. Most fortunately, he was leaving a few hours later with a load of wine for a company in Lisbon, and our journey there was uneventful.

I am, Sir

Your obedient servant,

Henry Burton

Flying Officer

The letter must have been sent on from his squadron to the Air Ministry, as there was a sheet of AM-headed memo paper with a somewhat irate note from a certain Group Captain Jenkins, telling his assistant to contact F/O Burton immediately and to get fuller details of the affair, including the names of all the people concerned.

But the next note was to the effect that F/O Burton had been killed in an accident, and someone had scribbled over it:

Don't bother the family, we've got too much on our plate already.

There was much in this for us to think about, and we could sympathise with that irate staff officer. Why, we wondered, had Henry given away so little information? But on the bright side, we now knew the area where he had landed, the name of the haulage contractor who had taken him, and his French friend Jeanfils, to Portugal; and, for what it was worth, they also knew the name of the German who had been killed. Some vital bits, however, were missing – the name of the old man who had owned the treasure, the name of the Frenchman who had collaborated with the German, and for good measure, the name of the village, near where the treasures were buried. But things were now looking much more hopeful and I said to Granny, "I think we do have enough information now, at least to have a stab at things, and I'm sure you will agree that we should try to do something, and do so right away. Now, for the present, I haven't yet made any plans for a summer holiday, and what better holiday could I have than to try to explain this family mystery? So, shall

I find out what dates are possible when I go to the office tomorrow?"

She gave me an emphatic nod. "Yes, dear, you do that, and I am very glad that you have decided to do this so quickly; as a family we have been idle about this matter for far too long. Everything got arranged easily, and I was home next evening with the news that I could take a holiday at a time to suit myself. There are advantages in being not too senior in a firm!"

When we were talking over my plans a few days later, Granny said to me, "You know, I do so wish that I could come with you, as I have a conscience that, as I have said, we have left this affair on the shelf for so long. What annoys me is that we don't know everything, yet I'm sure that Henry would have written down the whole story somewhere; maybe he took his notes with him when he went back to his squadron, and they didn't realise their importance when sending his belongings back to me."

As she said that an idea suddenly occurred to me. "Granny," I said, "it is very odd that he left nothing for you about his time in France, especially as you are French, so is it possible that he had a secret hiding place for confidential papers? This leads me to ask if there were any other papers missing after he died, which he should have had…"

"No, not so far as I can remember…Oh!...Wait a minute…yes, after Henry was killed I needed my marriage certificate to validate my claim for a widow's pension from the RAF, and I couldn't find it and had to get a duplicate. At the same time I found that my birth certificate was also missing…are you thinking what I'm thinking, that he really did have a hiding place?"

"Yes, Granny, I certainly am. It seems very likely that Granddad may have had some secret compartment for his important papers, so where could it be?"

"Well, the obvious place," she said, "is somewhere in that big desk in the study, but I've never heard of anything like that in it."

"Let's go and look!"

The desk was made of solid oak, which looked as though it had been around forever, and Marie told me that it had been bought by his grandfather, so that dated it back as late Victorian or earlier. I looked it over carefully, and ruefully felt that it was far too plain to have any secrets. There were no projecting bosses or knobs to be turned, or anything which could double as a handle, yet I had a gut feeling that there had to be something, so I turned to Granny. "It doesn't look very hopeful, does it, but before we give up I'd like to take a few measurements, and see if there is any space unaccounted for."

I had almost finished the job without finding anything out of the ordinary until I measured the depth of the drawer above the knee hole, and found that it was nearly five inches too short. Excitedly, I ran round to the back of the desk and got down on my hands. There – at the back of the knee hole – was a tiny gap between two boards and, when I inserted the blade of a small knife, I was able to open up a small door to reveal a roll of papers, secured with an elastic band. I gave a whoop of joy. "Bingo! Just look at this, Granny."

And we excitedly spread out the papers on the desk. "Look!" said Marie, "there are my certificates, birth and marriage, along with his documents and…what's this?"

The 'this' turned out to be a number of foolscap sheets with Granddad's rather sprawling writing, and with the heading: France and Portugal 1942/43.

"You've done it," Marie laughed, "now we are really in business. It is wonderful to find this after all these years, but I wonder why he hid it away?"

Then she buried herself in the paper. It didn't take her long to finish reading it, and say, "This is wonderful, if only we had thought to look for this, these sixty odd years ago. It is only an aide-memoire, but it contains most of what we need. Here, read it. And what we read was:

France and Portugal 1942/43

I promised Agnes I would put something down, but I haven't had time to make it a proper report, just a few notes in case I forget anything – although I can't imagine why I should. I think it is best if I number them, so that things are kept separate.

1) I landed by parachute near the Etang de Laguibe in the small hours of November 30th but my pilot unfortunately came down in the middle of the lake and drowned.

2) I was fortunate enough to find a tiny village, maybe about eight miles away, and the first man I contacted was a M. Emile Jeanfils who had a friend in Bayonne who ran a motor haulage business, and who helped escaping servicemen at times.

3) Jeanfils was an odd job man and, on the next day but one, he had to do a job for an elderly man who had a large house in the village – really, a small chateau, and he took me with him. He was a M. Martins who had owned a jeweller's shop in Biarritz before the war, and who now lived alone except for a couple who looked after him, but they were away for a few days.

4) His only relative, M. Jeanfils told me, is a married daughter who lives in Avignon.

5) At about 3 o'clock that afternoon, when Jeanfils and I were in the kitchen, a car drove up with a German, Major Hassell, and Pierre, a young Frenchman, and from their conversation it was obvious that they had a homosexual relationship – ugh!

6) They must have known that the old man had many valuables in a large safe, as they forced him to open it, and then shot him – no doubt to hide their crime. This can't have been their first enterprise, as Hassell said something to Pierre about this being a 'nice addition to what we have collected already'.

7) But M. Jeanfils knew where the old man kept a shotgun, and he shot the Major but not fatally, and I finished him off with his own gun.

8) We discovered that the safe contents appeared to be extremely valuable, what with bags of jewellery, other bags of uncut jewels and a single gold bowl. We decided that the best thing to do was to bury the lot somewhere, and return them after the war to the daughter. Maybe then we could also bring Pierre to justice.

10) He was a devil and had been pleased when Mr Martins had been shot, but very distressed when his German lover was killed. Jeanfils, however, was reluctant to shoot him, as I would have done, saying that his parents were good people.

11) So Jeanfils warned him that if he said anything about the affair it would be the worse for him, and, as a further bit of security, I got him to handle the gold bowl, so that his fingerprints would be on it. I told him that it was solid as it had a London hallmark.

12) We did bury the treasures, in a place where we could find them again. The site is in a wood, a few miles out on the road towards Bayonne, and is some thirty paces south of a large stone which is easily seen from the road. Now that Mr Jeanfils is dead, to return these valuables to the daughter of M. Martins is a duty I must perform, as, so far as I know, Jeanfils had no near relatives who could help.

13) Jeanfils took me that evening to Bayonne where we met his friend Jacques Juvenal who took both of us to Lisbon in one of his vehicles, which was delivering a load of wine. We were damn lucky, but this part of my story isn't very interesting.

14) I wouldn't like to leave this lying around so I'll put it into my little safe – I must tell Marie where it is when I next see her.

15) I decided not go into any details in my report to the CO, as the less said the better until the war is over and I can get the stuff dug up and given back to the girl.

When I had finished reading it, I looked up to see Granny's eyes bright with excitement, and I felt just the same. To have found these papers after they had been hidden for some sixty years was pure magic. But there was still a problem. I realised that there were still some pieces missing, and the puzzle was not yet completely solved. "Tell me, Granny," I said, "it is true, is it, that he said nothing to you after writing this?"

"No, he didn't. The reason was that he was called back from leave a day or two early. They had some kind of tummy bug in his squadron, and they were suddenly very short staffed. He phoned me to say that he couldn't come to see me as we had arranged, but was full of beans and promised that I would see him again in just a few days time...and that was the last time I spoke to him."

She stopped, and blew her nose, saying, "Damn it, even after all these years I still get weepy to remember these days...but when he left I was still quite ill, although now on the turn and beginning to get better. I feel sure that if he had been given even one more day of leave I would have been well enough for us to have had a real talk, and that might have meant that there would have been no mystery for us to solve now. You would read that he was going to tell me about this compartment when he next saw me, and that is why I never heard about its secret and why we have been ignorant about this for so very long."

"Well," I said, "let's look on the bright side...now we know almost everything except for three rather annoying gaps. He hasn't told us the name of the village, or the surname of Pierre, the gay Frenchman, and exactly where this stone is. He mentions that it is visible...but, damn it, we don't even know what road it is on."

"However," I went on, "I'm sure I'll be able to sort these things out, as I'll be able to talk to people...thanks to you, Granny, who insisted on making me bilingual. I can tell you that often I could have seen you far enough, but now I am just enormously grateful."

"Thank you, kind sir!" she smiled, "but tell me, are you going alone, as you did mention something about your girlfriend, Rachel, going with you when you got your holidays?"

That was something which had upset me about a month ago, but now I had managed to persuade myself that I'd had a fortunate escape, and I said, "I'm afraid, Granny, she is now ancient history, so far as I am concerned, or maybe it would be more accurate to say that I am the ancient one, as she met a young British Airways pilot who seems now to be number one in her love life."

"I'm sorry," said Granny, "she was quite a nice girl...but not nearly good enough for you! I never said anything, but I confess that I hoped that nothing would come of your friendship. She was shallow, lots of fun, I'm sure, but believe me, it wouldn't have lasted!"

"If you say so, Granny!"

***

Next morning I got a somewhat unpleasant surprise when a young friend of mine, Adam Brown, a reporter on *The Herald,* phoned me at the office, and said, "Hello, Charles, I want to do a little piece about you. I hear that you are going to France to try to retrace the steps of your grandfather's escape from France in 1942. Come on, give!"

I didn't need to be a genius to know where he had got his information, as his grandmother, I knew, was a close friend of Great-Aunt Agnes. The last thing I wanted was publicity...but I wondered what damage could be done, so I said, "Well, it isn't really much of a story, and I bet what little you have came from old Agnes... what did she tell your Granny?"

"You're a clever chap, Charles. That of course is precisely where I got the story, but all she said was that now, after the death of your father, you wanted to find out anything you could about your grandfather's time in France. And why have you suddenly decided to do this?"

I crossed my fingers and said, "Oh, it is just a sudden whim, and I got details from the Air Ministry, which tells me where he landed, after bailing out. Tell you what, you can interview me when I get back. I'll possibly have more interesting things to tell you about then."

"OK, I'll hold you to that, and I'll just put in a little piece for now with no details. Don't forget to see me when you get back!"

I breathed a sigh of relief. He had obviously heard nothing about the papers we had discovered in the desk, and what he had seemed innocuous. I phoned Granny at once, and she was even angrier than me. I could see that there were going to be some sharp exchanges between the sisters-in-law, and that Agnes would be told to shut up in no uncertain terms. Certainly, the piece he had in the paper next day – Saturday – was much longer than I had hoped. It went into some detail about things, mentioned about Granddad's bailing out in France and his escape from there to Portugal, and said that his grandson was going to try to trace details of his escape, and what happened in France and that I would be interviewed on my return. It also said that my family believed that he'd had some interesting adventures in France and the whole story would be reported later. Because of all the suggestions in the article, I decided on Monday that I owed it to the senior partner in my firm to tell him what I was up to and, to my surprise, Mr William Henderson was most interested. So much so that he took me out to lunch, nothing fancy, just beer and sandwiches, but nevertheless it was confirmation – if I had needed it – that I was now recognised as a valuable member of the partnership. I talked while we ate, and told him everything I could about the matter. When I had finished, he steepled his fingers, and thought for a few moments. "Do you know, Charles," he said, "I wouldn't think that your enterprise is entirely without risk. I don't at all like the idea of that young gay Frenchman having been let off Scot free. Just remember that statement by the German which indicated that they had stolen other items. Is it possible, don't you think, that the young man could have been their custodian, and so could have surfaced, after the war, with a nice little nest egg? So, I wonder, what is he up to now? I realise that he must be getting on for eighty but he must still worry, occasionally, about these fingerprints of his on that gold bowl, and certainly would worry if he heard of your investigations."

"But," he went on, "don't let me worry you. As I've said, I have a certain reputation for being a pessimist and it is, of course, most unlikely that you'll stir up any trouble. Anyway, I'll bet that old Martins' daughter – or more probably her offspring – will be astonished to find that they are quite rich!"

He paused, and looked at his watch. "Time we were off. But no, one other thing occurs to me, where there is a lot of money about, it always pays to be careful. I know, of course, that this adventure of your grandfather took place almost sixty years ago, but there could be another problem. Is it possible that there are still people around, apart from Pierre, who wonder where M. Martins' valuables went? If so, would they want them for themselves, rather than you giving them back to their rightful owners?"

He stopped again for a moment before going on. "I can tell you, Charles, that in a sort of a way it is as if you have dropped a stone into a pool of water – so there are ripples. So far, of course, you have only made a single enquiry to the Air Ministry but now there has been this innocent piece in *The Herald* – and that may have spread that little ripple. However, I wonder who will be interested. Probably, any worries are stupid but still, just as a back-stop, I think I'll give you the name and address of our correspondent in Paris, so that you can get in touch with him if you strike any problems…or rather, better still, I'll give him a ring this afternoon when we are back in the office."

But I was not convinced by these ideas of problems ahead. "Surely," I laughed, "it is highly unlikely that there is still anyone who is interested, and who could wish me harm? The only one I can think of is Pierre – don't know his surname – whom Granddad described as being a teenager at that time, so now he is getting on for eighty – if he is still alive. The only others are the descendants of M. Martins, and they will be firmly on my side!"

But Mr Henderson wouldn't be deflected, and when we got back he phoned his friend, M. Phillipe Duchene, at once. I was amused to hear that he believed he could speak French, and I congratulated the unseen M. Duchene on understanding the dreadful and tortured language he was subjected to by my boss. But I could just comprehend that he was trying to introduce me and I hoped that I didn't look too superior as I picked up the phone.

M. Duchene's first words after I spoke were, "Thank God for a Scot who can speak French. Don't tell my old friend William that I had come to believe that it was genetically impossible for any of you up there to speak a foreign language!"

We talked for a while as I explained my quest, and at the end Duchene said, "It's an interesting story, and certainly I can't imagine that you are going to run into any trouble. But if you want help at any time, please don't hesitate to give me a ring. Better still, should you be in Paris, do please come to see me, and you would be most welcome to spend a night with me. My wife died last year so I am on my own and it would give me a great pleasure if you do come. Just one thing more, I'd better warn you, young Charles, that when I ring your office in future, you are the chap I'm going to ask for. There will be fewer misunderstandings that way!"

That was not the only surprise of the afternoon, as about an hour later I got a call from Granny who sounded very excited. "You'll never guess, Charles, who called a few minutes ago to speak to you…it was the chap in the Air Historical Department of the Defence Ministry who sent you that report by your grandfather. Apparently, there has been a development, and he wants to talk to you…he gave me his number, here it is, and his name is Squadron Leader Howard Chisholm."

"Did he give you any clues about what has happened?"

"No, and I didn't tell him that I am the widow of Flying Officer Henry Burton, as I felt that it was now your affair. But hurry home tonight and tell me all about it!"

I rang him at once, and the Squadron Leader explained that his department was always careful about releasing copies of documents, especially to foreigners, where British servicemen or women have been involved in affairs where people have died – apart from the times when they are carrying out their normal duties of combatants. "Trouble is," he said, "that now there are armies of lawyers engaged in digging up old incidents, and doing their worst to besmirch our service people. This case of your grandfather is ancient history, but now, within a few weeks, first of all you ask for his report. That is quite understandable…and now, today, we have another enquiry, this time from a gentleman in Paris, who has sent it by fax with a request for urgent treatment, and to send the details back also by fax. This, for us, rings an alarm bell, despite the fact that it seems impossible that he can be trying to make some kind of case against your grandfather. The only other thing we can worry about is whether the enquiry is because of this treasure which your grandfather mentions...can I ask you if your family have done anything about it?"

"That is very odd, Squadron Leader," I said, "as I'm sure you know, my grandfather was killed within a few days of writing that report which you sent me, and nobody has done anything about it until a few weeks ago when my father died, and I became interested. Incidentally, the lady to whom you spoke this afternoon is my grandmother, so she is also most interested as you can realise. We have, in the last few days after getting the report from you, been wondering if we should pursue the matter, and I am going off on a trip to France at the end of next week, in the hope that I can do something by way of retrieving these buried valuables, and returning them to the descendants of the old man who was killed, and there was a quite innocent mention of this in *The Herald*. What has prompted us to do something is that my grandmother and I have found an old cache of papers, including a much fuller report, giving names in a secret drawer in my grandfather's desk, so I'm now hopeful that I'll succeed."

"But, tell me," I went on, "do you know anything about the Frenchman who has made this new enquiry?"

"No, but the address is that of a lawyer's office in Paris."

That certainly rang alarm bells for me, as with lawyers getting involved, the other people...whoever they were... meant business. So I thought for a moment before going on, and then said, "Look, Squadron Leader, could you do me a favour? If you do, I promise to do you one in return! Can you delay sending this lawyer the report for, say, a couple of weeks, as by then I'll either have succeeded or failed, and when I get back I can then give you the full report that the old Group Captain was so keen to get back in 1943, and also the details of whatever I have been able to find in France."

"It's a deal!" he said, "I can certainly do that, and a delay in this department is nothing out of the ordinary! For now,

I'll just drop him a line by fax so that he knows we have noted his request for urgency…saying that we'll have a look for the papers and be in touch as soon as possible."

"You can do one more thing for me," I said, "tell me the chap's name, and the address of his office. I am a lawyer myself, and have a legal friend in Paris who may be able to tell me something about him."

And the Squadron Leader gave me the address, and the name of the man, a M. Mathieu Jeannot, and then said, "Well, I can only say good luck. It is fascinating for me to find one of these old bits of paper in our files, coming alive, so to speak. Be sure to phone me whenever you have any news!"

I realised that the affair had now moved up a further notch, and went straight round to Mr Henderson's office, who was fascinated by this new development, and suggested that the best thing was to contact M. Duchene in Paris at once and, to my relief, passed me the phone. When I spoke to him, he was most interested, and said, "If you can remember your Alice in Wonderland, this is a similar situation… curiouser and curiouser. You see, this gentleman M. Jeannot is one of the leading avocats in Paris – certainly one of the most expensive – and his firm does quite a lot of work for the government…so why is he interested in a little affair like this? It certainly is all very strange."

"Look, Charles," he went on, "I would suggest that you take the time to come and see me in Paris on your way south. I think I'll be able to make some helpful suggestions as you will have to make enquiries at the Maries in some of the towns down there, and unless you ask the right questions they will be obstructive. Also, I may be able to prepare the way for you."

Just then, Mr Henderson broke in and asked me to hold Duchene on for a moment. "Look, my boy," he said to me, "this affair has now become urgent, and so far as I am concerned I think that you should head off for France immediately. Don't worry about things here, just give your outstanding papers to me, and I'll have them dealt with. I won't tell anybody here the reason for your sudden departure…just urgent family business will be enough! So make your arrangements now to see Duchene."

I made some rapid calculations, and said to him, "M. Duchene, I have just been given leave by Mr Henderson to start for France immediately. I need a car for my investigations, so I'll use my own, leaving this evening, and get as far south as I can before stopping for a short sleep. I would then hope to get to the Channel Tunnel by mid-morning, so I should get to you by early afternoon."

"Good, good, now I suggest that we meet at my house, rather than in the office, you can park your car here, which is impossible there, and we can have the evening to get to know each other. You can then head off for Bayonne the following morning, having had a good rest and a good night's sleep. Don't bother trying to phone me with your time of arrival, I'll go home for lunch, and there are a lot of things I can do till you get here."

He continued by giving me his home address and instructions about how to get to it. When I hung up the phone, Mr Henderson looked at me with a rather wry smile. "You know, Charles, I used to like puzzles, and this is a very odd one. I can hardly think what this is all about, but just keep your eyes peeled."

***

Marie was almost waiting on the doorstep to greet me when I got home. "Come in, dear, your drink is already poured out, so start NOW and tell me all about it!"

It was two drinks later before we finished talking; this new approach from a lawyer in Paris was a worrying development, and Granny said to me, "Do you think that all this could have stemmed from that piece in *The Herald* on Saturday?"

"I don't think so," I said, "I'm still cross with Great-Auntie, but I don't think it can have done any harm. I can't see a Parisian lawyer subscribing to *The Herald*, can you?"

"I suppose not," she said, "but all this makes me angrier than ever that we didn't do anything about this business earlier, it is absurd to be worrying now about events of nearly sixty years ago."

She stopped, and laughed. "You know, having said that, it is surprising how small events can cast a long shadow, and I don't think I have ever told you just why your grandfather was on that ill-fated flight, have I? No? Well, he had in fact been about to come home on leave, as the replacement planes were being sent to Gibraltar by relief crews, but one of the navigators developed mumps, and Henry was asked to replace him, and to delay his leave for a few days. Just think that if that young man had stayed healthy, none of this would have happened, and Henry might still be beside me now."

She stopped again, and gave me a rueful smile. "Damn it, I know that rambling on about times gone by is a sure sign that one is getting old...and I hate it!...so let's get back to your trip and whether we can get any new ideas. But on that subject I wonder if you know that Mr Henderson was once an intelligence officer in the army, and I think that he had a brief period in the Foreign Office, so that may explain why your affair interests him."

I could only shake my head, as I knew nothing of his early life, but it certainly did explain his liking for puzzles. However, back to us that night, try as we might, we couldn't come up with anything useful but before I left, Granny did something which, for her, was quite out of character. Ever since I came of age, she had let me live my own life with no restrictions, but now she said, "Charles, I am worried, I don't like unanswered questions, so will you do something for me? I would like you to give me a ring every evening, just to tell me that you are well, and to hear what you have been doing? Is that too much to ask?"

"Of course it isn't," I said, "I'll love to talk to you each night, and to fill you in."

"Not so much of the night," she laughed, "the evening is what I said!"

***

CHAPTER TWO

I wanted to get off as soon as I could so I'm afraid that I displeased Granny by refusing the elegant dinner she was preparing, and insisted on just a large plate of soup – Scotch Broth – one of the few local dishes that she approved of. I had very little to do by way of packing, just some changes of shirts and underwear, as I didn't think I would need any formal clothes, but I was careful to remember to take photocopies both of Granddad's report to the Air Force and of his notes which we had found in the desk. I was quite well equipped as I also had made French translations of both of them. So, with a rather sentimental parting from Granny, and her final admonition of "Don't do anything silly!" I was on my way not long after six o'clock, in what was then my pride and joy – a new 6-cylinder Ford Mondeo which I had acquired in celebration of my move up in the firm. It was a good time to travel, as the M74 and then the M6 were not too busy, so I made good time…even although, due to my nippy little car, it was often at somewhat illegal speeds.

I didn't want to get to France without a good night's rest behind me, so soon after I passed Birmingham and joined the M1, I pulled off not long before midnight at Exit 14. I had stopped previously at this service station at Newport

Pagnell, and knew that there was a welcome lodge in the complex where I could spend the night. It was a good decision as I got a late night snack which, along with a couple of Scotches, settled me down for the rest of the night.

I didn't hurry myself in the morning, and it was nearly ten o'clock before I got on the road again, with my fingers crossed that there wouldn't be any hold-ups on the M25. This precaution must have worked, as I had a clear run, getting to Dover in about three hours, then through the Tunnel and into France a further hour later. The second miracle that day was that I managed to get off the Peripherique in Paris by the exit that M. Duchene had recommended…and those readers who have taken on the challenge of this road will appreciate why I mention this as being a miracle! Then having done so, I found his house without too much difficulty.

His voice, when I had spoken to him on the phone, had seemed youthful, so I was surprised to see that he was pretty elderly, and I had to restrain myself from greeting him as M. Poirot, as he was small and rather self important, and would have been perfectly type cast in that role. And he wouldn't have been miscast either, on the score of not having sufficient 'little grey cells', as I soon realised that he was keenly intelligent. When I say 'soon', one must remember that this was France, so there were all the preliminaries to be gone through and a bottle of wine opened, before we got down to any serious discussion. But I thought at first that it would be a good thing to tell him that my grandmother was French, and when I told him something about her, he looked up with interest. "Do you know," he said, "I have always avoided going up to Glasgow to meet the people in your firm, but now I shall certainly make it my business to do so. Your grandmother sounds like a lady after my own heart that I should very much like to meet. But for now, we have business to attend to, and this is a delightful puzzle. Here we have this old mystery, which has lain untouched for some sixty years, and yet first you, and then a short time later my avocat friend, Mathieu Jeannot, start looking into it. That does suggest that your actions may have come to the attention of somebody with contacts in France. Can you think of any candidate for that role?"

All I could say was, "No, Monsieur, the only people I have spoken to are my grandmother, and my great-aunt, and, of course, Mr Henderson, and none of these can be considered as possibles. But there was one small leak of information, as my great-aunt mentioned to an old friend of hers that I was going to France to retrace my grandfather's footsteps, and a little piece went into our local newspaper, *The Herald*, which is a Glasgow paper. Here, I've got a copy of it in my pocket."

Following in his Grandfather's footsteps

We learn that Mr. Charles Burton, son of the late John Burton, whose obituary was published in our edition of 19th. April, has decided to try to complete a piece of his family history.

In November 1942 his Grandfather, who was then Flying Officer Henry Burton, was flying in a Beaufighter from England to Gibraltar when it developed engine trouble and he and his pilot had to bail out in France, close to Bayonne, near the Spanish border. His pilot was killed, but he managed to make his own escape, first to Spain, and then to Portugal, before getting back home. It would appear that he may have had some adventures while in France, but unfortunately he was killed soon after that in a flying accident before he could write down a record of his adventures and it now is a project of his grandson to visit this area of France to see if there are still people there who can remember his grandfather, and tell him what happened, and how he escaped to Spain.

We understand that he is hoping, before he leaves, to get some assistance from the Air Historical Department of the Air Ministry, who may have some useful information about the ill-fated flight. If he is successful it should make an interesting story, and Mr. Burton has promised to allow us to interview him on his return, and to tell us all he has managed to find out."

M. Duchene read it over carefully, then said, "Well, that seems quite harmless, and anyway I can't see old Jeannot subscribing to a local rag…" I hadn't the heart to interrupt him, but I wondered what my friends would say if they heard their favourite paper which, apart from the tabloids, was one of the leading daily papers in Scotland, being described as a 'local rag'.

"Well," he continued, "we are left with the puzzle of why an avocat in Paris is looking into this old affair. As I mentioned to you, he is one of the highest paid members of my profession, and has a clientele which includes many of the richest, and most powerful people in France. In addition to that, he has many contacts with the government…but I'll have more to say about him later."

He stopped there and for a moment looked at me rather ruefully, but then he smiled. "Let's leave it there for now, I've arranged for us to have dinner in a little nearby restaurant, so let's go there now."

***

It may have been a little restaurant, but the food was wonderful – as too was the wine – and I was very contented when, back in his house again, we sat down once more with glasses of cognac in our hands. He started very thoughtfully. "Now, Charles, you explained to me on the phone yesterday why this old affair has been ignored for so long, but that makes any investigation now very difficult. It is obvious that everything stems from the murder of the old jeweller, M. Martins, the death of the German Major, and the treachery of Pierre, the young Frenchman, so your researches must start there. But, for now, please explain what has happened so far."

I began by giving him copies of Grandfather's two reports; first, the English originals and then the French translations I had made. He read the French text first, and then the English one, no doubt to make sure that I hadn't made any mistakes, before turning to me and commenting, "It certainly is a remarkable story, Charles, and it is a great pity that the affair was not investigated immediately after the war, or at least when your father was a young man. And now, we have this strange coincidence of both you and M. Mathieu Jeannot contacting your Defence Ministry to get details of a small affair which took place in 1942. First of all, I think I'd better forget my legal training and give you a frank description of Jeannot…all I can say is that he is shit!"

I just had to laugh as up to that point everything had been so polite and formal, and now I was glad to see that Duchene laughed with me before he went on. "So now you know that while he is covered with honours, and also loaded down with money, he exhibits all that is worst in the legal profession. If you look at the major trials he has been involved in, they have all been of defendants who are extremely rich, or were backed by a powerful organisation, and a common link is that all his clients were as guilty as hell, despite the fact that they all got off! The trials also show a pattern, either of the main prosecution witnesses changing their stories or disappearing, or the sudden appearance of new defence witnesses.

I know that he has been investigated, but no mud has ever stuck to him…more's the pity! Anyway, the problem we now have to solve is why some very rich Frenchman or big company should want to employ him to look into this old affair. The likeliest candidate, of course, is this man Pierre, who was allowed to go free, but not before your grandfather got his fingerprints applied to a gold bowl, but he doesn't sound like a man who could have got rich enough to pay Jeannot's fees…but we mustn't forget him."

"Anyway," he went on, "your first port of call must be in the Bayonne area, and I suggest that you should first contact the Mairie there, and see if they have, or can tell you where to find, details of the people who lived during the war in the little villages in the area south of the Etang de Laguibe. In particular, you should endeavour to find the name of the village in which M. Martins lived, and then look for people in it with the Christian name of Pierre."

But he stopped there and went on rather doubtfully. "Yes, you may of course be lucky, but a lot of records went during the Occupation, but even if they have, you have a second string to your bow. We know that old Martins had a jeweller's shop in Biarritz, and there must still be people there who knew him, and also knew where he lived. It shouldn't be difficult to find which was his old shop, and that could be your number two project."

It was obvious then that he thought that there was nothing more we could usefully do till we got more information, but I still felt curious about this, possibly crooked, lawyer and I wondered about him. "Tell me," I said, "is it possible that he is working for the French government?"

I thought that he would laugh at the idea, but I was interested to see that he did not dismiss it out of hand as he said, with a question in his voice, "Probably you don't know, but we have something of a political crisis on our hands just now. Two weeks ago, our Minister for Education was found guilty of some rather questionable behaviour and the opposition is running around trying to find if they can find any mud to throw on any others in the government team. So, the thought does occur to me that, just maybe, one of our ministers isn't as squeaky clean as he or she should be, and that Jeannot is looking into things but…but how the hell could this old affair be a factor? I may say that I have been running a list of government ministers through my head and, so far as I can remember, there is only one Pierre among them, but he is about forty, and had a distinguished career in the army before going in for politics. Anyway, we'll leave that idea. As the Americans say, leave it on the back burner for now…but I for one will not forget it."

At that point, he began to discuss with me where I should stay and, very politely, began to sound me out as to what price bracket for accommodation I had in mind. He was obviously disappointed by the price level I indicated. "You know," he said, "it is a great pity to economise while on such a short stay in France as yours. I know nothing about the hotels in Bayonne, but Biarritz is nearby with some of the finest hotels in France. If you want to push the boat out for a day or two, try to get in to the Chateau de Brindos, which is a little way out of town towards the airport. It really is a luxury restaurant with about ten bedrooms, but it is very pleasant, and has a Michelin Star for good measure."

I laughed and said that if I won the National Lottery I would consider his advice, but he wouldn't be put off. "I can tell you, Charles, that it is better to have one night there and spend the next night sheltering under a hedge, than to have two nights in a run-of-the-mill hotel. Just remember that," he smiled, "and on that note of good advice – which I can see you are going to ignore – I would like to mention one other thing, which is that many people, even now, find it distressing to be reminded of the days of the Occupation, and their attitude now is to forgive and forget…or, failing that, just ignore. So you may find actual animosity when you try to dig up an old scandal. I am sorry to have to give you this warning, but I'm afraid that I must do so. Anyway, on that rather sad note, I suggest we break up for the night, as you will want to be fresh for your journey tomorrow."

But that remark about bedtime reminded me about having to phone Granny, and I explained to Duchene about my promise. "Of course, my boy," he immediately replied, "please do so now before it gets any later. Do you want to be private, or to use this phone here?"

"Nothing secret!" I laughed, and went over and put in my call…I won't say that Granny was angry, but she was slightly displeased at the lateness of my call. "Charles, I had almost given you up, what kept you that you didn't call earlier?"

"My only excuse, Granny, is that I have had a most interesting and very helpful evening here with M. Duchene and I'll be off to Bayonne in the morning."

"That's good," she said, "I am glad that things are getting themselves organised so easily. Look after yourself, my dear, I shall be thinking of you…bonne nuit."

***

Breakfast with M. Duchene was delightful, and of a type which I was used to, as Granny had always refused to let us have British-type cooked breakfasts. Somehow, however, here in Paris, it tasted better than ever, the croissants melted in my mouth with fresh Normandy butter giving them added flavour, and the coffee… well, it was even better than Granny's – and that is saying something! As I said my somewhat inadequate "thank you for having me", M. Duchene stopped me. "My thanks are due to you, Charles, I have very much enjoyed meeting you, and I look forward to hearing your news. Just remember that if you run into any difficulties, don't hesitate to tell me, and I'm sorry to say it again, but please be careful, I don't at all like the background to this affair."

So it was with this admonition ringing in my ears that I set off, and first I had to chance my luck again on the Peripherique. But, somewhat to my surprise, I managed to find the correct exit for the Autoroute to the south west and could relax as I drifted along the superb French road at a pretty steady 80-90 mph, a little over the speed limit, but not sufficiently illegal to interest the cops. The journey was nearly 400 miles, by way of Orleans, Tours, Poitiers, Bordeaux, and then down the coast to Bayonne. I had looked up my Michelin Guide, and I saw that a Hotel Lousteau was within my price range and also looked easy to find as it was in a big square in the Place de Republique – just back from the river Adour and, when I got there mid-afternoon, I found it with no difficulty.

My first port of call was to the Mairie, where I explained my problem to the young man at the enquiry desk. I had worried on my drive down how to explain what I was after, and I decided to use just a little of the truth. "I have come here," I said, "on a rather odd mission. You see, my British grandfather was in the Royal Air Force, and his plane got engine trouble quite near here, and he and his pilot bailed out, coming down near the Etang de Laguibe. He did manage to escape, thanks to some very helpful people, but sadly he was killed in an aircraft accident not long after getting back to England. I am in France now on a different matter, but I felt that I would like to come here, just in case any of the people concerned are still alive but, although I have a few names, I don't know the name of the village where they lived, only that it must be a few kilometres south of the

Etang de Laguibe…so can you show me the voters' rolls for the villages in that area during the war?"

"You are in luck, Monsieur," he said, "I know exactly where to find these old papers, as I was asked for them only this morning!"

For a moment, I just didn't know what to say…obviously I had roused a hornet's nest into action, and the opposition – whoever they were – were a step ahead of me. However, I decided that I should exhibit nothing of this to the young clerk, and all I said was, "That's extraordinary, do you know who it was?"

"No, he said that he was a lawyer, trying to settle up an old affair – he was an elderly chap and had a young assistant with him. Anyway, I'll go and get the papers for you now."

He was away for a very long time, and when he came back, there was an elderly man with him, and they both looked annoyed, and also worried. It was the older man who spoke. "I'm very sorry, Monsieur, but the file which held these papers has been tampered with, and the relevant pages have been replaced with blank sheets. This is most unfortunate, and my colleague should have checked the file when it was returned this morning, but I can sympathise with his mistake, as I also saw the man who asked for the details, and he seemed entirely respectable. Tell me, is this matter important for you?"

For a moment, I was so disappointed that I couldn't think clearly, but then I realised that it might be counterproductive if I made a fuss. Who, I wondered, was looking over my shoulder? So I just said, "It is rather important, but it can wait. However, perhaps you could be kind enough see if copies of these sheets are available elsewhere? I shall be in Bayonne for the next few days, so I'll drop in to see you again in the hope that you can find these copies for me."

It was then late afternoon so I dismissed the idea of taking a drive up to the area of the Etang, preferring instead to get back to my hotel, have a quiet rest and just think things over. Instead, I am afraid, I went up to my room and turned on the TV and found myself looking at a dull episode of a soap…so dull that I nodded off, and didn't come round till dinner time.

After my meal I went into the little bar, and I found myself talking with a young man who was a lawyer in the town, and we spent an hour or so talking over the differences between the professions in France, as compared with Scotland. It was after that when he asked what I was doing in coming to Bayonne, and I felt that I could confide in him – to some extent – so I told him what I had told the clerk in the afternoon, namely, that I was just endeavouring to follow in my grandfather's footsteps. However, I didn't tell him about the missing papers as I was beginning to think that the less said the better. But we parted on good terms, and he said that he had several elderly clients, and that if I got stuck in finding information about wartime days, he could ask one or two of them to see if they could help. He gave me his telephone number, and I felt that he might well come in useful if I wasn't getting the information I wanted, so I told him not to be surprised if I contacted him again.

I did, though, remember to ring Granny, and before I could say anything, she said excitedly to me, "Charles, you'll never guess, but I've had that nice Squadron Leader from the Air Ministry on the phone this morning to tell me that he had been forced to send a fax to that lawyer in Paris, giving him a copy of Henry's report. Apparently, a representative from the French Embassy in London got in touch with the Foreign Office yesterday morning, asking them, as a matter of courtesy, if they could expedite the matter…and he had no excuse for delay…so had to send it off immediately. Apparently, he then tried to call me, but I was out for the day with friends, which explains why we didn't hear of it until today. I must confess that this worries me even more, as there are hidden forces working against us, and we don't know who they are. However, let's look on the bright side, if the opposition is an arm of the French government, at least we are not up against an illegal organisation."

She had been talking so quickly that I hadn't had a chance to tell her my news, but she suddenly stopped for a moment, and said, "Sorry, Charles, I do run on, don't I? But I worry about you…so I hope you'll forgive me. Now, what is your news?"

"My news," I said, "well, I am afraid it adds yet another puzzle to the pile we have already. You see, I went to the Mairie in Bayonne this afternoon to get the voters' rolls of the villages we are concerned with, only to be told that a lawyer had been in a few hours before me with the same request. That was bad enough, but when they got the files out for me, the relevant sheets had been replaced with blank paper."

"That settles it for me!" said Granny. "An organisation like this must point to a government department, no individual could have arranged these things – the intervention by the French embassy, and then this affair in Bayonne today. It's too complicated for me, but do give M. Duchene a ring right away and see if he has any ideas – and be sure to let me know as soon as you get any news."

I did so, but he was as baffled as Granny. She did agree, however, that everything pointed to an official organisation. "Everything," she said, "must stem from that little article in *The Herald* which appeared last Saturday, as the reaction has been remarkably swift. No doubt the Embassy scans all the main newspapers for any references to France, and it took them only until yesterday to arrange for M. Jeannot in Paris to ask for a copy of your grandfather's report, and then this morning to get somebody to dispose of the voters' rolls, which you wanted to refer to. So, my boy, what are your plans now?"

"There are two things to do," I said, "the first is to find the shop which Martins used to own, and see if anybody there can tell me where he lived. The other is that I met a young lawyer who was having a drink in the bar of my hotel, and he has offered to put me into touch with some of his elderly clients. So all is not lost…and I'll be in touch as soon as I have any news."

***

I drove the short distance into Biarritz after breakfast next morning, and parked the car in a side street off the wide road, La Prospective, which had a magnificent view out to the Atlantic Ocean, over a stretch of parkland. It took me no time at all to realise that it was a beautiful town, and I knew that it had been 'the' seaside resort in France, before the British found and made popular the Cote d'Azur on the Mediterranean coast. I asked a friendly looking elderly man if he could tell me where the best jeweller's shops were, and then struck pure gold when I said that I was looking for the shop which had been owned by a M. Martins before the war. His eyes lit up, and he beamed at me. "Know it? Of course I know it! Your mentioning that shop takes me back to 1939 when I was courting the lovely girl who was to become my wife. She had never got round to accepting my proposals, but then at the beginning of September, when the war broke out and I got my calling up papers, she relented, and I took her straight round to M. Martins' shop so that I could buy her an engagement ring. I knew that he would give me a fair deal as he was well respected in the town. I can still remember now how helpful he was and I have a strong suspicion that he sold it to me cheap, as I was wearing my uniform as a poilu, and got a far better looking ring than I thought I could afford. That is over sixty years ago, but I am very glad to say my dear wife still wears that ring today, beside her wedding ring."

He scorned the idea of giving me instructions, and insisted that he would lead me to it, and soon I found myself looking at a most elegant shop, with its windows filled with expensive-looking jewellery and timepieces. The name board had the proprietor's name in large, gold letters – Louis Duvier – but above the entrance door was a little sign – *Successor to M. Georges Martins*. I could see that my guide was curious about why I wanted this particular shop, but I felt that I had told too many people already about my quest, so I contented myself by thanking him as profusely as I could. Inside the shop, everything was as elegant as the exterior, and a suave young man came forward and asked if he could be of assistance. I'm afraid that I disappointed him when I said that I was not there to purchase, but was seeking information about the erstwhile owner of the shop, M. Martins. I said that I knew that he had been dead for many years, but I wondered if by any chance they knew where he had lived, as I was anxious to get in touch with his daughter, or her family. As I said this, an elderly man came out from the rear of the shop, saying, "I couldn't help hearing what you were saying, but I'm sorry to say that we cannot help you. As you may know, M. Martins died about sixty years ago, and he was long dead before I joined the firm…and none of my assistants have been with the firm since long after that."

I couldn't help getting the feeling that he wanted rid of me as soon as he could, and I also noticed another of his assistants looking rather doubtfully at him, so I took a chance and said in rather a loud voice, "That is unfortunate, you see

I am visiting Bayonne for just a few days to try to retrace the steps of my British grandfather, who was in the Royal Air Force during the War. He and his pilot had to bail out, in November 1942, quite near here and M. Martins helped him escape, so I wanted to express my thanks to any of his family whom I can get into touch with. If by any chance you can trace where he was living, I would be most grateful if you could contact me, I shall be in the Hotel Lousteau, probably until Sunday."

That seemed almost to alarm him, and he said very firmly, "There is no chance I can help you, Monsieur, I am sorry." So that was that, and I didn't risk looking back at the assistant who had been looking doubtful. I just hoped that he got the message about where I was staying in case he did know something, and cared about it enough to contact me.

I did one more thing that morning by going into a map shop and getting a large-scale map of the district, and I asked them if, by any chance, they had any maps of the district as it had been in the 1940s. To my surprise, the assistant smiled at me and said, "You're in luck, Monsieur, we were doing a clear out last week, and we came across a box of old maps, and nearly threw them out, but we decided to hang on to them, just in case we were asked for them…just give me a minute, and I'll see if this area is among the old maps we still have."

He was back in a surprisingly short time with a dusty sheet, which turned out to be a large scale map, dated 1938 – 1 cm to 1 km – and it covered just the right area for me so I bought one of each of the maps, one old and one new, and took my treasures back to my hotel room and had a careful look at them. In fact, there wasn't a great deal of difference between them, except for the new roads which had been built, and the boundaries of both Biarritz and Bayonne had spread over the years, but the area where Granddad had landed seemed unchanged…until I noticed one oddity. In the old map there was an indication of a small village with the name Urdes, but it didn't appear on the modern map so, when I went downstairs to have a drink before lunch, I asked around in the bar if anyone could tell me why this village had disappeared, but they were all young people and none of them seemed to know anything about it…or in fact be in the least interested.

So, in the afternoon, I drove north out of Bayonne through the village of Tarnos, and then to Ondres where I consulted my map and found a road which would take me to the Etang de Laguibe where Granddad had parachuted into France. I turned off down a minor road, and soon saw a direction post to the Etang, which was only a short distance away. I got out of the car when I arrived and made my way to the water's edge, but it was rather disappointing. I had felt that I would get some sensation of times gone by, but there was nothing. It was just an uninteresting stretch of water, and it was difficult to imagine that night when my grandfather had come down where I now was, and saw his pilot drowning far out in the middle of the water. In reading my grandfather's papers I had wondered why he didn't seem to have made any effort to save his friend, but now I saw that the Etang was much larger than I had thought and anybody who had landed in the water on that winter's night in full flying clothing, would have drowned very quickly.

I drove a little further along the road and found a turnoff to the right, but as I drove down it I saw nothing of interest and, a few miles later, it joined the main road to Bayonne from the west. So I retraced my steps, and then found another little road, marked on the old map as leading to Urdes. It obviously had very little traffic but, after about a couple of miles, I came to the ruins of a small house, then, a little further on, the ruins of another few houses. Everything pointed to this being the lost village of Urdes and what clinched it was when I went a bit further on, and found the ruins of what had been a quite substantial house. I parked the car, and fought my way through a jungle of weeds to what had been the front of the building, then going up what remained of the entrance steps, and I saw the remains of the tiles, which must have floored the hall. But it was all so derelict that again I had no sense of the drama, which had taken place all these years ago, despite the fact that this must have been old Martins' house.

What was also disappointing was that the road south from the old village was quite uninteresting, and there were no landmarks leading as it did through farmland, with an occasional field of vines. I decided there and then that it would be a great help if I could find somebody who remembered things as they had been in days gone by, before I tried to retrace the footsteps of my grandfather and his friend M. Jeanfils to where they had buried the jewels, and the all-important gold bowl with the fingerprints. Just to make sure that there were no indications to help me, I turned the car and drove back slowly up over the road again, and the only point of possible interest seemed to be an entrance to a private road, leading to what looked like a very large house, which was nearly a kilometre away. There was also what had been a patch of woodland, but the trees had been cut down years ago, and only some scrub and bushes remained. I was curious enough to get out of the car to have a look around, but soon decided that this could not have been the place, as there was certainly no large boulder to be seen as a marker point.

Anyway, I decided there was nothing more I could do there that day, so I retraced my steps to the car, and headed back to Bayonne to see if I could tie up one other loose end. I was curious to find out whether the transport firm of Jacques Juvenal still existed and so went back to the Mairie to see if they had old lists of trade firms. They did have, and the assistant from the previous day was glad to be able to do something for me now. However, although details of the firm were showing a 1940 list, there was no reference to them in any post-war ones. I had a nasty feeling that maybe Grandfather's escape with M. Juvenal might have come to the notice of the Germans, and I wondered what had happened to the firm and to him and to his family and colleagues.

So I decided then that it was time for tea back at my hotel, and perhaps also to do some constructive thinking…well, I did get the tea, but I am afraid that again I fell asleep before I could do anything else!

***

CHAPTER THREE

It was when I was about to come down for dinner that my phone rang and I was told that a Maurice Lefarge wished to speak to me, so I rushed downstairs to find – as I hoped – that it was the assistant from the jewellery shop. I went over and shook his hand enthusiastically. "I am very glad to see you, I did get the impression this morning that you wanted to speak to me, but it didn't seem wise to do anything about it at the time."

"You're right, M. Burton," he smiled. "I did want to speak to you, but I didn't dare to do so! There is something very odd going on, and –"

But I stopped him there. "Look, we'd better speak in private, how about my getting a bottle of wine sent up to my room, and that we talk there?"

He nodded his assent, and soon we were organised with a bottle and glasses, and seated in the comfortable chairs in my room. I thought that I had better start the ball rolling, so I said, "Did you hear, this morning, my explanation as to why I am here in Bayonne?"

"Yes, I did, you are trying to find an address for the family of old Martins, so that you can thank them for the help they gave to your grandfather, that's it, isn't it?"   "That is it, and I can't think of any reason why this enquiry of mine seemed to worry your manager."

"Well, I do know the reason, but it makes no sense at all! Let me say at once that the manager, M. Louis, has often talked about old M. Martins, and I'll be very surprised if he doesn't know what his address was, back in wartime days. But the puzzle began early yesterday afternoon when a very respectable, quite elderly gentleman, came in with a rather tough-looking young man and then, after a brief conversation with M. Louis – which I didn't hear – they were taken through to the office at the back of the shop. It happened just then that a lady came in who wanted me to show her what we could offer by way of gold bracelets...now she is one of our better customers, so I didn't show her any of the run-of-the-mill stuff. We went into the security store at the rear – which is next to the office – to get a tray of our choice bracelets from the safe. As I was doing this, I couldn't help overhearing the elderly man say to M. Louis...and it was so out of character with his appearance, 'Now, is that quite clear? If the young man from Scotland comes in and asks where old Martins used to live...well, you don't know...and make bloody sure that none of your other assistants speak to him! It will be better if I do not tell you the reason for my request and, although I call it a request, you will be very sorry if you choose to disobey.'"

"I wish," M. Lefarge went on, "that I could have heard the rest, but although that bit was quite clear, his next words must have been spoken quietly, and although I'm not quite sure, I think he said, 'Perhaps I should tell you that I represent the...' Sadly, I couldn't make out anything after that, so all I could do was to take the tray of bracelets back to my customer and I am glad to say that she did buy a very expensive one from me! Soon afterwards, I saw M. Louis show the men out and, when the shop was empty, he called us together and said that the men to whom he had been talking were with the government, and that he had been warned not to answer any questions from a young Scotsman – a M. Burton – who might come in to the shop. You know, if he had gone on to tell us a better story, I might have believed him, but what he said was that you, M. Burton, had been sent here to make up a sensational story for a Scottish paper called the *Herald*. He went on to say that you were trying to invent details of old wartime events involving escaping air crews and that you didn't mind libelling the dead, so long as they were French, in writing these ridiculous stories. He then said that they suspected that you were working on a story involving old M. Martins, the original owner of the shop, and so it was important that we did not help you by way giving any details of old addresses, either of him or his family. He then pointed out to us, not very convincingly, that any stories about him might be picked up by our local papers and have a bad effect on the trade in our shop."

"What worried me," he went on, "was that when he spoke to us he didn't look concerned about the affair, he just looked plain frightened, and I couldn't equate his story with what I saw of you this morning when you came into the shop. But, before I go on, perhaps you can tell me just why you are here?"

For a moment, I didn't quite know what to say, but then I decided that as he was confiding in me, I should do the same to him – to some extent at least! So I said, "M. Lefarge, what I told your M. Louis this morning is quite true, and I am here to retrace the steps of my grandfather, who was in the RAF in November 1942 and had to bail out of his crippled plane somewhere near here. What I want to do is see if I can get into touch with the family of M. Martins, who helped him to escape to Spain. However, that isn't the complete story… certainly I do want to thank them…but also I may be able to help them to recover a treasure in jewellery which a German officer tried – and failed – to steal from him. He failed because my grandfather and a Frenchman with him were able to surprise the German and to kill him. But the whole affair seems to have cast a long shadow, and even that isn't the entire story, but some of it I must still keep to myself. I am hopeful, however, that if I can meet the Martins it will all be resolved quite soon."

M. Lefarge looked thoughtful. "You know," he said, "what puzzles me is how keen they are to keep this old address from you, as old Martins died in 1942, so he hasn't been there for some sixty years, and anyway it is no great secret as there must, even now, be at least a few people who remember it…as I do!"

"You know it!" I broke in. "That is wonderful…but how on earth do you happen to know it?"

"Easy, you see I sometimes have to go through the old stock books, which we have going back as far as 1935, as we are often consulted by heirs who have inherited jewellery, and are interested to find out when items were purchased, and at what price. Now these books also contain correspondence about things like this, and up till 1941 they were from M. Martins, so I have often seen his address on these letters…and I pinched one this afternoon!"

He stopped there, and fished a sheet of paper from his pocket and handed it to me. I unfolded it, and the heading read: M. Georges Martins, Chateau Urdes, Urdes. It was just as I had expected. That old ruined village and the house I had seen was indeed where Martins had lived, and where Grandfather had come to. It was also the one which had now been erased from the map. "Tell me," I said, "do you know anything about Urdes? It's shown on old maps, but now it seems to have disappeared."

"No, but I believe that there was some kind of German purge there during the war, apparently a German officer was murdered, and the few who lived in Urdes just disappeared. I know that sounds awful, but very few people were involved, it was only a tiny village, with just a group of about four houses and Martins' chateau. My late father did mention it, but apparently there never was any explanation from the Germans. One day the chateau and the houses were there, the next day they were demolished, and it would seem likely that Martins was killed during that operation. These things, and many others like them, happened, I am afraid, during the time these bloody Germans were here. Nobody could ask questions at the time, and after the war very few people bothered."

I hope that I said an adequate thank you to Lefarge, but his information horrified me. I had always imagined that the village would have continued, despite the death of Martins, the squire, but now it seemed as if everyone had either been killed or taken into captivity – and what had happened to Pierre, my prime suspect? Anyway, I did my best with some more wine, and he went on his way quite happily. But then it was back to work again and before I had dinner, I first phoned Granny, and then Duchene in Paris. Granny was interested, but still worried for my safety. Duchene, however, was pleased. "That is most interesting news and, to use an English phrase, the plot thickens! But as for any explanations of these events of today, I'm ashamed to say that I have none."

We talked for a while, and then agreed that the best thing for me to do – now that there were no old villagers to talk to – was to think and try to come up with ideas as to how I could now possibly find the present address of Martins' family. The best idea I could come up with was to take up the offer that the young lawyer had made the previous evening, and see if he could introduce me to some of his elderly clients. So, after dinner, I gave him a ring, and I was glad to find that he was still friendly, and offered help at once. "Look, M. Burton, one of my old friends is coming round this evening in less than half an hour to play chess with me…come to my house right now and you can have a chat with him before our game. He is, I may say, one of these lucky oldsters, in that he is nearly ninety but still manages often to beat me at chess."

It took me longer that I had thought to find his house, so I got there just a few minutes before the old man, M. Etienne Marchand, and when I was introduced to him, he looked at me with keen interest. "Tell me, what is a young Scotsman doing here? You all seem these days to be just passing through on your way to some of the cheap Spanish costas."

So, once again I had to relate a somewhat shortened version of my story, and the reason why I wanted to get in touch with the descendants of M. Martins. I could see, and hear, that he was interested. "Well now," he said, "it may surprise you to learn that I attended the wedding of Martins' daughter, it must have been in either 1938 or 1939 – certainly before the war – but I haven't the slightest recollection of the name of her husband, although I do remember her name, Julie. She was a pretty young girl – can't have been more than twenty, maybe less – but the wedding was a very grand affair in the cathedral."

"But you can't remember the name of the husband?"

He shook his head, and my heart sank. Certainly knowing that the girl was called Julie was something, but without a surname I was little further on. But then he laughed. "You must forgive me, M. Burton…but I am teasing you! You see, while I don't remember the name, I can easily find it! My dear wife, you see, has always made a point of keeping all the papers dealing with the weddings we have attended, and

I'm sure this one will be in the file she has. If you are in a hurry I can give her a ring now."

It was as easy as that. He did phone his wife, and when she rang back in less than ten minutes, he passed me the phone to me, and she told me that Julie Martins had married Jean Lebrun on 22nd June 1939, and she even had a letter from her thanking them for their wedding present. Sadly, however, it had been written before the marriage, so the address on the letter was that of her father in Urdes, and neither she nor her husband could remember where Julie had gone to with her new husband. So for that we had to rely on that statement in Granddad's notes, which said that she lived in Avignon. Anyway, I thanked her, and then M. Marchand, for the help they had given me, and congratulated him on his wife's filing system.

"Nothing to it!" he smiled, I'm lucky too as my memory still isn't too bad, fact is I can still remember what we gave the girl, it was a silver epergne which I bought in an antique shop in Biarritz. How's that for a nearly ninety-year-old man! Anyway, good luck in your quest, and if you find Julie, please give her my regards…but I haven't seen her since 1939, so I wonder if she will remember me?"

I left them to get on with their chess game and hastened back to my hotel so that I could phone M. Duchene again as it had occurred to me that he might be able to help, and save me a lot of time. So, when I reached him, I said that I now knew the details of Martins' daughter's marriage – her new name, but no address – and that we had now to rely on she or her family still being in Avignon. I then said that I intended to go there first thing in the morning and was just about to ask for his help, but he was ahead of me. "Charles, I'll ring my correspondent there in the morning and ask him to do some checking up to see if any of them still live in the town…and that shouldn't be too difficult."

He then gave me the name and address of the Avignon firm, and also the name of his lawyer friend, a M. Chevalier, and told me to ring him as soon as I got fixed up in a hotel."

"It is a fair distance," he went on, "must be the best part of six hundred kilometres by way of Toulouse and Narbonne, but it is Autoroute almost all the way, so it is quite an easy journey. Better make an early start, and I'll tell him to expect your call in the early afternoon. By the way, I can recommend that you stay at the Fimotel which has the advantage of being on the orbital road round Avignon and is easy to find. I was there a year ago, and it should do you very well. My advice is to leave your car there, and take a taxi when you want to go into the town as parking is difficult. This case is getting most interesting, be sure to ring me tomorrow evening!"

***

Next morning I took his advice, had an early breakfast, and was on my way not long after half past seven, and I got to the Fimotel in time for a late lunch, feeling rather pleased with myself. And I was even more pleased when I rang M. Chevalier, to find that he had been busy and had all the information I required.

"I know, M. Burton," he said, "that you are pressed for time, so just get paper and pencil and I'll tell you what I have found."

I still have the notes I scribbled down – notes which were going to have a remarkable effect on my life!

Mlle Julie Masters had married M. Jean Lebrun in June 1939 who was then an accountant, working in the Banque Lyonnaise.

An only son, Gaspard, had been born in 1944 and had married a Mlle Yvette Laurent in 1974

A daughter, Michelle, had been born in 1980

M. Jean Lebrun had died in 1972

M. Gaspard Lebrun had died in 1988 (as the result of an accident)

Mme Yvette Lebrun had died in 1990

As I scanned this information, I realised that the only people on the list, who were still alive, were Martin's daughter Mme Julie Lebrun, who must now be about eighty, and her granddaughter, the young Mlle Michelle Lebrun. Finally – and best of all – there was the address of the house where Mme Julie lived, and I could only hope that the young Michelle lived there also.

I thanked M. Chevalier profusely for his help, and said that I would be in touch again before I left Avignon, and hastened down to the foyer to call a taxi. I took nothing with me except the sheets of paper – with the official statement by Grandfather, and the notes he had written – both in the original English and in French translation, and I wondered what the old lady would think of me, turning up more than some sixty years after the murder of her father. I was taken through the town and into a residential area of substantial houses, and in a quiet cul-de-sac of terrace houses. My taxi stopped outside Mme Julie Lebrun's house and, just in case they were out, I asked the driver to wait. It was with a sense of keen interest that I rang the bell and, a few moments later, the door was opened by a very pretty young girl who looked rather doubtfully at me and I reckoned she was wondering just what I was going to try to sell to her. “Don’t worry,” I said, “I’m not going to try to sell you anything, but tell me, are you Mlle Michelle?”

“That’s right,” she smiled, “and you…?”

“Well, it is a long story, but for now, just let me tell you that my name is Burton, and my grandfather was in Urdes in November 1942 when your grandfather was murdered.”

Her reaction astonished me, as she started back, with her arms akimbo, and shouted at me, “You bastard! How can you have the nerve to come here – even although it is some sixty years since your grandfather murdered mine! Whatever it is you want to say, I don’t want to hear it…we have long memories…and I’m not going to have my grandmother upset by seeing you…or anybody from your bloody family!”

I was so surprised that I had moved back a little from the door, and this allowed her to slam it in my face before I could say anything else. My chagrin was not helped when I saw that my driver was laughing at how I had been received but, when he saw my face, he had the good sense not to say anything. I had no alternative but to go back to the cab, and I said to the driver, “Just wait a bit, will you, it is all a misunderstanding, and I’m going to post a note through the letterbox.”

He gave that Gallic shrug of the shoulders which is the one bit of Frenchness impossible for a foreigner to learn, but it obviously meant: “There is one born every minute!”

As I sat down in the cab, the only explanation I could come to was that the Germans had spread some false story, so as to clear the name of their Major Hassell, and that they had blamed Grandfather in some way. I decided that I had better try to clear things up right away, so I got out Grandfather’s two statements, both in English and in French, and wrote a short note in French:

"Mlle Michelle, somebody must have told your family an absurd tale, do please

just read these two documents. The first is to the Air Force by my grandfather after his escape, and the second is some notes, which he wrote a few days after that, just before he was killed. These notes my family have only now found, which is why we have not in bygone years tried to contact your grandmother with a view to finding, and returning, your grandfather's valuables, which the German Major tried to steal. This is the only reason why I have come to France and I'll wait in my taxi till you are ready to speak to me."

Under the sardonic gaze of the driver I rang the bell, before posting this and Granddad's notes, through her letter-box, and returning to the taxi to await results. It took longer than I expected before the door opened again, and she came out, and said, "It would seem that I may owe you an apology, M. Burton, do please come in, my grandmother is very keen to speak to you."

I felt I had better make things less serious, so I smiled at her. "I'm glad, Michelle," I said, "that I am no longer a pariah, do you think it is now safe for me to pay off my cab?"

For the first time I got a tentative smile from her. "I think, Monsieur, that you can take a chance on that..."

As I paid off the driver, he gave me a dirty leer. "Bonne chance, Monsieur, she's lovely, but my God, she does have a temper!"

It was with that ringing in my ears that she led me into the hall, and then stopped and gave me just a tiny smile. "My grandmother is recovering at present from a nasty fall, just last week, when she sprained her ankle quite badly. It is getting better, but she is in bed this afternoon. Come, follow me..."

And she led me upstairs and into a front bedroom, a big sunny room, where I saw an elderly lady with a cap of silver hair, holding the papers in her hands, and looking up at me with an expression of keen interest, but still with a shadow of doubt. "Come over and sit beside me, here, on that chair. The unfortunate misunderstanding with Michelle when you arrived is because my husband and I were led to believe, back in 1942…and subsequently all my family also were…that it was an escaping British airman, a Flying Officer Burton, who killed my father, and then stole his valuables, aided by a Frenchman M. Jeanfils whom I had known as a young girl, so you can appreciate her feelings when you showed up on the doorstep. I should think her only surprise was that you didn't have horns and a tail! But now you have come with a very different story, which contradicts all we have believed for some sixty years. It is hard to change such long held opinions, but despite that I am almost convinced that your story is true…no, that's wrong, as in fact must be true!"

She paused and shook her head, as if to shake all the lies from it, then went on, "So, you are the grandson of Flying Officer Burton? It seems incredible, as I never thought that we would see any of his family. I'll tell you later how my husband and I came to Britain after the war, hoping to find him, and to confront him with his crime. Well, we tried, but of course found that he had been killed. Anyway, I suggest that Michelle gets us all some wine, and I shall then tell you the story we have been led to believe until now…then, after that, it will be your turn."

There were a few minutes, during which I had the good sense to remain silent, while Michelle brought in a tray of glasses, and a bottle of red wine. It was after the three of us were served that Mme Lebrun turned to me and said, "These were awful days, that early winter of 1942…you and the Americans had just invaded North Africa, and the

Bosche had moved south in France, and had taken over this previously unoccupied part of the country, and we…all of us…couldn't help wondering if the agony would ever cease. I knew, of course, that my father was then living alone, but he refused all our invitations to leave Urdes and come to stay with my husband and me here. He was an independent old man, very fit for his years, and seemed to enjoy being solitary. Anyway, my husband and I got a visit one evening in 1942, I think it was on the third or fourth of December, from a Major Kreitzer who was stationed here in Avignon, who told us that their local HQ in Biarritz had been in touch with him with a request that he come to see me and, sadly, to tell me the bad news that my father was dead. He explained that a British airman, a Flying Officer Burton and a local Frenchman by the name of Jeanfils, had broken into his house, possibly with a view to get money to aid their escape from France, but that my father had disturbed them during the course of their crime, and came up to them with his shotgun, and told them to leave – just to leave – as he made no effort to restrain them. But that wasn't good enough for that pair, as they easily overpowered him and took his gun. Just as they did so, the German officer in charge of the district, a Major Hassell, called to see my father as he often did, and the British officer at once shot him with my father's gun, and then shot him a second time with the Major's revolver. He must have then decided that the only way for them to avoid discovery was to shoot my father, and this he then did, using the shotgun and also the German gun to confuse investigations, after which they opened a big safe in the living room of the house with my father's key, and went off with the treasure in jewels which he kept there."

"Just try, M. Burton," she went on, "to imagine how I felt when I heard this, he was very persuasive, but then we both wondered how he could be so precise about the events and said so."

"That is easily explained. He told me that there had been a witness to the whole affair, as a young man who lived in the district, Pierre Dupont, had also come to the Chateau that afternoon, and happened to be outside the living room window, and saw everything..."

"Pierre Dupont!" I broke in, "that's the bloke I want to find, and so far I only have had his Christian name...but now–"

But then it was her turn in interrupt. "I'm afraid," she said, "as you will hear, that information isn't going to help you, just be patient and listen to the rest."

She paused, as if to gather her thoughts, before going on. "I can still visualise that damn German officer, so immaculately dressed in his smart uniform, even with an Iron Cross, and he was so proper that it was difficult not to believe just what he said. Anyway, he then went on to say that if only the young Pierre had come to the German HQ immediately they might have caught, what he called, the murdering pair, but he was afraid lest he be blamed, and he had delayed for a vital hour or two, and although they at once endeavoured to trace your father and M. Jeanfils they were too late."

"He then went on to say that it was a great pity, as if they had known just a little earlier they might have prevented their escaping with my father's jewels. But he told us that they had managed to escape that very night to Spain, taking the loot with them."

She stopped again, and said, "Do you know, I can still remember that he smiled after he said that, and he told us, almost with relish, that there would be no more people escaping to Spain by the method they had used. Apparently, they had suspected a transport concern in Bayonne, called Charrier, and had gone there that night, but not soon enough, as your grandfather and M. Jeanfils had already crossed the frontier by then. But they were able to interrogate the other people there who told them the names – Flying Officer Burton and Emile Jeanfils – and also that of the driver Jacques Juvenal, who had driven them to Spain. I shudder to think what methods they used to get that information from the others in that firm, and from Jacques' wife. I knew them quite well from the days when I lived at home but she wasn't there after the war."

She paused again, then went on, "As I have told you, he was very persuasive, and he finished by saying that the German authorities would not let the matter rest there…that we French people were under their protection…and, when Britain was defeated, they would make every effort to bring the miscreants to justice, and try to recover what had been stolen. At the time, we really had no alternative but to believe the story as there was no way that either of us could get to Urdes to investigate matters on the spot. I did in fact write to a friend in Biarritz but although she had no hard information, she had heard a rumour about a German officer being killed by an escaping British airman…but was frightened then to investigate further. My husband dealt with my father's estate, and I'll tell you later about a time after the war when we went back. So please forgive your reception by Michelle, she has been as brainwashed as I have been for all these long years. But for now that is enough from me, and before I give you the rest of the story, please tell us how you came to find this paper, and what you plan to do."

So I told them all the reasons why the matter had been left for so long, and our finding the papers after so many years in the secret compartment in the desk, and then I came to the odd events of the last few days…the enquiry to the Defence Ministry from the French lawyer, M. Jeannot, the approach to them from the French embassy in London, the theft from the Mairie in Bayonne of the voters' rolls for the wartime years, and the warning to the shop manager in Biarritz not to give me M. Martins address. "It is all very odd," I said. "None of these things could stop us finding out the various pieces of information eventually, but they would cause delay, and I wonder if whoever it was just wanted me to give up the chase as not being worth the bother? But now that I have found you and Michelle, there are two more things I can do, the first is to try to locate the spot where my grandfather and M. Jeanfils buried your father's valuables, and then bring that bastard Pierre Dupont to justice…now that I know his surname as well as his Christian name it should be possible to find him, and you will remember that his fingerprints should still be on that gold bowl. I know that you didn't think we could bring him to book, but I don't think the long time which has elapsed will matter, as they are now very smart at enhancing latent prints."

But she shook her head sadly. "No chance of doing that I am afraid…and I'd better tell you now that my husband and I began to make our own researches into the affair and, in 1944, as soon as that part of France was freed, we went back to Urdes, only to find that the Chateau was a ruin, and the four little houses which made up the village had been demolished. Nobody then knew where the six old people, and also of course M. Jeanfils and Pierre Dupont, were…they had all disappeared at the end of that November two years previously. It was as if the place had never existed, and because of what you have told me this afternoon, I think I now know the reason why they decided to make the whole affair a kind of non-event. You see, M. Burton, they must have been terrified lest the story of Major Hassell's homosexuality came out, as for the Nazis that was a cardinal, almost a sub-human sin. But there is a snag in that idea. You see, if they were terrified lest that tale get out, why did they let Pierre Dupont go free?"

"Go free?" I exclaimed, "but from what you said earlier, isn't he dead?"

"No, he was very much alive at that time…you see, that same friend of mine in Biarritz to whom I wrote in the winter of 1942, was in Marseilles in the summer of 1943, nine months after my father was killed, and she happened to see Pierre in the street one day. She had a few words with him, but he seemed ill at ease, and quickly broke off the conversation."

"So," I said, "he was alive then, and – "

But she broke in. "Just hear the rest of it. We had no time to do any further researches in 1944, as we were busy with the arrival of my son, Gaspard, who was born in December of that year. But by the summer of 1945, the war was over and we took ourselves to Marseilles for a little holiday to stay with my husband's young brother who was then a hospital doctor…but who also from time to time did some jobs for the gendarmes by way of examining, and reporting on, the corpses of accident or murder victims. We had told him, of course, of the story of Father's death and, while we were staying with him, there was one of these extraordinary coincidences. He was called out one evening to make a report on the body of a young man who had drowned, seemingly after accidentally falling into one of the docks. It was treated as a simple case of death by drowning, and a head injury on the body could have been caused by his hitting a wall as he fell. Police enquiries showed that on the previous evening he had been with a crowd of his friends in a dock side cafe´, and that very likely they had all had too much to drink. There really was nothing for the gendarmes to investigate, and two of his drinking companions went to the mortuary and confirmed his name as that of their friend Pierre Dupont…so that was that."

"Anyway," she went on, "that was in 1945 and in the autumn of that year, soon as the war was over, my husband and I went to Britain to try to find your grandfather and to get our revenge. It didn't take us long, while we were in London, to find that he had been killed and that his widow lived in Paisley, up in Scotland near Glasgow, and we decided that it really wasn't worth the journey, and who were we to appear out of the blue and bring distress to a young widow?"

"It is a pity you didn't," I broke in, "as if you had I'm pretty sure Granny would have approached the Air Ministry then, and you would have got Granddad's report, and things might have been cleared up all these years ago."

"You're right," she said, "it would have been great to get to the truth then… however, better late than never, what are your plans, and what help do you want from us?"

"Easy, first of all we should try to find these valuables of yours, it shouldn't be too difficult to find a standing stone, somewhere a few miles from your father's old house, and I'm only sorry that we can't bring that bastard Pierre Dupont to book."

It was when I said that I noticed that Michelle was sitting up and looking intently at her Grandmother. "Look, Granny, doesn't it occur to you that the death of Pierre was, shall I say, rather convenient for him! He must have known that you and Granddad would come looking for him after the war, so is there any chance that his death was faked? And remember also the suggestion that he and his German lover had stolen more things, could he have run off with them?"

For a few moments that silenced both Mme Lebrun and me, but then she looked up. "Michelle, I must confess that I did wonder at the time, but it seemed so unlikely then that

I didn't pursue the idea...but maybe now we should try and look into it."

Then she turned to me. "M. Burton, I happen to know that Michelle is preparing a large pot au feu for our evening meal, I wonder if I can persuade you to join us? You see, I have more to tell you but for now I should like to have a rest for a little while. However, I can come down and join the two of you at, say, seven o'clock...is that agreeable?"

I needed no persuading because, for much of the afternoon, I had been glancing at Michelle whenever I felt I could do so without her seeing me, and I was coming to realise what a very attractive girl she was. She was not a conventional beauty, as her face tended to be a little severe, but whenever she smiled it was as if her face lit up, and she became almost a dazzling beauty.

"Mme Lebrun," I said, "I shall be more than delighted to stay and have dinner with you and Michelle...but only on one condition."

"What's that?" she smiled.

"Very simple, M. Burton is far too formal, will you call me Charles?"

"Of course, and you'd better call me Julie, everybody else seems to do so! And don't drink too much with Michelle before I come down to join you! We have a lot to talk about, and will need clear heads to consider this idea of hers and also the puzzle of who is trying to hinder your enquiries... that is very odd."

***

CHAPTER FOUR

I went downstairs with Michelle, and she first took me into a big room to the front of the house, but it was one of these rooms which was obviously intended for the reception of guests, and I wasn't sorry when she turned and said, "This room is far too stuffy, let's go into the family room…" She led me to a pleasantly untidy little room, with windows looking over the garden, and with very comfortable looking chairs. We sat on either side of the empty fireplace – no need for a fire, as it was a warm afternoon – and she looked at me with a smile. "I hope, Charles, that you have forgiven me for your reception, but ever since I was a little girl I have heard of this wicked British airman, Flying Officer Burton, and so I was horrified when you introduced yourself. But now I find it absolutely fascinating, just to think that we may now get to the bottom of this awful affair, which has been a source of grief to my family for all these long years."

By this time I was agreeable to forgive this most attractive girl just about anything, so that little bit of forgiveness was easy to do. It was after I made my little speech that I went on. "But, I can tell you one thing, Michelle…I do agree with you in viewing the supposed death of Pierre with suspicion, and if he did manage to get away from Urdes with some of the loot that he and Major Hassell had acquired, then maybe it is just possible that he could afford to pay to get a new identity, as a precaution in case any enquiries arose after the war."

"Yes," she said thoughtfully, "and if this is true he has done a pretty good job of it...but surely it must be impossible that he has now heard of your investigation and can be behind the effort to put you off the chase?"

We talked a little more about the affair, but without achieving anything except to feel even more puzzled, but then our conversation turned to ourselves, and she enquired how I came to speak French so well. When I finished, telling her about Granny, who had come from Nice before the war, and how I had been brought up by her, she suddenly surprised me by changing to English, and while she made the odd mistake, she was fluent, and spoke with a quite delightful accent. "Come on, Michelle," I said, "you speak English beautifully, why is it that you too speak a foreign language so well?"

"Don't flatter me," she smiled, "I know that my English isn't perfect, I'm sure I should have worked harder at it, but maybe you'll allow me to make use of you while you are here...let's use English, and please correct me where I make any mistakes...is it a deal?"

"Of course, and to begin with do please tell me about your life from infancy to the present day...that will give me a chance to find out why your English is so good. And don't think I'll be bored, I shall be fascinated, so long of course that you don't censor your story too much."

"And what, M. Burton," she laughed, "makes you think that there are any episodes in my young life which require censorship? I am, of course, as pure as the driven snow!"

"If you say so," I said very seriously, "and I'll do my very best to believe it!"

"Just you do that, and first I'd better tell you why I can speak English, you see, my father, Gaspard, married an English girl – "

"But," I broke in, "when I was trying to trace your family and where you lived, I saw that your mother was a Mlle Yvette Laurent – "

It was now her turn to interrupt me. "That's right, but, you see, my Laurent grandfather was French, and he went to England when France fell in 1940 and joined the Free French. His good luck was that he married a wonderful English girl, and they had a very happy life together. My dear mother was their only child, and they gave her the rather French sounding name of Yvette and although she was brought up in England her French father saw to it that she could speak French. Anyway, she and my father met in the early seventies when they were both doing postgraduate work at the Sorbonne, he in his field of biochemistry, and she in French literature, and they spent all their married life here in Avignon. So I grew up in a bilingual household, and you and I have been equally lucky in that respect."

We beamed at each other in a spirit of mutual congratulations, and I went on, "You know, when all this nonsense is cleared up, both you and Julie must come and see my grandmother and me in Scotland. I know that she would love to have both of you to stay, and it would be especially interesting for her to have the opportunity to meet Julie and to talk about old times, as they both grew up in France before the war changed everything. It would also be a treat for her to be able to talk with real French people as, despite the fact that she has lived in Scotland for more than sixty years, she still considers herself to be French…and to be proud of it."

"I agree with that entirely," she smiled, "and I would very much like it if Granny and I could come to Scotland, as so far I've only been to England." As she said that, the day suddenly became brighter. I was coming to realise this girl was really something very special. She then went on to tell me briefly about her school days, and then her time at the University of Lyons, but I noticed that she never mentioned anything much about her private life. I had the good sense, however, not to press her about that. *Sometime, but not just yet…*

Anyway, I didn't in fact have much time to enquire, even if I had wished to do so, as we heard the sound of Julie beginning to stir, and Michelle went off to help her downstairs, and then I followed her so as to provide an extra pair of helping hands. She was in fact fairly mobile, as her ankle was well strapped up, but she was glad of some help, and we were soon able to settle her in one of the chairs. When she sat down she gave a sigh of relief. "That's better, I do so dislike lying in bed when there is so little the matter with me…now, Michelle, you know what I want!"

"Yes, Granny, I certainly do, and I should think that Charles will be of a like mind!" She bustled off for a few minutes to see to things in the kitchen, but her main duty was to come back with a tray of glasses and to dispense our aperitifs. There was a choice, but we all settled for Ouzo, something which I never drink except when I am in France, but seemed then to like it very much. It was while we were still on our first glass that we began to talk again about the death of Pierre…had it really happened?…and Julie surprised me by saying that she thought that Michelle and I should go to Marseilles next day and speak to her Great Uncle, Dr. Xavier Lebrun, who, by an odd coincidence, had done the autopsy on Pierre, or whoever was supposed to have been.

She paused there before going on. "It may seem absurd to you, Charles, that I can remember Xavier's involvement, but if you go and see him tomorrow…all will then be revealed! I can tell you that my dear brother-in-law, Xavier, has often annoyed me with his obsession for accurate filing, and never throwing out old papers. But this may well be useful for us now because my bet is that if we can get him interested he may be able to turn up his original notes on the case. I know that he was involved as I was with him at the time. However, it is never easy to get him motivated to do anything so, if you agree, I'll phone him now and tell him enough to make him interested. He will be astonished to hear your name, and that you are the grandson of our pet villain. But I'll tell him briefly that we have been wrong about the past, and after that I'm sure he will be interested to meet you. I'm also certain that you will be invited for lunch…and I can tell you also that it will be worth eating, as since he was a boy, cooking has been his hobby. You will find it, Charles, quite a pleasant run down to Marseilles, it is only about a hundred kilometres and is Autoroute almost all the way, so you should get there in not much more than an hour, except for the last bit in the city traffic."

She picked up the phone and, after the introductions, said to him, "Would it be convenient if Michelle came for lunch tomorrow? There is something about which we want your help."

There was an obvious assent, and then, "She will be bringing a young man with her, M. Charles Burton, a grandson of Flying Officer Henry Burton – "

But she didn't get any further than that, and I could hear what was obviously a very surprised enquiry, but she broke in, "Let's keep everything as a surprise till they get to you tomorrow, but for now just let me say that we have been wrong for all these years about what actually happened on that day when my father was killed. Why they are coming to see you is because it is possible that you can help us to solve a very old puzzle."

And, despite all his entreaties, that was all she would tell him. But then Michelle picked up the phone to arrange when we should arrive, and after that he must have made some enquiry about her relations with me, and I was surprised to see her look a little embarrassed, saying, "Don't be silly, I only met him a few hours ago!"

But then she looked up at me, and I saw her blushing which – I felt – was a hopeful sign. Dinner was a splendid meal, cold Vichyssoise followed by the pot-au-feu I had been promised, and washed down with a superb wine from a little way to the north, a Chateauneuf-du-Pape from the Rhone valley, which was pure ruby magic. Michelle smiled at me as she saw how much I was enjoying the wine, and I explained that Granny had given me a careful education about wines – particularly from France – and that almost all our holidays had been spent in France, several of them in Burgundy, others in the Bordeaux area or in her home town of Nice where I could learn about the very underrated wines of the south. They then enquired as to whether I had any relations there...but I hadn't...Granny had been an only child, and she had lost touch with such few cousins as she'd had.

Not long after we had finished dinner I saw that Julie was looking tired, so I excused myself, saying that as Michelle and I were off to Marseilles in the morning, an 'early to bed' was the order of the day for me. As regards our journey to Marseilles, she said that she would pick me up at the hotel at ten o'clock. "It will be easier," she said, "if we take my car, as I know the way. The bit on the Autoroute is easy, but it gets complicated once we get to the city."

This I could happily agree with, but I firmly refused her offer to run me back to the hotel, and got her to ring for a taxi. After I had said my thanks to them for the splendid meal, Julie said to me, "Charles, I am going to enjoy this quest of yours, which has now become one for Michelle and me as well. Do you know, I feel years younger tonight than I felt this morning!"

That remark of hers must, for some odd reason, have reminded me of a thought I'd had. "Do you know," I said, "I wish I had seen a picture of this man, Pierre Dupont, so that I could visualise him…did you know him when you lived in Urdes?"

"Oh yes, he was some years younger than me, and when I got married he must have been about seventeen, he was somewhat of a misfit and, as I remember it, he never seemed to play with the other village children. He was, of course, called up when the war broke out, but there must have been some medical problem, as he never went away. His father was very elderly to be a father, and had been a gardener in the chateau until he retired, and after that he and his wife – aided I presume by Pierre – ran a tiny small holding on the outskirts of the village."

"And what did he look like?"

"Nothing very remarkable, but he was tall – about a hundred and eighty centimetres, maybe more – quite slim, a bit weedy in fact."

"And what about his hair colouring?"

"Very fair as I remember it…yes, that's right, he was blond."

As she spoke, I was getting a quite clear picture of this slim, fair-haired youth, who must have attracted Major Hassell, and it somehow made me keener than ever to pursue the quest…especially as I was to be accompanied on the morrow by this lovely girl. So, it was with that happy thought that I said good night to her as she came out to see me off in my taxi, and I took a chance by leaning forward to give her a chaste kiss on her cheek.

"Good night, Charles," she said very quietly, "see you in the morning."

And for a moment she gently stroked my cheek, then blew me a kiss as I got into my cab.

It was then only just after nine o'clock, so it wasn't too late to make my telephone calls both to Granny and to M. Duchene; they were delighted to hear of my progress, and shared my interest in finding out all we could about Pierre.

"Just wait till tomorrow!" I said to each of them.

***

Next morning I was out in the forecourt of the hotel long before ten o'clock, which was just as well as she too was early – if not quite so early as me. I settled down comfortably in her nippy little car – a sporty Peugeot 206 1.4GLX – and for a while we talked trivialities as we zoomed south down the Autoroute, but then she began to tell me about her great uncle, whom we were going to meet. "He and my grandfather," she said, "were very different, in some ways, yet almost identical in others. My granddad was tall and well built, a very keen rugby player when he was young, and he skied to almost Olympic standards. As for Xavier, his younger brother, he was quite short and tubby, and hated team games, in fact almost all kinds of exercise. So, you see, they were opposites as regards physical things, yet in their work they were very much alike…both dedicated to what they did in their respective fields. Granddad – like my father – in biochemistry, where they both did world class research, and Xavier as a physician in his young days as a doctor, until, in mid thirties, he changed to specialising in psychiatry."

As she said that we reached the end of the Autoroute, and joined the city traffic, and I could see why she had suggested that we take her car, and let her drive. I had often been in France before and I knew how macho the male drivers were but Michelle was up to all their tricks, and it didn't take long before we turned off into a quiet street where her great uncle lived, and stopped in the middle of a terrace of houses. "Right, here we are," she said, "that wasn't too bad, was it?"

I can't remember what my reply was, but it would seem to have been adequate, as she took my hand as I got out of the car. "Good, I hate nervous passengers, go and ring the bell, as I've got some things to get out of the car which Julie has sent…she always likes to send him some odds and ends of fancy grub when we come down. So, I went up to the door and rang the bell, and almost as I did so the door opened and I saw a little man smiling at me who could have made an excellent Poirot. He was short and tubby, as Michelle had said, with rosy cheeks and a pair of pince-nez perched somewhat insecurely on his nose. "So," he said, "you are the grandson of our favourite villain, that's a real turn up for the book! Come in now…and you too Michelle…I'll get some coffee ready and we'll have it out in the garden."

It was when we were all settled that he turned to me. "Don't keep me waiting any longer, Charles, as I can hardly believe dear Julie having you in her house, let alone allowing you to come here with Michelle. What is the true story of the affair?"

I had brought with me copies of Granddad's notes, and I gave them to him without any comment; he quickly scanned them, then, "Well, that is quite extraordinary, but why has it taken your family some sixty years to come here?"

So, again, I had to explain everything to him, about the delay, and then the oddities in France, and I saw him getting more and more excited. "That's an amazing story," he exclaimed, "and I wonder what on earth has stirred things up here in this country? What can there possibly be which is so important to keep concealed after so many years? I know that there is that gold bowl which you hope to dig up which has young Pierre's fingerprints on it…but as Julie knows, he has been dead since 1945, she and my brother were staying with me when I did the autopsy, so I can certainly confirm that he was very dead then!"

"But is that the case?" Michelle broke in excitedly. "We have all assumed that he did die then, but could another body have been substituted for his?"

"Surely not," he said, "remember that the body was identified by two of his drinking companions who had been with him that night when he fell into the dock and was drowned."

"That is what everyone has thought," she said thoughtfully, "but if his drinking companions were criminals…what then?"

"That's a thought…" and it was some time before he went on, "but what chance do we have of checking up on that after so long?"

There was a pause in the conversation, and I broke in. "Tell me, M. Lebrun, can you remember anything noteworthy about the corpse of that young man?"

He shook his head sadly. "No, I'm afraid not, but what I do remember, as I have said, is that your grandparents, Michelle, were staying with me at the time. You must appreciate that these were bad times in France, and there were many instances of summary – so called – justice, where *colabos* were executed, or, as I prefer to say, murdered. So I was kept busy, and while I was doing police work then I saw many dozens of accident and murder victims and, after so many years, how could I even try to remember just one of all the corpses I saw then?"

But then he obviously had a sudden idea, and got up excitedly. "Just wait till I get my files out, but I'll need the date before I can find my notes on the case…now, as I remember it, my brother and Julie came down to see me, I think in July of that summer of 1945, that is some help, and maybe I can do better!"

He bustled away and came back in a few minutes with a large, leather-bound book and he turned to me. "I can tell you, Charles, that my family always make fun of my keeping records of everything…this is a visitors' book and everyone who stays here has to write something in, so let's see when they came."

He turned over the pages to what was obviously an early part of the book, and suddenly said, "There it is, come and look, Charles!"

And I read:

4th. July 1945

Dear Brother,

Julie and I have very much enjoyed our week with you and young Gaspard is very much better after your treatment of his cough... If your practice of medicine is as good as your hobby of cooking, your patients are going to be very fortunate.

Jean

"That narrows the dates," he said happily, "now it shouldn't be too difficult to find what we are looking for." And he bustled off again, coming back in a surprisingly short time with another leather-bound book. He sat down and hurriedly turned over the pages, and it took him only a couple of minutes before he almost shouted, "Here it is," and I could see him excitedly scanning a page. "And do you know, that seeing this triggers an old memory for me, as I can remember the exact day very well indeed. You see, I had cooked a rather special Sunday lunch for Jean and Julie, a Fillet de

Boeuf en Croute, and I was very annoyed by being interrupted, as it was then just a few moments after I got it out of the oven. All I could do was to bolt my helping down before dashing off to the morgue as the police didn't like being kept waiting, and in these days I needed the money they paid me for this kind of work."

He then seemed to go back a little on the page, before looking up with a beaming smile. "Well, well now, wonders will never cease, have a look at this, Charles."

And he passed the book to me, and pointed out the page. I still have a copy of this page in front of me as I write this, and the very brief notes that I read, translated into English, were:

2nd. July 1945

Report on the body of a young male recovered from Dock No. 14.

Death was by drowning, and there were no signs of suspicious injury. A contusion on the left temple had probably occurred when he had fallen, and had hit his head on the wall. From the body temperature and the state of rigor I estimate that he had been in the water since late the previous evening.

165-78-n

Note on 3rd. July:

The body has been identified as that of Pierre Dupont, aged 20, by two young men, Maurice Durand and Gerard Seurat, both friends of the deceased, who had been with him on the previous evening:

I read it carefully, then read it again, and said, "I see that the body was identified as being that of Pierre Dupont while both your brother and Julie were still with you. After all, the Germans had already told you that he had seen your father being killed. But now things has have changed and we'll need to see if Julia can help us."

"However, I was not greatly interested, and I should imagine they too felt the same. There was nothing in the German story to implicate him and none of us had any reason to believe then that he had been other than an observer. As a result, however, although we did discuss the coincidence of my doing his autopsy, we just didn't bother further."

"I can understand that," I said, "and your notes don't really help much…they tell us nothing about the corpse."

"You're wrong," he smiled, "just look again…"

It all seemed straightforward, but then I noticed the cryptic note: 165-78-n, and I pointed to it, saying, "What does that mean?"

"That," he said, "was a shorthand of mine, which I used for a while just when I started practice, and it is fortunate that I was using it then. It wasn't long before I realised that nobody was interested in my additional notes, so I gave up entering anything but the most essential items. But in this case these notes tell me that he was short and fat, with black hair!"

It was Michelle who was brighter than me when she suddenly laughed, and said, "Of course, Uncle Xavier, he was a metre-sixty-five high, weighed 78 kilos, and the 'n' is for black hair - is that right?"

"You're a clever girl," he laughed, "now does anybody know what Pierre looked like."

She turned to me. "Charles, you asked Julie about this last night…had you second sight?"

"No," I smiled, "but it did occur to me that a description was our only hope, and this information has clinched our suspicions, as Julie told us that Pierre was tall and slim with blond hair. So that body was not that of Pierre, despite the fact that these two, so called, friends of his wrongly identified it, so I wonder who they were, and why the charade was executed?"

It was again Michelle who put her finger on the real puzzle. "There is something very odd here. Just remember that in November 1942 we have the young Pierre fleeing from Urdes, and he must then have come to Marseilles. So how could he – just two and a half years later – have got into a position where he could not only acquire a convenient corpse, but also get two friends to identify it wrongly? That calls for an organisation of some kind."

"You're right," said Xavier thoughtfully, "and we may be able to find out something if we can get some information about the two, very convenient, friends. I still have contacts in the Gendarmerie, so I'll give a friend of mine a ring, he is an Inspector Emil Manchon and he is always boasting about how efficient their filing system is, so here is a chance for him to prove it!"

But, unfortunately, it wasn't as easy as that, as his friend was at a conference which would go on all day, and then finish with a formal dinner in the evening, so although it was taking place in the city, he could not be contacted until the next day. That was all we could do for the present and Xavier took us back into the house where a wonderful meal appeared as if by magic. He had a battery of hot plates, and also a refrigerator the size of a large wardrobe, so we had a chilled consommé´ to start with, then tender fillet mignons, and a bowl of fresh fruit and ice-cream to follow.

Back in the garden again with coffee, I turned to Xavier. "It is most unfortunate that you decided to become a doctor, if only you had been a chef, you would have been world famous!"

He didn't get a chance to reply, as Michelle said, "Just keep quiet. Charles, after that wonderful meal I for one am going to close my eyes and have a spot of shut eye."

Xavier looked at me with a wry smile. "My boy, when you get to my age you will realise that when a woman tells you what to do, it makes good sense to obey her… anyway, I confess that a little sleep would be very pleasant."

It was after four o'clock before we surfaced, and after some chat, Xavier disappeared for a few minutes and then came back with a trolley laden with an elaborate afternoon tea. Michelle looked at me, and burst out laughing. "I should have warned you, Charles, that you should have starved yourself for a couple of days before coming here, but never mind, we can both starve tomorrow to make up. I, for one, am going to do full justice to this afternoon tea which is, I may say, the only good thing, my great uncle thinks, that England has invented!"

It was after consuming that magnificent tea, and when we were about to leave, that I suddenly got an idea. I turned to Xavier and said, "I wonder if I could borrow your casebook for a few minutes. I'd like to get Michelle to take me down to a photocopy shop as I would like to send a copy of the page with your case notes on that autopsy to my lawyer friend, Phillipe Duchene, in Paris. He is now very interested in the affair and – "

But he interrupted me. "You young people never seem to use your eyes. Didn't you see, Charles, that the sheets in my casebook are in duplicate? In the days before photocopiers were invented we got along very well with carbon copies!" He showed me the book again. "See, the carbons are tear-out sheets…" He ripped out the copy and gave it to me. "There now, that should keep him happy, and I am glad that this information is being spread around…I'll call Julie tomorrow as soon as I hear from my friend in the police."

On the way back to Avignon I tried to put all thoughts of the affair aside, and I said to Michelle, "I was thinking of asking you and Julie to come out and have dinner with me tonight, but after that enormous tea I think that a glass of milk and a piece of bread and butter will be all I can cope with."

"Don't worry," she said, and proceeded to squeeze past a slow moving old Citroen 2CV before answering me. "You will find that Julie knows all about Great Uncle Xavier's grub, so she knows that neither of us will be hungry."

Well, maybe we weren't, but nevertheless we both managed to enjoy the large plates of French onion soup, which was the sole dish which Michelle and Julie produced, and it was after that we got down to business, and discussed the findings of the day. "It really is a shame," said Julie, "that Jean and I didn't take more interest when Xavier told us that Pierre was dead, but our interests then were for each other, and for baby Gaspard. Also, of course, everyone was trying to forget the war and the bad years in France, and it just never occurred to us to make more enquiries…but if only we had, the whole thing would have been resolved all these years ago. But it will be fascinating, to see if the two *friends,* who wrongly identified the body, are still alive, and can be traced. But we'll need to wait till tomorrow when Xavier speaks to his policeman friend."

Our conversation then turned to other matters, and to our plans for next day, and Michelle suggested that we go to Arles where I could see the great Roman arena, which was very much okay for me, and I said "That will be super, but there is one sight much nearer home which I must see."

"What?" she said.

"Why, the Pont d'Avignon! I could never miss going there, and singing one of the very few French songs that we Brits know!"

"You're on," she smiled. "You can *sous le pont* with the rest of them in the morning before we head off for Arles."

***

Next day we had a very pleasant morning sightseeing, both in Avignon and in Arles, and afterwards took some grub and a bottle of plonk with us to the Parque Naturel de Camargue to have a picnic, admiring herds of the famous white horses as we ate it. It was a beautiful late spring day, and I was quietly very happy as I turned away from the horses, and looked instead at the lovely girl beside me. She must have seen what I was doing, and said, "You seem very thoughtful, Charles, what are you thinking about?" I felt that it was a case of now or never, so I said, "I was thinking about you, and how very glad I am that we have met."

"Good," she smiled, "I was hoping you would say something like that, as I too am very happy to be beside you here."

For a moment we just looked happily at each other and then we both leaned forward to kiss. Her lips were soft against mine, but then she suddenly drew back, and looked almost doubtfully at me. But then, she must have put behind her whatever the problem was, and we kissed again…then, as we embraced, her lips parted, and it was as if time stood still. We were in a secluded hollow, and for the rest of the afternoon we just lay beside each other, telling each other about ourselves, and being a little embarrassed at being so frank and candid after having met only two days previously. At least I could be pretty frank, not very surprising as I had little to hide. I'd only had my three years in St Andrews

University away from Granny's eagle eyes – where I had taken an Arts degree – before going in for Law, and even there I'd had only a few girlfriends, and none of them very serious. Then some time afterwards I had met Rachel, my most recent one, and I had sometimes wondered if I really did love her, but now she had broken it off, and was certainly in the past. However, while Michelle seemed to tell me everything about her time in Avignon, and her early years at the University of Lyon, she brushed aside my enquiries about her last year there, just a year ago. She must have seen a question in my eyes, as she suddenly looked embarrassed. "Yes, darling, there is something which I am not yet ready to talk about…will you be patient?"

A nod and a kiss was my reply.

***

CHAPTER FIVE

We got back just before six o'clock to find Julie in a state of high excitement, and she hurried us into the sitting room to tell her tale to us. "You'll never guess," she said, "but Xavier phoned not long after you left this morning, as he had managed to get into touch with his Inspector friend earlier than he expected. What he did not expect to find was that both of the friends who had identified the body as Pierre were not only known to the police, but were notorious! The first man – Maurice Durand – is high on the wanted list for the Gendarmerie – if only they could prove something against him – and he is reputed to be a very senior member of the Union Corse. As for the second – Gerard Seurat – he was well known as a hitman for that organisation until he was killed in a gunfight many years ago."

Now I had heard of the Union Corse, but knew nothing about it, and Julie must have seen my puzzlement as she stopped to explain. "Of course, Charles, you won't know much about that organisation and I can tell you nothing good about it – only bad! Like many dreadful societies it began with high ideals, but these were soon forgotten. It started getting on for two hundred years ago in Corsica and in the island at that time the rich were very rich, and the poor were very, very poor. So to begin with, they were not unlike your Robin Hood, stealing from the rich to help the poor…but that didn't last very long, and for the last hundred years or more it has been an organisation like the Mafia, and, with its power base here in mainland France in Marseilles. I can tell you that no policeman would dare make enquiries about Union members, especially about those near the top, unless they have cast iron reasons to do so…and this affair of ours regarding the identification of a corpse in 1945 is certainly too trivial even to be considered."

She paused for a moment, and Michelle broke in. "Damn it, we're having the same problems that Charles found in Bayonne – blockages along the way – but, if the cops can't do anything, why don't we approach M. Durand ourselves? Maybe he won't answer, but it would be interesting to see what his reaction is."

"Michelle, my dear," said Julie, "don't even think of doing that. We don't see much evidence of the Union here, but Xavier knows them all too well, particularly from the number of 'honoured dead' he has seen. He told me to ensure that neither of you were foolish enough to contact Maurice Durand as, if your enquiry was in the least awkward to him, you wouldn't see the week out. Charles, believe me, that line of enquiry is closed, and must remain so, and I must ask you – although very reluctantly – not to pursue the matter of my father's jewels. In fact my advice to you is to get out of France right away, I'm afraid that he has terrified me with his tales about the Union Corse."

I didn't know how the hell to answer her, but Michelle certainly did! "Granny, we can't leave things like this, with a question mark hanging over our lives. Surely, even although we don't pursue Durand there is nothing to stop us all going to Urdes and see if we can find the treasures that Charles' grandfather buried for us? Surely the Union Corse cannot now be interested in some old jewels which were buried nearly sixty years ago?"

Julie didn't reply immediately, and I could see how upset she was, so I said to her, "Look, this affair has been left for so many years, surely a delay can't matter now? So why don't we defer doing anything about the jewels for a few weeks or even months, by which time the people who have been watching me must surely have given up? If we lay off doing anything about the wrong identification of Pierre, they will then have no reason to bother us. After we have waited for a while, I can then come back without any contact with you and Michelle, and I know just the chap to bring with me…he had five years in the army, and ended up in the SAS, so I reckon he will be a match for any members of the Union if by any remote chance they are there. Not that we'll be likely to meet any, as we can arrange to come into France from Spain, and I reckon that we can survey the roads from Urdes to Bayonne, at about the four mile or so distance that Grandfather mentioned, without arousing any interest whatsoever. I'm sure that it will then be easy to find the standing stone that he wrote about, and we should be in and out of the country in no more than a day, hopefully with your jewels. And afterwards, if that is what you wish, we can then forget all about the fingerprints on the gold bowl, and let sleeping dogs lie."

I don't know what Michelle would have said then, in reply to my suggestion, but the phone rang and she went over and picked it up. I was so wrapped up in the affair that I didn't pay any attention to what she was saying, but then she put her hand over the mouthpiece and called over to me. "Charles, how would you like to forget all about this, at least for a few hours, and come with me to a party tonight? This is my friend Claire…her brother has just got himself engaged, and they would like me to come to the celebrations, and will be delighted if you will agree to come with me."

It seemed to me an excellent idea to get away from our problems, so I nodded, and gave her a thumbs' up. When she finished the call she said to Julie, "I'm glad this has come up, Granny, we were all getting too het up, let's leave the affair till the morning – okay?"

Julie agreed, a little reluctantly, just saying, "All right, my dear, but just remember that you and your happiness are far more important to me than any of these old jewels. We've got by without them for about sixty years, so I'm not prepared to see either you or Charles taking any risks to get them."

Michelle looked over at me, and I could easily read her thoughts. "I'll wait for a short time just to please Granny... but then...?"

It seemed a good time then for me to head back to my hotel to get changed for the party, but Michelle said, "No need for that, your jeans and that sweatshirt you are wearing look quite clean and will do just fine. It isn't, I assure you, any kind of formal affair. We are asked to get there at nine o'clock, so we've got time to get ourselves ready and have a simple meal here..."

"But there is one snag, Michelle," I said, and I explained about my nightly phonecalls to Granny and to M. Duchene in Paris.

However, it was Julie who answered. "Phone from here, Charles, and I can tell you that I would like to speak to your grandmother. She sounds a very nice person."

I called Granny first, but the line was engaged, and I turned to Julie. "It's just not long after six o'clock in Scotland, the time when the cheap calls come in, and although Granny is French, she has picked up some of the saving ways of the Scots, and she always keeps her social calls to this time. Anyway, I'll try Paris before speaking to her."

M. Duchene was there, and he became very thoughtful when I told him about the identity of the two who had given the wrong identification of Pierre Dupont. "Look, Charles," he said, "I don't want to sound alarmist, but I suggest that you do nothing further on this trip to France. We are in a weak position, as we do now know who all our antagonists are, they can't be only the Union Corse as the buried jewels would just be peanuts to them…no, it must be something to do with the identity which Pierre Dupont acquired in 1945. Just as a suggestion, maybe some top man in the Union at that time had taken young Pierre under his wing – for obvious reasons! – and arranged his change of identity to protect him from any possible investigations. What I wonder now is what he has been doing all these years, and whether, by any chance, he is now an important member of the government or of some official body. There has to be some reason why the embassy in London became involved in getting your grandfather's report."

"Take my advice, Charles," he went on very seriously, "and give up for now. As for me, I am off for a couple of days, staying with an old friend in Versailles, and after that my young sister has persuaded me to join her in going to Portugal for a week of sunshine in the Algarve. So that will mean a ten day delay in my researches but, when I get back, my first job will be to examine the CVs of all the important men in the country that I can think of…we know that Pierre was about twenty in 1945, so he was born in perhaps 1925, and that narrows the field enormously. So, off you go home right now and get back to Scotland, I'll be in touch as soon as I get back."

I then managed to get hold of Granny and she too gave me just the same advice, to which all I could say was that I would think about it. As arranged I then passed the phone to Julie, and they had a long conversation, at the end of which I heard her say, "That is very kind of you, I would love to come, and I'm sure that Michelle will agree…she is between projects now. Anyway, I'll talk to Charles about his arrangements and we'll be in touch tomorrow."

When she hung up the phone she turned to me. "I like your granny, and she has asked us to come to Scotland with you, as she is concerned about us as well as about you…how about you, Michelle, would you like to have a little break? We can discuss the arrangements tomorrow and decide then when we shall leave."

I confessed that I was delighted and said, "That will be super, I would like that very much, and it doesn't matter about your being away as we can leave things alone till M. Duchene in Paris does his research, before taking things further. It really is a very strange affair."

By common consent we didn't talk any more about it, and had a simple pasta meal and then talked of other things till it was time for us to leave for the party. We walked the half mile or so to her friend's house along busy pavements for most of the way, it was a pleasant evening, and I felt on top of the world when she whispered, "Hold my hand, darling, I am so happy to be with you." As we were nearing our destination I happened to notice a smart yellow Renault car slow up as it went past, and the two occupants seemed to be looking towards us, but then it drove on and I thought no more about it.

It was a jolly good party, and I enjoyed meeting so many of Michelle's friends, but it was rather worrying to see how many highly eligible young men seemed to be keen on her. Late in the evening we got down to party games, and Michelle and I contrived to win a bottle of wine for producing the best charade. The word we did was Marseilles, and we warned them that although the word was French, that they might need to think of English words and pronunciations when they saw our performance. This wasn't as ridiculous as it sounds, as they all spoke very good English, and one of them got it almost at once. The first syllable we acted was of a harassed mother who was obviously buying a bar of chocolate, and was insisting on her own brand, and the second was the same woman going out to buy some things in a shop which was giving special offers, hence, Mars and sales equals Marseilles! Not very clever, but good enough for a party where we were all the better from drinking perhaps a little too much of an excellent Burgundy.

So we were a happy, and just slightly inebriated couple as we left the party after midnight, and walked back hand in hand through the now quiet streets. What certainly saved my life, and maybe that of Michelle as well, was my hearing a car draw up close behind us, and seeing its reflection in the angled window of a shop we were passing, and I felt suddenly uneasy…cars are by way of being a hobby of mine, and I recognised it as a yellow Renault Laguna of the type I'd seen previously when we were walking to the party. Then, to my horror, I saw two men getting out and running towards us with knives in their hands. I jerked my hand free from Michelle's, and shouted, "Danger! Run for home…"

I turned round and did what the man running towards me least expected, I ran straight at him and must have used some folk knowledge from the bad old days of the Glasgow Gorbals, when I smashed the bottle of wine we had won over his head – he must have been dazed, but he still had the knife, so I then used the second part of my folk knowledge when I thrust the broken bottle right into his face…and then did so again. He gave an anguished scream, and collapsed onto the pavement, blinded with streams of blood, which stopped the other man, who was just about to grab Michelle, and I used the moment to pick up the knife that my man had dropped. I reckoned that the most important thing was for us to get away safely and worry about justice later, so I shouted, "Get away from my girlfriend, and I won't stop you getting this man to a doctor – he certainly needs it!"

For a moment he was irresolute, but then quickly grabbed her hand. Then, just as quickly, he released her, putting his hand into a pocket, and I was quite sure that he was about to produce a gun, as he said very quietly, "Just stay where you are, you bastard, Maurice is not going to be pleased, so now it is your turn…!"

I am pretty sure that he would have then shot both of us, but we were saved by a most welcome sight and sound – that of a crowd of late-night partygoers emerging, in a rowdy throng, from a house just a few yards down the street and coming towards us. It must have been a very good party and about ten of them, boys and girls, began to weave their way towards us. They weren't interested in the body lying on the pavement and moaning in pain – they probably thought that he was just another drunk – and I knew that this was certainly a case of safety in numbers. I jumped across to Michelle, seized her hand, and pulled her into the drunken crowd, then, just as an excuse to join them, I pretended to be as drunk as they were and produced the broken bottle saying, "Look at this, I dropped our bloody bottle!"

There was a volley of ribald suggestions – quite unprintable! – but they seemed unsurprised when we joined them in making our way down the street. I risked a glance back, and saw the man helping his injured companion back into the car, and they drove off with a scream from its tyres. It was not more than about a hundred yards till we came to the little street where Michelle's house was, and we left our companions with a shout of thanks. It was only then that we began to run like hell till we got to the house, and only when we were safely inside did Michelle suddenly burst into tears, and I could feel her trembling as I held her close – and I'm pretty sure that some of the trembling came from me.

After a few moments she drew back from me, and said, "These men wanted to kill us, didn't they? It's all quite incredible, but I'd better phone the cops right away." She picked up the phone, and whoever she spoke to said that a patrol car would be round in a few minutes. But Julie had heard the commotion and called out to Michelle who ran up to her bedroom, and I heard the murmur of their voices, before she called to me to come upstairs. I found that Julie now looked a very old lady as she was, of course, devastated by what had happened to us.

"Don't tell me, she said, "that these two were common muggers, they could only be from the Union Corse… God, they do have tentacles everywhere, and they must have people in the police in Marseilles who told them of Xavier's enquiry of this morning, and he must have mentioned your interest in the enquiry." She paused there, and suddenly put her hand on my arm. "But to hell with the enquiry, the most important thing is to thank you for saving Michelle's life. I'm sure these two would have killed her as well."

She paused again and then smiled at Michelle. "You have my permission, my dear, to give him a kiss of thanks…he certainly deserves it!"

Michelle tried to look like a shy young maiden and said to me, "Will a chaste one on your cheek be enough?"

"No it bloody well won't!"

So I got my kiss, and we all laughed, but that didn't last long as we had all come to the same conclusion, that there was no doubt that the two muggers had spotted us early in the evening and had then waited till we were going home along quiet streets. Then, before I could speak, Julie suddenly brightened up again, as she came to a conclusion. "Charles, and you Michelle, we now have to decide what we tell the cops, and we have no time to waste as they will be here in a few minutes. I'm afraid that my vote is just to say that they must have been casual criminals. If we now introduce this story about the buried treasure back in 1942, and the possible involvement of the Union Corse because of the wrong identification of a drowned man back in 1945, it is never going to be kept secret, and we are going to be at the centre of story which will be plastered all over the tabloids...and all I want is to lead a peaceful life...can you agree to keep quiet, Charles?"

I didn't know what to say, everything was happening too quickly, but safety was the paramount consideration. "I'm not sure, Julie," I said, "and I don't think I told you what the driver of the car shouted to me...'Maurice isn't going to be pleased!' And you will remember that one of the villains in the Union is Maurice Durand. All I worry about now is your safety and that of Michelle, so I think we should, quite simply – run away!"

"Where to?"

"To Scotland with me. As we discussed earlier, you and Michelle will be safe there, and we can just sit and rest quietly, letting things die down here, and only then decide what we are going to do. You know that Granny will be delighted to see both of you...so, please say yes."

But we had no time to discuss the matter further because just as I said that, the doorbell rang, and I ran down to answer it, leaving Michelle to follow on with Julie. The police had obviously thought that the affair was important, as I found an inspector and a sergeant on the doorstep, and I took them into the formal front room as the best place for the interview, and we waited for a few minutes until Julie and Michelle got downstairs. The inspector was quite elderly, and was most polite to Julie, and to Michelle, and also said to me that he was distressed that a visitor to the town had had this unfortunate experience. I reported seeing the yellow Renault car on our way to the party early in the evening, and then seeing a reflection of it again as we walked back. I certainly surprised him then when I produced the broken bottle, still smeared with the blood of our assailant, and also his knife.

"You are a lucky man, Monsieur, to have had that bottle with you, and to think of it as a weapon, and do you think the man is seriously injured?"

"I would say," I said, "that he is certainly in urgent need of treatment to stitch up his face, so it might be a good thing to warn your local hospitals."

That idea interested him, and he got his sergeant to ring their HQ, so that a general alert could go out. He then asked a question and I didn't know how to reply to it. "Now, Monsieur, can any of you think of any reason why these two men should have attacked you?"

But it was Julie who answered. "Of course not, M. Burton here has only been in France for a week, and surely you cannot think that my granddaughter and I can be of any interest to a criminal organisation?"

Although that reply that seemed to disappoint him, he accepted it without demur, and said that he would be in touch next morning as we would probably have to be interviewed by an examining magistrate. But when he was about to take his departure I suddenly came to a conclusion, and looked at Julie, giving her a wink, before saying, "Inspector, I hope we won't be delayed long…you see, Mme Burton and her daughter and I intended to leave tomorrow for a short holiday in Switzerland, so we hope to be clear to get away by lunchtime?"

"Probably, Monsieur, but I can't guarantee it. Just wait till the morning, I'll be in touch before nine o'clock."

When they had left she turned to me. "I presume, Charles, that you think, as I do, that we must keep our plans to ourselves? It would be very unwise to let it be known that we are thinking of going to Scotland...the less everybody knows the better."

"You'll come?"

"Yes," she smiled, "I certainly shall, and I'm sure that Michelle will come as well. This whole affair is now quite beyond me, and I very much like the idea of getting far away, at least for the present. Now, as for what we do now, I hope that you will agree to spend the night here, I don't like the idea of your having to go back to your hotel, and equally I would be happier with a strong young man in the house."

"Thank you for the compliment," I smiled, "but most certainly I would prefer to stay here and it will he handier in any case if I am here when the Inspector comes to see us in the morning. So, perhaps as your minder I should go and check that all the doors and windows are locked, and after that I'll doss down here for the night on that sofa. I tend to sleep lightly, and if anyone tries to break in it will have to be in the ground floor."

By common agreement we once again deferred any further discussion till the morning. And while I checked on our security Michelle collected some bedding to put on the couch, and Julie too was busy coming back with pyjamas and a complete toilet kit, including a razor and shaving soap. She then made her own way upstairs, saying, "I'm sure that you and Michelle will want to re-live your adventure, don't stay up too late, we will have a lot to do tomorrow."

With that statement, I realised – and I think Michelle also did – that Julie knew what we were beginning to feel for each other, and that she approved. We didn't in fact stay up very late, but we did share a nightcap together in the shape of a cup of hot chocolate, and her goodnight kiss was very sweet. For me, it also seemed to be somewhat of a watershed in our relationship just to sleep under the same roof as she did, and I wondered how long it would be until we slept together…and on that happy thought I settled down. But although I was tired, I was suddenly wide awake, with a feeling of sheer terror. Until then I'd been buoyed up, feeling all macho, at having saved my woman, but now I just felt afraid. I had never before faced death, and now I wondered what we had got ourselves into…and then it occurred to me that I was a weakling compared with my grandfather. This thought seemed to give me a much needed kick in the pants and, with the feeling that I'd have to do better, I snuggled down and got to sleep.

Our troubles, however, were not far away, as next morning the Inspector turned up soon after eight o'clock, but fortunately Julie had wakened early, so we had all nearly finished our breakfasts, and so could again take him into the front room, and join him for coffee. Although he allowed himself the informality of taking coffee with us, he was very formal indeed when he got down to business.

"I must tell you," he said, "that I feel you may not have been altogether frank with me. You see, there have been two developments during the night, and the first of these will be very distressing to you, Mme Lebrun."

I saw Julie look up quickly. "To me?"

"Yes, it is my sad duty to tell you that during the night there was a devastating fire in the house of your brother-in-law, Dr Xavier Lebrun in Marseilles, and I am afraid that he is dead. Investigations are proceeding, but it is possible that some of the circumstances may give grounds for suspicions as to the cause."

She was a tough old girl, and her only reaction was that her eyes narrowed, and she turned to me. "Charles, that clinches it, you will have to tell your story to the Inspector as now, surprising though it is, I feel that the affair of last night must surely be involved with our story and poor Xavier has paid the price."

"I agree," I said, but then turned to the Inspector. However, first, you said that there was a second event in the night?"

"Yes, the man whom you injured with your broken bottle has probably been found...but he was dead. He had been shot."

That seemed an odd statement, surely either he had, or had not, been found, so why the qualification? "I don't understand, Inspector," I said, "why do you say *probably*?"

"The reason, M. Burton, is that although we have found the corpse of a young man, his hands have been cut off – presumably so that he cannot be identified by fingerprints – and gunshot wounds to his mouth will render identification through dental records an impossibility. Why we think he must be your victim is that enough of his face has been left to show the sort of cuts which you probably inflicted. So why can it be so important to keep his identity secret? Is it perhaps to hide who were behind the attack on you and Mlle Lebrun? Could the fire in Dr. Xavier Lebrun's house have been arson?"

Michelle and I looked at each other in horror, and we both realised that a possible reason for Xavier's house being torched was to destroy his casebook...and we were the only people who knew that I had a copy of the vital page in my pocket. Obviously, we would now have to tell the Inspector something about the affair, but I still had the feeling that only if we – Julie, Michelle, and I – dug up the jewels and the gold bowl by ourselves, would we be able to identify, to pin guilt and to get our revenge on the guilty party, whom I now felt certain had to be the erstwhile Pierre Dupont and whatever friends he had. But for some reason I didn't trust the police to do this for us...we already had evidence that the Union seemed to have contacts with them, so I said, "That is awful about Dr Lebrun, I only met him for the first time the day before yesterday, and he was a charming man. But if his death was due to arson I can't help wondering if an old affair which my grandfather was involved in could be casting a shadow today, although it may seem ridiculous, as it took place in December 1942 when he was in the RAF as a navigator and his plane came down not far north of Bayonne. His pilot was killed, but he escaped aided by a brave Frenchman."

Having said that, I went on to tell my story, almost complete, but although I mentioned the missing jewels I said nothing about them being buried, or about the gold bowl with the fingerprints and nothing about the copy of Xavier's casebook page. However, I told him of the German major killing M. Lebrun's father, and how my grandfather and his French friend killed him and I also mentioned the presence of a young Pierre Dupont who appeared to be his friend. I didn't go into any details as I had to assume that while the police might get hold of the *Herald* report and the RAF one, they would not get hold of grandfather's papers, and I felt I could edit what I told him. I also told him about the other German officer, back in December 1942, coming to see Mme Lebrun and blaming my grandfather for the murder of her father and then his stealing the jewels, which of course was nonsense as he certainly was not a thief. In his story he had also spoken about an eyewitness, Pierre Dupont – a man whom Mme Lebrun had known as he lived near her father's house. Finally, I explained that the Lebruns had believed that story until my arrival here, just three days ago, when I told them what had really happened.

He broke in there to enquire why none of my family had not come in search of the Lebruns, in all these long years… and that was a story which I had recently had a lot of practice in telling. Finally, I explained about our trip two days ago to

Marseilles to see Dr Xavier Lebrun. "You see," I said, "Mme Lebrun had told me of an extraordinary coincidence of she and her husband having stayed with Dr Xavier Lebrun in 1945 just when he carried out an autopsy on a drowned man who was supposed to be Pierre Dupont. So Mlle Lebrun and I went down two days ago to have lunch with him, just to ask him if he remembered the autopsy and we found that he did remember it, and was able to look up his old case notes and was surprised to see that there could be an error in the identification of the corpse as Pierre Dupont, as the description of the corpse didn't quite fit with recollections of his pre-war appearance, and he felt sufficiently interested to speak to your colleagues in Marseilles. You will know that Dr Lebrun did speak to them yesterday to see if they knew either of the two names of the men who might have given the wrong identification, and of course he found that the names are indeed very well known to the police. Now, of course, this did seem to make a tiny link with the Union Corse, because although one of them was dead, the other, a M. Maurice Durand, would appear to be in that organisation. However, that link appeared so tenuous that I didn't think it worth mentioning it last night and anyway, now with the death of M. Lebrun and the destruction of his case notes in the fire, we cannot possibly go any further."

"However," I went on, "back to Pierre Dupont, you should understand, Inspector, that all of us just wanted to speak to him, if he were still alive. We were not, I can assure you, going to make a fuss, but we were interested to see what pressure the Germans had put on him, to make him go along with the absurd tale. The only thing we wanted was to set the record straight in our respective family histories."

Well, he didn't look very convinced, but said, "It is a pity that none of you explained this last night, but I suppose that you could not be expected to make the link then, anyway no harm has been done. And I must confess that I find it hard to understand why this affair about Pierre Dupont is so important, so long after the event. Maybe it involves something entirely different, and we shall need to do our best to establish the truth, so if any of you can come up with other ideas, please let me know. But, because of these new events, you will appreciate that you cannot go off to Switzerland now, and in any case you will have to make arrangements about Dr Lebrun's funeral. As for the present I have been asked to tell you that the Examining Magistrate would like to see you, in the Mairie, at 11 o'clock this morning."

"We'll be there," said Julie, "but can you tell me if there will need to be any delay in my brother-in-law's funeral, because of the circumstances?"

"Probably not, but I shall have to discuss this with my colleagues in Marseilles, and it also depends on the instructions from the Examining Magistrate after your meeting with him this morning. As regards that, I am concerned for your safety, as there is a lot which we do not understand, so I shall send one of my cars to pick you up at a quarter to eleven, and bring you back afterwards. Also, until we are clearer about the background to this affair, I shall detail some of my men to keep watch on the house. I may say that your projected trip to Switzerland could in fact be very convenient, as it will get you away from this part of France. If you will take my advice you will tell nobody where you are going."

When he had departed, Julie and Michelle both felt that I had been right to edit my story to the Inspector, especially about the copy of Xavier's page, which was the only proof that Pierre had not died in 1945, and Julie said, "I do agree that I would not be happy at this stage to let the authorities in on the whole story. I can just visualise them digging up the jewels, and having an unfortunate accident when the fingerprints were cleaned off the bowl. Just remember that it isn't only the Union Corse who are interested in our affair, as the French Embassy in London asked your Defence Ministry to expedite sending a copy of your grandfather's report to that lawyer in Paris, so astonishing though it is I cannot help thinking that something, or somebody, more important is involved."

"But," she said, laughing rather wryly, "I'm damned if I can see what it could be, and I can hardly believe that the weedy young man – that Pierre Dupont – could become important…but I suppose that stranger things have happened."

"However," she went on, "I can tell you that I am very glad that we are soon going to Scotland, and I sincerely hope that the authorities do not wish to detain us for long, and that we can go off immediately after Xavier's funeral."

She seemed to me to be treating her brother-in-law's death rather casually, and I think she then realised that both Michelle and I were puzzled, so she stopped there and turned to her. "I can see, my dear, that you wonder why I don't seem too upset by Xavier's death, so I'd better tell you why I am not too sorry about it. It is of course awful, but now his troubles are over…you see, I haven't told you before – at his request – what he learned a month ago, that he had inoperable cancer and had no more than six more months to live. The prognosis was for increasing pain before the end came…but he asked me not to tell you. As a doctor he knew what he was in for, and I'm sure that a quick end would have been his choice."

"But now," she went on, "I must have a word with old Paul Jussot." She turned to me. "He is our lawyer, and was Xavier's as well, and he is an old family friend of ours here in Avignon. Probably he won't have heard the news as yet, and I would like to leave all the funeral arrangements to him. Once that is arranged, you can then warn your grandmother that when we are free to leave here…she can expect us tout de suite!"

She put in her phonecall, and her lawyer friend was most efficient, as he called back in less than an hour to say that he had been in touch with a firm of funeral undertakers in Marseilles, and the service could be held three days hence in the family church in Avignon, subject to Julie receiving permission from the magistrate at our meeting, and that he would deal with all the formalities and the funeral notices after we confirmed the position. By then time had moved on to ten o'clock, and we spent the next half hour or so in rehearsing our stories – still keeping to ourselves anything about the buried jewels, the gold bowl, and the copy page. In the event the magistrate turned out to be a kindly, middle-aged gentleman who knew Julie slightly, so he was politeness itself, with no awkward questions, and at the end of the interview he looked up kindly at her. "I do so sympathise with you, Julie," he said, "it is awful to have lost your brother-in-law in such a tragic fashion, and I have now received a second report from Marseilles regarding the fire. Their first impression was that it might have been caused deliberately, and that petrol might have been thrown into the house…but now they know that Xavier had a small laboratory at the back of the house, in which he kept a quantity of industrial alcohol for his experiments, and an accidental fire, starting there, would seem to have been the cause."

"But that is absurd!" Julie broke in. "He was most careful in all his work and would never have done anything to cause a fire."

The magistrate shrugged his shoulders, almost apologetically. "Strange things happen, and anyway that now is the police view. Just accept it, my dear, and remember that because of this there need be no delay in Xavier's funeral, and after that you can go off on your holiday as soon as you like."

"What you are telling me," Julie said sadly, "is that this explanation is convenient to the authorities in Marseilles, because of outside pressure."

He looked embarrassed, and whispered, "C'est la vie," before hastily indicating that our meeting was over.

When we got back to the house, Julie turned to me. "Charles, don't think we can alter things just now, we can't, but in a while once we dig up that gold bowl we'll have fingerprint evidence which may lead us to the guilty man."

I phoned Granny at once, and felt that I had no alternative but to tell her everything and her reply was predictable. "That is awful…do please leave things for now and come as soon as you all can…I am concerned about you."

"I'll do that, Granny," I said, "and we'll leave as soon as Dr Xavier Lebrun's funeral is over – in three days' time – but I am bringing two new friends back with me."

"You mean Mme Lebrun and her granddaughter?"

"That's right, but you'd better get used to calling them Julie and Michelle…here's Julie to speak to you."

It didn't take me long to realise that my idea had been a good one as, when she hung up the phone, she smiled at me. "What a nice grandmother you have, I shall look forward to meeting her, and I very much look forward to being up in Scotland without feeling that I have to have eyes in the back of my head. I know that the local police have been asked to keep an eye on the house, but it is up to us to be very careful."

She was a good organiser, and phoned a shop which knew her, and arranged for a load of food to be sent round, enough to keep us for the next three days, and she suggested…not quite ordered, but nearly!…that we should stay in the house, and not go out. In fact I agreed with her, but first I had to go to collect my car and to check out of the hotel, and Julie surprised me by phoning the Inspector, and arranging that I would be taken there in a police car, and escorted back. When I was at the hotel it occurred to me that I might be able to catch M. Duchene before he went off on holiday so that I could tell him about all my adventures. However, as there was no reply to my call, I reckoned that he was now staying with his friend in Versailles. But I had his home personal fax number and thought that he would probably go back there before going off to Portugal so I sat down and wrote quite a long note to him, and got one of the receptionists to send it off on the hotel fax machine. I felt it was important to make my message as detailed as possible and so gave him a full report of how Xavier would seem to have been murdered within a few hours of his making enquiries from the Marseilles police…although the police now denied that. I then explained about the page we had of Xavier's notes, which showed that Pierre Dupont was probably still alive. I also told him about the attack on Michelle and me, and the delay now in getting away from Avignon because of the interview with the Investigating Magistrate and of Xavier's funeral but that I now intended to take Mme Lebrun and Michelle back with me to Scotland, and that they would be staying with me and my grandmother. I pondered over the situation. *At least that will bring M. Duchene up to date before he goes to Portugal, and when he gets back we'll be in Scotland he can then get into touch with us, to tell us of his researches into the possible candidates for the new identity of Pierre Dupont.*

As my luggage was brought down to my car, I was impressed by the police, who insisted on doing a complete survey of the car, especially underneath, to ensure that all was well. But I was rather thoughtful as I drove back…the fears of the previous night had come back to me, and it wasn't at all pleasant to be considered as a possible target for terrorists. As soon as we got into the house, Julie said, "Now, for better or for worse we are prisoners here for the next two days, so please let's keep off talking about the affair – are we agreed?"

We were, but Michelle soon broke the deal. "Do you know what puzzles me about all this…it is as if there were two groups working against us!"

And she went on to point out the non-violent problems I'd had in Bayonne followed by Xavier's probable murder, and our attempted murder, as soon as we found out about Pierre's faked death.

"Odd, isn't it?" she ended.

It was, but we had no answers to her question.

***

CHAPTER SIX

Xavier's funeral, two days later, involved a lot of work for both Julie and Michelle. However, the helpful family lawyer had arranged a reception in a local hotel for those who had attended the funeral, and it was only then that I realised how very well known the Lebruns were. There must have been well over a hundred people in the church, and most of them came on to the reception. What was unpleasant, however, was that it was easy for me to realise that quite a few had only come because of the circumstances of Xavier's death, despite the fact that the press had not mentioned the possibility of anything suspicious. The police too had been discreet, and no mention of a possible link with the Union Corse had become public. But this did not stop some of the so-called mourners asking very pointed questions, and there were also many enquiries as to who I was and why I seemed so close to the family. As regards these questions, Julie just said that my grandfather had met her father during his escape from France to Spain in 1942, and that only recently had I got into touch with them.

We were a quiet group on the night before we left for Scotland. The funeral had been very trying both for Julie and for Michelle and they were glad, as they had been for most of the previous two days, just to relax and not talk. Anyway, as we sat there I was glad that we would soon be leaving and, when we finished dinner that evening, I suggested to Julie that we all have an early night, to which she smiled, "I'm ahead of you, Charles, I have just taken some sleeping pills, which I got some time ago when I had a minor medical problem. So I am off now, but I'd better warn you that I may wake early...but that will be a good fault as I like to get off bright and early when I am making a journey. We were in fact taking it easy, as while I would have driven quite happily all the way to Calais – about 550 miles – in the day, Michelle and I had decided that it would be too much for Julie, and instead decided that we would just head north, and stop somewhere along the road to the Channel coast whenever we felt like it.

In the event Julie did wake early, so we all had breakfast soon after half past seven and in less than an hour later we had organised all the various things in the house and I had begun to take the luggage out to my car. As I did so, our watching policeman came over to assure me that it had just been checked and was quite safe to use and, as I thanked him, I felt a great sense of relief that we were now getting away from all this nasty business, and to be far away in Scotland. It was when I was coming back with another load of stuff that I noticed an elderly man limping painfully across the street with the aid of a stick, and then tripping just as he passed behind my car. As he fell he dropped his stick just at the back wing, but he was none the worse and the cop helpfully assisted him back to his feet. I then saw him carry on down the street with a wave of thanks from his stick.

Soon after that, the house was locked up and Julie and Michelle were settled comfortably in the car, and I confess that I was so relieved to be free to go that I set off with an unusual burst of acceleration. But then I got a guilty conscience and glanced over at Julie. "Sorry about that, but I am so glad to be on our way. I promise to drive better for the rest of the journey."

"Don't worry about that," she smiled, "after driving with Michelle I know what to expect from you young drivers. Anyway, like you, I also am very glad to be making our escape."

It was because we had no need to hurry that we stopped about an hour after starting off, in order to sort out some luggage in the car which was rattling about. We pulled into one of these delightful Aires which the French have on their Autoroutes and which have no facilities except toilets – sometimes pretty primitive! – but rather pleasant picnic areas. Then, some time later, we stopped again in a service area, just north of Macon, to have some morning coffee and to top up the car with petrol. It was then that I happened to see a Fiat car, which I had seen at our previous stop. The reason I noticed it was that its registration number ended in 411 – my birthday is on the fourth of November – and I suddenly realised that each time we had stopped it had arrived just shortly after us, and then parked a few cars further on. It was an unusual coincidence, and it was Michelle who noticed that I was worried, saying, "What's the matter, darling?"

By then I had it all worked out…that cripple, crossing the road, had been no cripple but somebody acting the part, and I decided that when he fell – so conveniently – at the back of my car, he must have planted some kind of homing device under our back wing. "Just a minute, darling," I said, and when I got out of the car and looked, there it was…a small, round box like a powder puff container, so I tugged it off and took it back into the car with me. I felt that I had no option but to tell both of them my suspicions, and I felt especially sorry for Julie, as she had been so delighted to be away from all the problems.

To my surprise, however, she just looked on it as a challenge, saying, "Well now, I wonder why the bastards want to keep track on us? They can't just be interested in killing us, they could surely have managed to do that this morning if they had been serious, but I'm fed up with all this and want them off our backs, so let's lead them on a false trail!"

"And how do we do that?"

"Easy, why not just attach that infernal machine to some other car, and let them follow it!"

She was right, it was as easy as that, and by chance the car next to us was ideal, a somewhat elderly – but still fast – Alfa Romeo, with four tough young men as its occupants. I had heard them discussing the fact that they would need to hurry to get as far as Reims in time for the match, so I knew that they were going straight north for another two hundred miles, and to drive quickly as they did so. So it wasn't hard for me to bend down to examine one of our own tyres, and at the same time place the device under a wing of the other car.

When I got in again. I turned to Julie. "You are a genius, now let's have some fun!"

We waited for a few minutes till the four men came back from the shops and got into their car and, as they drove off, we followed them closely. I could see no signs of our followers in the Fiat, but obviously they didn't need to keep all that near since they had the device to follow. But a few minutes later, on a long straight stretch of the road, I could see them, following maybe about a quarter of a mile behind. In the meantime I too had been thinking. "Look," I said, "we've been planning to go to Calais, and then through the Eurotunnel, but let's fool them and instead head for Rotterdam and if we are lucky we'll be in time to get the North Sea Ferry overnight crossing to Hull in the north of England. I suggest that I now pass our sporting friends and get far enough in front of them so that we can get off at the next Autoroute exit without being seen, and lose them…okay?"

Things worked out very well, and I wound the Mondeo up to a most illegal 120 mph, before passing the Alfa just before the exit to the south of Chalon-sur-Saone. I waited until the very last minute before turning onto the slip road, cutting across the front of a large truck with a big trailer as I did so – much to the indignation of the driver. But it served the purpose of hiding us from the road, and we saw no signs of the tracking Fiat following us to the exit.

It didn't take Michelle long to work out our route, and we first of all headed north west, then north through Luxembourg and into Belgium, and finally into Holland and to Rotterdam. It was when we crossed the frontier into Belgium that Julie showed how worried she was when she said to Michelle, "You know, I never thought that I would ever have to say how glad I was to be out of France, but I am now. Somehow, I don't think that the tentacles of the Union Corse will extend into the Low Countries – or indeed into Scotland. So, let's enjoy ourselves!"

She fished into one of the many bags she had with her and produced a flask of brandy – sorry, cognac! – and a set of these silver cups of the type which nest into each other, saying, "Charles, I know all about the dangers of drinking and driving, but I think a tot for each of is may now be considered as being strictly medicinal!"

I hoped that it could still be considered in that light, as we were doing about 115 mph as I knocked mine back. My illegal speed was of course due to the necessity to make our reservations and to get to Rotterdam in time to catch the evening boat. But my mobile phone had been cleared for use on the continent, so that dealt with booking our tickets and, thanks to breaking speed limits all the way, we did manage to catch the boat. It was a good choice to come by this route as from past experience I knew that it is a well-organised crossing with dinner and breakfast as part of the ticket price, and the food and the accommodation were first class. We were given two adjoining cabins and, after dinner – a most pleasant meal with a nice litre of the house wine – Julie said to us, "Now, children, you must allow me the luxury of age when I say that I am tired and want to go to bed, and I am sure you will find things to amuse you for the evening. Don't worry, Michelle, when you come back to our cabin, I'm going to take another of these pills, so I'll probably be out for the count."

She paused for a moment, then said to me, "You know, Charles, I can hardly believe that it is only about a week since we met you, yet here you are taking us to drive a thousand and a half kilometres plus a sea crossing to stay with a lady whom we have never met…and yet I can tell you that I'm glad to be here with you, and it all seems quite natural! Run along now with Michelle, but please do remember that she is very precious to me."

I didn't answer immediately, as I took my courage in both hands. "Julie," I said, "I hope you won't mind when I say that although I have only known her for these few days, that she is now very precious to me too." She didn't answer, and instead just leaned forward and kissed my cheek. "Good night to both of you, have fun…"

There is, in fact, a surfeit of attractions on these ships, but all Michelle and I wanted was to find a nice quiet corner where we could be close together. It was maybe an hour later when for a while we'd just sat happily and quietly together, that she looked at me. "Darling, I'm thirsty, get me a drink, will you? A glass of that house white wine we had during dinner would be nice."

But when I came back it was with two quite long glasses of amber liquid, and she looked at them doubtfully. "What are these?"

"Just remember, dear, that we are headed for Scotland and, as I'm sure you will have heard, we Scots are permanently sozzled with our national drink...so you'd better start to learn now. You are about to drink a very good Scotch – Bell's Black Label and water. It will of course taste even better with some of our pure Scottish water, but this Vichy stuff is the best I could get here."

She took what looked like a doubtful sip, then surprised me by laughing at me, and taking a large swig. "You seem to think that I have lived a sheltered life in a French backwater, but I can tell you that I was twice in London while I was a student, and I was introduced to a number of your crude British drinks. None of them, of course, have the quality and finesse of ours, but I suppose I'll have to put up with them – and particularly your own Scotch – while we are in Scotland. But I promise that I'll behave myself and pretend to like it!"

"Oh, but I quite agree with you, darling," I said, "that Scotch has an awful taste. But the reason that it is so popular with men in Scotland is that it tends to concentrate feminine minds on most pleasant pastures and activities."

"Does it now?" she laughed. "Well I can tell you that you have just wasted your money! Shall I tell you why?" She leaned forward and kissed my cheek very gently. "You see, for the last hour my mind has been concentrating on exactly those activities which you had in mind!"

But she then gave me a rather doubtful smile. "Darling, let's go back to your cabin, but at the same time I suggest that this time you do not do what we both want to do."

"As to what I am now thinking," I said, shaking my head seriously, "I wouldn't have thought that my thoughts would be so very predictable!"

She leaned over and took my hand. "That, my sweet, is what I am afraid of. You see, I do want to make love with you very much, but I don't want our first time together to be cramped into a bunk bed, as we would have to be tonight. I have in mind a large double bed with a mattress soft enough even for that delicate princess who felt a single pea, about ten layers down, and if you could rustle up a chamber orchestra to play love music, that would also be very pleasant. You see, I want our first night together to be something which I can remember with happiness for the rest of my life…is that okay?"

I had a quick look round and as nobody seemed to be looking, I leaned over and kissed her cheek, as I thought what a wonderful girl she was, and said, "You've achieved a miracle, darling, as, much to my surprise, I find that I agree with you. But will you trust me to – shall I say – just enjoy the view when we get back to my cabin?"

She didn't answer, but just gave me one of these wonderful smiles, taking my hand, and then led me to my little love nest – about 10 ft. x 5 ft.! As to what happened there is very little to hide, but nevertheless it was a night that I shall long remember. It began – thanks to North Sea Ferries – with some delightful music on the channel that my set in the cabin happened to be tuned to. I seldom turn on muzac as a background, but I did so as we went into my cabin, and all we could do when we heard it was to look at each other and laugh. It was what could be said to be a most appropriate choice, as the song which was being played was that evergreen golden oldie, *Just the way you look tonight,* and most certainly Michelle looked wonderful as she shed her clothes. I suppose we spent the time that night as our grandparents – and maybe also our parents – probably did, in what they called petting in the days before the Pill. But the bond between us was certainly stronger when a few hours later I ushered her the six feet or so from my cabin to hers.

***

We were all up bright and early in the morning, and had time for an excellent breakfast before having to get back to the car to disembark. I had crossed my fingers that it would be a nice day to welcome them both to Britain, and it must have worked as it was one of these magical early summer days when everything looks clean and fresh in the bright sunshine. As we drove out of Hull I invited Michelle to look at a road map I had in the car, saying, "You will now see the truth of the old saying *East is East and West is West, and never the twain shall meet!* Just look at the map, there are good roads up the east coast, and also up the west coast, but the only Motorway link between them in these parts is the M62 there, which would be a considerable detour to the south. So, we have a choice of going all the way up to Edinburgh before heading west, or else go up the A1 as far as Scotch Corner – which in fact I think we should – and then take the cross country A66 road to Penrith on the west coast road, where we can catch the M6 Motorway, which then leads us up to Glasgow."

Julie too looked disapprovingly at the map, and I could see that she found it hard to resist comparison with the Autoroute system in France. But I did manage to get in a little dig when I pointed out that whatever the failing of our motorways, at least they were free – unlike her Autoroutes. We had no need to hurry that day, so soon after we turned off at Scotch Corner, I stopped for coffee at a favourite pub of mine, the Morritt Arms at Greta Bridge, and I managed to impress Julie when I showed her the Dickens Bar with the appropriate murals, as reminders of his visit there in 1839. The coffee too was hot and strong, and I could see that Julie was beginning to think that – just maybe – civilisation had not completely stopped at the north side of the channel.

As regards lunch, we had bought sandwiches on the boat, and so it was after just one more comfort stop that we got to Paisley by mid-afternoon. I had of course phoned Granny from the car to confirm our arrival time but despite that, she was still waiting, almost on the doorstep, to greet us. It was interesting to see the two old ladies, at first looking a little doubtfully at each other, but then suddenly embracing with a flurry of continental kisses. Then Granny looked over at Michelle, and smiled. "Come over here, my dear, and give me a real kiss. Charles has told me a lot about you, but I can see that he hasn't done you justice."

At last, Granny turned to me. "You are a clever boy, Charles, to have brought these delightful people to see me, and I can tell you that there isn't going to be a single word of English spoken in this house tonight; it is going to be wonderful to pretend that I am in France again."

At this remark, Julie laughed. "I'm glad, Marie, to hear you saying that…all you clever people so completely bilingual…while my English is okay but rather basic. So you must do what you can to improve it while we are here, and put up with my mistakes."

"That's as maybe!" said Granny. "We can think about doing something about that tomorrow, but for today it is French or nothing!"

I had expected that we would have a quiet evening together, but soon after that the phone rang, and I answered it to find that it was my boss, Mr Henderson. I had of course intended to let him know that I was now back, and would be free to start in the office again come Monday, but I was surprised to find that he already knew all about my doings in France, and when I asked him how he knew he just laughed. "There are no secrets where M. Duchene is concerned, you see he spoke to me the other day, just before going off to Portugal on holiday, he had gone back to his house and got your fax from Avignon. So he sent me a copy of it, and it is quite incredible what has been happening to you and to the Lebruns. Tell me, have you brought Mme Lebrun and her granddaughter back with you?...good...well now, I have some more news which will be of interest to all of you, so why don't you bring them all round for drinks before dinner."

In fact, his house is only a few hundred yards from Granny's, in an area of Paisley called Castlehead, a development of houses built in late Victorian times which still formed one of the most desirable areas of the town. So it wasn't far away, and no problem for us to go, but I wondered what on earth this news of his could be, and why he wouldn't tell me now.

"It's a good story," he went on," and I'm not going to spoil it by giving it to you piecemeal, so shall we say six o'clock?" I excused myself, and told Granny what was suggested, but she would have none of it, and picked up the phone herself.

"Hello, William, this news of yours had better be good! But these folks have just arrived after a long journey, so I'm not having them going out tonight. So why don't you and Rosemary come round here for drinks...or better still, come and stay for dinner. I always overestimate how much food to make, and there will be enough Boeuf Strogonoff in the Aga to feed a regiment."

"That's better," she said. She hung up the phone, and went on to explain to Julie and to Michelle who Mr Henderson was...the Senior Partner in the legal office I was in, and a colleague of my late father. When she had finished, she turned to me. "Charles, I don't think I have ever talked much to you about William's career before he joined the firm, have I? No? Well, he took his law degree in Edinburgh in the late 1960s, but then decided that he might like a few years in the army, so he took a short service commission where he found himself doing some kind of Intelligence work. He would never speak of what he did, even to your father, but I can see that your adventure has brought back some of the excitement of his youth."

When he and his wife arrived, he very graciously welcomed Julie and Michelle to Scotland, all in his appalling French, and it was Julie who saved the day. In her not very fluent English she said to him, "I too am pleased to meet you, but do please speak in English. You see, I am so unhappy to find all you clever bilingual people, and my English isn't up to much. So I have decided to talk nothing but English in my holiday, so I'll try to understand what you say…will you help me, please?"

Granny looked over at me and winked, and I reckoned that she had warned Julie – despite her previous edict about speaking French – that if he got started on French we'd never get him off it! So, mercifully, we did talk English that night, and I could see that while Julie's didn't speak it very well, she understood most things, and only seldom did she have to ask for clarification. The gist of Mr Henderson's story was that he had not only had a fax from M. Duchene before he went on holiday, but that he had received another one from him that very afternoon. He brought it out, and passed it over to me. Its address was one which I afterwards got to know very well:

Le Meridien Penina Hotel
Portimao
Portugal
FAX 351 282 420 300

My dear William,

As I said, the people in my office have been busy in the last few days in examining the CVs of our more prominent politicians, and they have found one candidate for our rogues gallery who meets so many of our criteria, that I have no doubt they have found the new identity of the supposedly late Pierre Dupont. It will surprise you to know that he is indeed very well known, as M. Vincent Fouquet, the leader of the small political party Le Parti de Socialisme et d'Amical, which you may have heard of, but you may not know that it currently occupies a pivotal position. This is because our present government is a minority one and only the votes controlled by our M. Fouquet keeps them in power.

Anyway, here is his official history, although of course we suspect that the early years belong to the other man who was murdered in order to give Pierre Dupont a new identity:

Born: 24th. August 1920 in what was then French Indo-China. Little information about his early life, and his parents would seem to have died during the war. There is no record of any relatives, and he was held by the Japs in one of their islands during the war until his prison camp was overrun by the Americans, but only after most of the occupants had died. There is a record of his arriving in Marseilles in a hospital ship on 25th. June 1945, so it would seem that he was immediately befriended by the Union Corse, and then murdered by them a few days later, when Pierre Dupont took his identity.

The next record of him is as a student at the Sorbonne where he studied Law, becoming active in the many political parties of the Left which appeared at that time.

He finished his studies in 1951 and soon joined the legal firm in which that damned lawyer, M. Mathieu Jeannot (who asked for details of F/O Henry Burton's reports) is now a Senior Partner.

I have not yet got full details of his career in Law, but I do know that he was involved in several cases by way of defending Union Corse members. But that may have stopped some twenty or more years ago when he went into politics full time, and the line which he always plugs is the importance of a complete rapprochement with Germany, and to distrust Britain as a country which will never be a friend of France. Because his party now holds the balance of power he is the present Minister of the Interior, and I am sure that the last thing the French government wants is for any mud to be thrown at him...as if he were to be disgraced the government would probably fall.

As to his personal life, he has never married, but no scandal about homosexuality has appeared. It may, however, be significant that although he lives in a quite modest apartment in Paris he has a luxurious country house...really a small estate about 20 kilometres north of Marseilles, and a near neighbour of his is the Union Corse chief, Maurice Durand (one of the two who wrongly identified the body as Pierre Dupont).

As regards his personal appearance, he is tall and slim, and with jet black hair. So, if he is Pierre, then he must have dyed his blonde hair right from the beginning, and has continued to do so, even although his hair must now be either white or grey.

Please speak to Charles Burton as soon as he and the Lebruns arrive. The matter is now so delicate and important that I suggest I also come to Scotland as we must have a conference. It would be most unwise to do anything further about the affair without having a serious talk...and I think also that it might be wise to appraise your government of the problem. Franco-British relations are bad enough at present without Charles digging up proof that M. Fouquet – a gov-

ernment minister – is not what he seems to be, and causing a political scandal.

I look forward to seeing both you and Charles, with the Lebruns, as soon as is possible.

I think that we were all so astonished that we didn't quite know what to say, but it was Granny who got in first when she threw back her head and laughed. "You know, I have spent a lot of my time trying to get young Charles here to speak without swearing, but now I am going to break my own rules and say that this is just bloody stupid! In this affair we started off with a simple idea of digging up a box of jewels and a gold bowl with some fingerprints…which had been buried some sixty years ago by my late husband, giving a clue to an ancient crime…and now, after all the excitement in France, we have a suggestion that in addition to the Union Corse, the governments of France and Britain may be involved."

But then she stopped suddenly and turned to Julie. "My dear, it was stupid of me to laugh just now, as what happened to poor Xavier was unforgivable, and also what nearly happened to Michelle and Charles…most certainly none of this affair is now a laughing matter."

"It most certainly is very far from that," said Julie, "and in fact I happen to know quite a lot about M. Fouquet. I don't usually take much to do with politics but, at the time of the last election, Xavier came and stayed for a weekend, and did his best to tell me something about all the participants, and he hadn't a good word to say for Fouquet or for his party. Like me, he believed that Britain is our surest ally, and again, like me, he doesn't trust the Germans." She stopped there for a moment, and turned to Michelle. "I seem to remember, dear, that you don't like him either?"

"That's right, there was a small group in the campus at Lyons, which supported Fouquet, but they were part of the lunatic fringe, like the neo-Nazis. So I shall very much look forward to seeing that bastard getting what he deserves, not just because of his past, but also because of his present!"

But then Mr Henderson, experienced as he was in chairing meetings, interrupted smoothly. "You are all, of course, quite right, he deserves all that he will get, thanks to us, and at least we are now one stage further on...with that information we can be quite sure that Pierre Dupont changed himself into Vincent Fouquet, and I have been able to take things a little further since I heard that you were here. What I have done was to phone M. Duchene to say that the wanderers have arrived, and I now have had a call from him to confirm that he is cutting his holiday short and will fly to Glasgow tomorrow. Now the normal scheduled flights from the Portuguese Algarve mean taking first a short hop to Lisbon from Faro, the local airport, then coming on to London, before getting a shuttle to Glasgow, all of which takes most of a day. But M. Duchene's sister has an apartment in the Penina hotel complex and so she knows many people there, including some of the airline pilots. What she has managed to do is to arrange that he will get a seat which happens to be free on one of the charter flights direct from Faro to Glasgow so you, Charles, can meet him at Glasgow Airport and bring him here, to Paisley, in time for lunch tomorrow...how's that for organisation!"

"If I too may be permitted to swear," I said, "it is bloody marvellous! And I can tell you that I very much value his advice." And I hope that no pause was noticeable before I thought of my career in the firm and went on, "So, what with his advice and yours, how can we go wrong?"

It was then Granny again who took the floor. "Right, that's enough about the affair for now, we can't do anything more tonight, so let's enjoy our aperitifs, and then cross our fingers that my meal hasn't been spoiled with this delay. You must appreciate, William and Rosemary, that there are three French-born people here, and we have our own priorities… and food and drink always come first!"

She needn't have worried, as the meal – as always with her – was superb, and we did manage to keep off business for the rest of the evening. But before they left, Mr Henderson took me aside. "We'll see after our talk tomorrow with M. Duchene, what to do about your coming back to the office, but my gut feeling is that this is something which must be resolved as soon as possible, which will probably mean that Julie and Michelle will have to stay here until everything is resolved. So for now just come to the office when it is convenient for you to do so."

He then turned to Granny. "Now, Marie, as you know, Charles is picking up M. Duchene from the airport tomorrow at noon, so why don't you all come and have lunch with us, and we can have our conference after that in the afternoon."

It was while we were thinking of getting to bed that Granny took me aside. "I can't tell you how happy I am for you. You don't need to tell me that you and Michelle have fallen in love – that is very obvious. Perhaps I can now tell you something I've never dared to put into words before… that I have always dreamed that you might fall in love with a French girl, and now you have, and she is everything I could have wished for you. Hang on to her, my dear, she is very special…"

***

CHAPTER SEVEN

At Glasgow Airport next morning it wasn't difficult to pick out M. Duchene among the other passengers from the aircraft. They had all been having a sunshine holiday, with all the goodies of cheap booze and lots of the sun and sex which the brochures promised...and were dressed that way. He was dressed as if for a day at the office, in a smart suit and even carrying a briefcase. But maybe he too had let his hair down in Portugal, as the amount of luggage he had with him must surely have contained some casual clothes.

After lunch we spent a lot of time together in the afternoon...he, M. Duchene, William and Rosemary Henderson, Julie, Marie, Michelle, and I, but for a while we really got no further. At least we now knew who the major villain was, but as to how we should proceed, that was another matter. The first problem, of course, was to find the site where the treasures had been buried, but, from what I had seen, all the woods seemed to have been cleared from the stretch of road down from the old village of Urdes towards Bayonne which I had seen. But there was, of course, the possibility that there was another road, and if we were to involve local people and engage in a major search of the district in the hope that we could find the large boulder that Granddad had written about, it would surely attract interest from the wrong quarters. Also, apart from that, there was the worrying question of possible friction with the French government.

At last Mr Henderson said, “I think that we need some expert assistance. Probably, Charles, you know that I was in the army before I came into my office but possibly you do not know that I spent a few years in an intelligence outfit. I have, of course, had no involvement in that field for some thirty years, but at that time I became friendly with a man, some years younger than me, who is now quite senior in the diplomatic service. He seems to have a wide field for his activities, and occasionally goes on trips abroad to our embassies, although he says that he just goes there to count the spoons! Fortunately for us, he is at present based in Glasgow and I think that he might be interested in our problem. If you will excuse me now, I’ll go and give him a ring.”

He came back after about five minutes to say, “Well, that is arranged, and my old friend Peter Armstrong and his wife Sue are coming here to dinner tonight, and I can tell you that if anybody can help – he is the one to do so.” So it was with some keen interest that I waited for the evening, and the arrival of the mystery man and his wife, and when they did so I could see that whatever they were or did, they certainly made a handsome, early middle-aged couple.

After all the introductions it was Granny who took charge of things despite the fact that Rosemary Henderson was the hostess. “It is very kind of both of you,” she said, “to come to try and help us in this family problem, but how about leaving things till after dinner? I’ve just walked through the hall and there are some very attractive smells coming from the kitchen, so don’t let’s delay dinner too long, and just leave any serious talk till later.”

But there was still time for some small talk as we drank our aperitifs…and what made things easy was that both the

Armstrongs spoke colloquial French. It was also obvious that they had been very well trained in the field of putting people at their ease and Julie and Granny, usually sticklers for formality, were now happily using Christian names, and they with Michelle, Rosemary, and Sue Armstrong, were soon involved in a cheerful French conversation, and in most intimate revelations! As for we men, Peter talked, thank goodness, usually in English, and although our conversation was mostly about trivialities, I decided, even from the little he said, that – like Mr Henderson – his army background showed.

After dinner we stayed round the table, and it was as if we were at a board meeting, this time with Peter as the chairman, and it was with our coffee that we took turns to tell our parts of the story. First of all, Granny with the events of 1942, then me about my getting Grandfather's report from the Defence Ministry, and our finding his notes in the secret compartment in his desk, and then the unfortunate article in the *Herald*. I then produced these papers, and there was a pause while Peter and Sue read them, after which I went on with my meeting with M. Duchene and my subsequent odd experiences in Bayonne. He didn't just accept what was said, but queried several things in great detail, and after all that came my meeting with Julie and Michelle, and they told their tale, including the 1942 visit by the German officer and then the visit to Marseilles in the summer of 1945 when Xavier did the post mortem on the corpse of a young man who was given the name Pierre Dupont. Then we covered the trip to Marseilles by Michelle and me to see Xavier, and the discovery that Pierre Dupont had not died in 1945. Lastly, we covered the death of Xavier, our adventure in Avignon, and the attempt to track us when we left.

Peter was quiet for a few moments after we finished, and before he could speak, Julie broke in. "You can appreciate my feelings in this matter, we have been living quietly for some sixty years, knowing nothing of all this, but since we have turned over this old stone, my dear brother-in-law is dead…almost certainly murdered…although the authorities may think otherwise. More than that, an attempt has been made on the lives of Michelle and of Charles here, and they even tried to find out where we were going after leaving Avignon by putting a tracking gadget on our car. I for one would happily give up the whole affair if I were not convinced that such action wouldn't buy our safety…if we did stop now I am sure we would spend the rest of our lives looking over our shoulders…so, Peter, what should we do?"

"I am very much afraid," he said gravely, "that I must agree with you about your continuing danger…they must have suspected that you were coming here, but put this gadget on your car just as a check…and so we must first take steps to ensure your safety. I'll come back to that later, but as to your enquiry I think that we must proceed with all haste and bring matters to a head. There would seem no shadow of doubt that Pierre Dupont did manage to acquire the identity of Vincent Fouquet back in 1945, and no question about it has ever arisen since then. But he and his colleagues must have kept some kind of watching brief on newspapers in Britain, and that little paragraph in the *Herald* must have been a severe shock to him, and it also seems certain that he has the resources of the Union Corse at his disposal. However, if we do manage to get conclusive evidence against him, and make it public, then his usefulness to them will come to an end, and that will then probably spell safety for all of you."

He paused for a moment to drink some coffee, then he turned to Granny. "But now the first thing we must do is to find the location of this buried treasure, and here we have the advantage of the opposition. Let's just look at the relevant sections of these papers…in your late husband's report to the Air Ministry, he reported…" Here he riffled through the sheets. "Yes, here it is…'we buried it nearby with the intention of returning it to the old man's daughter after the war' – so although the opposition got a copy of that report, that is all they know as regards the location of the treasure, and of the vital golden bowl. But fortunately we – and we only – have these notes which were lost for some sixty years, and here in these notes your husband said…'we did bury the treasures, in a place where we could find them again'. The site is in a wood about three miles out on the road towards Bayonne, and is some 30 paces south of a large stone. But what is surprising, Charles, is that when you went down a road to Bayonne there was no sign of woods, and you didn't see any large stone, so we shall have to find out whether there is – or was – another road, or else what changes have taken place in the road you saw, and then see if we can work out what things were like back in 1942. It does seem that these, so-called, treasures are still there to be found, as if our arch villain, Pierre Dupont – alias Vincent Fouquet – had already found and dug up the items, including the incriminating gold bowl, then he would have had nothing to worry about, and would have had no need to bother you…for him it would have been a case of the least said and done the better."

"So?" he smiled, "Where does that leave us?"

"It means," I said, "that despite the risk I'll need to go back and do some more research on the ground. It must be possible to find traces of where the woods were, even after all these years, and I'll have to ask some locals if they can remember what that road was like in the 1940s, and if a large stone means anything to them."

But Peter held up his hand. "I've got a better idea," he said. "You see, I don't at all like the idea of making enquiries in that area as I am sure the Union Corse are taking this matter very seriously indeed, and a secret shared is no longer a secret. So now I am going to ask all of you to trust me for just a few days, as I have an idea which may help in solving the problem. Having said that, I must also say that I'd rather not tell you at this stage just what I intend doing! So if you can you all bear with me…I would hope to have the information in four days, by Thursday morning of this week…will you be patient till then?"

He was so convincing that none of us queried his request, and he then surprised us by showing how seriously he intended looking after our security. He first turned to M. Duchene, saying, "M. Duchene, I am sure that all these folk are most grateful to you for finding out all this vital information, and also for giving so much of your time in coming here, but at present I am going to suggest that you leave things in our hands. Be assured that we'll keep in touch, but for now I would suggest, in order to simplify the security arrangements here, that it would be as well for you to return to Paris. We'll see that you are looked after here till you get a flight tomorrow morning, and I cannot see that you will be in any danger once you get back home."

I had expected him to object, and was surprised when he said, "I agree, Mr Armstrong, "I've done my bit in digging up all this information about Vincent Fouquet, so I'll get off the playing field and into reserve for now. But the key to everything is in France, and I'll bet that I have to get involved at some stage, before it is all over."

Peter then turned to Granny. "I can tell you that I don't at all like the involvement of the Union Corse in this affair, as they are just as ruthless as the Mafia where their interests are concerned…and for some reason, which surely must involve this buried golden bowl, they appear to be desperate to get it before you people. Because of this, if you will allow me, I intend to get two of my people to keep a watch on your house here, at least for the present. I wonder also if you and Julie and also the young people could agree to staying indoors for the next few days…it would make things easier for me."

I saw Granny and Julie give rather doubtful nods of assent, but this didn't appeal to me at all. "But what about Michelle and me?" I said, "I've brought her here to see Scotland, and surely you can't expect us to stay indoors as well until next Thursday…I suppose that is the earliest time for you to complete your investigation?" "Yes it is," he said, "as I need the cooperation of some other people, and I cannot see our getting the results earlier than that."

"Okay," I said, and I wondered if I could get off with a really splendid idea. "But if Julie will trust me with Michelle, why don't the two of us sneak away, and let me show her some of the beauties of Scotland. Once we are away from here there is no chance of them finding where we are, and we should be quite safe, and get back on Thursday morning."

"That would seem sensible," he said, "but what do Michelle and Julie have to say about it?"

For a moment Julie looked doubtful – as also did Granny – but then she smiled. "Yes, why not, it will do the two of you good to get away from all this nonsense, and from all us old people, for a few days…but what about you, Michelle, do you want to go off with Charles?"

And the answer to that was written by her smile. With that arranged, Mr Armstrong phoned some unit of his, and I realised that he was arranging for a permanent 24-hour watch to be kept on our house, and then he mentioned something about a search team to come here immediately. With that in train, he addressed us as if he were the officer in charge of our unit, and explained what we had to do. Firstly, none of us would be allowed to go back to our house tonight until it had been checked for booby traps.

But as he said this, Granny stopped him. "Look, Peter, surely we are getting into the realms of fantasy. We have only been out of my house for about three hours, surely you can't think that anything has been done in that short time?"

"Marie," he said, "I spent quite a few years of my life in fighting terrorists of various kinds, and the most important lesson I learned was not to underrate the opposition, and also to start taking all necessary precautions at once. Now I don't think that you were away this morning from your house sufficiently long enough for them to start, but this evening is different as already you've been here for quite a while. However, when my boys get here it will only take about ten minutes to make sure that everything is safe. Then – and only then – should you, Julie, Michelle, and Charles go back."

It was only about half an hour later when two cars drove up, one of them with the two guards for our house, and the other with the two-man search team. I had with me the necessary keys, including, of course, the keys of the alarm system, and went with them to identify the house. It was very educational to see how they went about things. First of all they examined the outside, which was easy given the addition of an almost full moon. We had security lights, which came on with darkness, and there were no obvious signs of forced entry. Then they asked me where the main electricity switches were – they were in a cupboard beside the front door – and got me to explain how to turn off the alarm system, after which I was told to wait in the car until they went in. There was no problem to begin with as they opened the front door, but then I realised that something was very wrong as the alarm system should have given a 'Beep...Beep...Beep...' until it was switched off, but now there was silence.

"Stay where you are!" one of the men called out. "Something is wrong!" And as they said that all the outside lights went off as they switched the power off at the mains. It was only a few minutes later till the security lights came on again and they called me into the house. "All clear now, Mr

Burton, and it would seem that this was just a warning – look at this." And he pointed at the door from the hall into the dining room where, to my astonishment, I saw a big sheet of paper crudely fixed to the beautiful, polished mahogany by a six-inch nail, driven right through the panel to the other side. The message on it was:

> J U S T A F R I E N D L Y W A R N I N G
> L E A V E U S A L O N E
> O T H E R W I S E Y O U M A Y N O T
> L I V E T O R E G R E T I T

They did a quick check around the house, but then one of them said, "I think we can assume that this affair was just a warning, but we may find out something about them if we examine their methods. As regards the fault on the alarm system, I'll be interested to see how they dealt with immobilising it."

That didn't take long, but then they suggested that I sit down and read the papers till they were finished – it was quite clear that they wanted me out of the road! However, at last they finished a complete survey of the interior and the exterior of the house and, after about half an hour, when they were satisfied that everything was safe, the two of them came and took me back to the Henderson's house, leaving the two-man security team to keep an eye on things. Obviously, they had reported to Mr Armstrong, no doubt by a mobile phone, so he knew that something had been amiss. He said to his men, "Well, well, tell me all about it."

It didn't take them long to explain what had happened, and although he looked puzzled he didn't then ask any questions, but just said that he would arrange for Julie, Granny, Michelle, and the Hendersons to be escorted to the house with me, and that he and Sue would also come with them.

Back in the house, very predictably, Granny was furious at the damage to her dining room door, but I could see that this only served to stiffen her resolve to see the affair through to the end, and she nodded with approval when Peter suggested that we should all talk some more about the affair. So, once more, we all sat round a table, this time our dining table, and he said, “It’s a puzzle isn’t it? Why, Marie, did they break into your house, and leave that message? Well, my answer is that while I am sure they want rid of you, they don’t want to get involved with murder, at least for the present – that would have started a full scale enquiry. But it was a clear warning saying “LEAVE US ALONE!” and the question we now have to answer is whether we do what they want, and give up the quest…but that is odd as there is a puzzle about why they say that, since what they want above all else is to find that golden bowl before we do. You see, if we were to give up now it would leave them still with the possibility of the bowl being found at some later date. So maybe they would be happy to keep us alive, if it could be arranged that when we dug up the bowl they could then be able to steal it from us. Now if that is true, then the warning is just to annoy us and be a spur to go on with the search. It is all very confused, and the question which must be answered by you, Marie, and you, Julie, is whether or not we still go on with the quest. It must be your decision because your involvement is much more personal than that of either Michelle or Charles.”

I was sitting beside Michelle, and she took my hand and gave a tiny nod of her head, and it was quite clear to me that she was agreeing with him. As for the two old ladies, they answered almost in the same words and although I can’t remember exactly what they said, it added up to ”We can’t let the bastards off with it – to hell with it – let’s go on!”

"I commend your sentiments," he smiled, "but if there is nothing more we can do now, shall we call it a night? As for tomorrow I'll be round at about nine o'clock, just to see if any of you are having second thoughts."

***

After breakfast next morning Peter came as arranged, and he was told that we were going on with the chase. As regards Michelle and me, the gist of his remarks was that he wished us to take some extra precautions, and he was sending a car for us to use while we were away on our trip, just in case they had watchers looking out for my Ford Mondeo, the registration number of which was familiar to them. So, soon after that a red Ford Focus arrived and was driven to the back of the house by a man with a most impressive black beard. I couldn't help laughing when he came into the house, peeled it off in a secluded back room, and told me I was to wear it when we departed. Peter then managed to get me on my own, and asked if I had as yet made a hotel reservation, and he surprised me by asking me not to use the house phone, but to do so on his mobile phone, and he smiled, saying, "Ask no questions and you will be told no lies!"

He was also kind enough to leave me to make the call without Michelle overhearing what I said. The car was parked out of sight at the back of the house, so we could load up in privacy, with Michelle having to lie down in the back of the car and behind the front seats, before I drove off in my disguise. I had been told to go a considerable distance before stopping to let Michelle appear, while all the time looking out for a following car, but there were no problems, and just before we joined the M8 through Glasgow she popped over beside me, saying, "Do you know, darling, you really look quite handsome in that beard, do you think you could grow one."

"I'm sure I could," I said, "but just think how tickly it would be when I kissed you – and I intend to do that rather often in the next few days."

"Good!" she smiled, "I shall hold you to that promise. But with all this excitement I haven't asked you where we are going, and there is one important thing which obviously you have not yet found out about me!"

"And what would that be, darling?"

"Don't try to soft soap me with that darling stuff…you see, I too have a mind of my own, and I can tell you right now that we shall only go to this destination of yours, if I too approve."

"I'm delighted," I said, "that you have a mind of your own, and all you now have to do from now on, is to ensure that it always agrees with mine!"

"Come on," she smiled, "enough of this nonsense, where the hell are we going?"

As we had been talking we had just then come to the turn off the M8 on to the M80 leading to Stirling, so I fished out a map and gave it to her. "Have a guess, darling…see, there is where we are now…"

For a few minutes she studied the map, and then I saw her smile. "I think I know where you are taking me, it must be to St Andrews. Isn't that what you British call, taking coals to Newcastle? I am sure that at least some old girlfriends of yours up there, from your university days, will be lining up to see you, and that is not at all what I was looking forward to about this trip."

"Don't worry," I said, "I phoned them this morning, and they will be discreet, at least for today! And don't hit me," I laughed, as I saw her pick up a rolled newspaper, "at least not while I am driving a car!"

"I shall wait, my ex-darling, until we stop, but just look out then!"

My good luck as regards the weather was continuing as the sun was still shining and the sky was blue as we drove into the Auld Grey City, and I hoped that the magic I always felt there would also come to Michelle. I had, of course, used Peter's mobile phone in the morning to phone Russacks Hotel and to reserve a double room overlooking the 18th Hole of the Old Course, and when we got checked in and they had shown us our accommodation Michelle looked at our large double bed with a happy smile.

"But there is just one problem," she said, "I am sure that bed will be quite adequate, even although that princess might have found fault with it, but there really is not enough space in the room for that orchestra I asked for…"

But then we found ourselves in each other's arms, and she whispered, "Well…just maybe…I can make do without it!"

But then she wriggled away from me. "Let's see what else there is. For starters, what's the view like?"

I took her to the window, saying, "This is one of the most famous views in the whole world. That stretch of grass there is the 1st and 18th holes of the Old Course, the 18th green is there to the right, and that building is the Clubhouse of the Royal and Ancient Golf Club."

"Should I be impressed?" she teased me. "I thought that golf courses had sandpits called bunkers, and there is nothing out there to make things interesting. What a dull course it is!"

"My sweet," I laughed, "you can consider yourself lucky that I haven't decided to give up this room and take you straight back to Paisley. Anyway, I shall not lose hope of you just yet, but I can see that you are in serious need of some education. As regards these two holes, while it is true that they don't have any bunkers, they are still among the most famous in the world." I had in fact made some advance preparations, and arranged with the hotel when I phoned them that there would be a video in the room with tapes of Open Championships, and the one on the machine was that of the 1995 event, so I wound it on to the bit near the end where Rocco and Daly were involved and Rocco holed that ridiculous approach at the 18th to tie the game. It was so different then, tens of thousands of people milling around, and probably a TV audience approaching fifty million, and I think that some of the magic got through to Michelle – aided, perhaps, with some drinks I got from the mini-bar.

Anyway, we resisted the attractions of that lovely bed and went down for lunch, followed by the obligatory sightseeing tour of the old town, and there is indeed a lot to see. We started with a walk up the Scores, past the Martyrs' Memorial, and then into some of the University buildings and the old University Library, once the Parliament Hall of Scotland, outside which was the oak tree planted by Mary Queen of Scots. Then, after the town, I took her through the ruin of the old cathedral, at one time the greatest church in Christendom north of Rome, but now a sad and ruined reminder of the days of the Reformation. I think what impressed her most in our walk was the fact that a few of the students we saw were wearing scarlet gowns – reminders of the fact that the University had been founded by the Pope in 1411. "I love traditions," she said, "so often nowadays people seem almost to be ashamed of them, but this is great."

"If you want traditions," I laughed, "that means another little walk. You see the old pier down there? Well, the tradition is to walk down there with your chums – or with your boy or girlfriend. You have to go out on the wide track to the very end, then climb that ladder you can see there, and come back along the top of that wall. It was – and probably still is

– a popular enterprise after Chapel Service on Sunday mornings, and the good Lord must approve as, so far as I know, nobody has yet fallen off the wall on to the rocks below."

"Let's risk it!" she smiled, and when we were on our way back, along the high narrow wall, she suddenly stopped. "What is that old building there?"

"That, my sweet, is the old Castle, but we'll leave that till tomorrow. You will have all sorts of things to look at there, from bottle dungeons to tunnels, some dug by besiegers, and others dug by defenders. It has a gory history. But today, while the sun in shining, let's walk along the beach, the West Sands, which you saw from our hotel room, and we'll do the East Sands tomorrow. What I want to show you then is the Maiden Rock, which we can climb if you feel brave."

There was nobody around and, despite the narrowness of the top of the wall, she put her arms round me and whispered, "Well, tomorrow is another day, but I'm certainly not risking anything happening to me today as having screwed up my courage to go to bed with you tonight, I'm damned if I want anything to prevent it, such as a broken leg, so, my boy, you be careful too!"

Well, nothing untoward did happen…and after dinner, as we sat in the lounge with our coffees and cognacs – I hadn't dared to suggest malt whisky! – and looked out at the last of the golfers coming in as the light faded, I thought that it was all pure magic. She felt some of it too, and took my hand, saying, "I can see why this place means so much to you, it really is very special." She leaned closer to me. "I can tell you, darling, that I am now quite resigned to there being no orchestra…shall we…?"

Well, we did, but not immediately. When we got back to our room she surprised me by sitting down in one of the armchairs. "Get me a drink, darling, and get one for yourself also. For the last few days I've been trying to pluck up the courage to tell you an unfortunate bit of my personal history, and I'll never feel right until I get it off my chest."

She was so serious about it, that I didn't quite know what to say, so I just got us two whiskies and water and said, "Here we are, Scotch will give you all the courage you need, and why don't you come and sit on my knee – a bit of togetherness seems what is called for." She gave me a doubtful smile, but did as I suggested, and it was with a glass in one hand and the other cupping one of her lovely breasts that I smiled at her. "Come on, darling, get whatever it is off your chest."

"I'll do that," she said, and gave me a tiny smile, "but please don't take your hand off my chest as I rather like it there! As you can probably guess, it is about my last year at Lyon University. Up till then I'd had a number of boyfriends, but it was just part of my growing up, and my feminine hormones getting busy – I am sure that you were just the same with your girlfriends here. But then I got what began just as a crush on one of the junior lecturers, a very suave young man – late twenties – from Paris. He seemed such an attractive man of the world, that I was delighted when he took me aside one day after classes, and asked if I would have dinner with him. Well, we had dinner, and after the third occasion he took me to bed, and I thought that I was no end of a sophisticated young lady. He was, of course, married, but he assured me that he loved me and that he would arrange a divorce from his wife…starry-eyed idiot that I was, I accepted all that. I don't know how long things would have gone on had I not been in the library one day, hidden behind a pile of books, when I saw him come in with another of my fellow students, a gorgeous blonde girl, and they sat down quite near me. I won't try to tell you all they said to each other, but the gist was that she agreed to spend that night with him, and he promised to get rid of me as soon as he could."

She stopped for a moment and then, to my surprise, she giggled before going on. "Oddly enough, I wasn't in the least sorry to hear him speak in this way, I was just bloody angry and – most fortunately – I had bought a large tray of raspberries before coming to the library, and I went over and smashed them into his face before he knew what was happening. I can tell you that I was delighted to see that he was dressed in what I knew were a new pair of mohair trousers, and a cashmere jersey, and it was with unholy delight that I saw the juice dripping down on it, I very much doubt if cleaning could ever get it and the trousers right again…and that still pleases me, even although all that took place more than a year ago. The affair certainly made me look a bit of a fool, but it did get to the ears of the University authorities, and I believe that they made their own enquiries and found that he was no end of a Lothario. Anyway, he suddenly disappeared from the campus a few weeks later, which was the end of the affair so far as I was concerned, but I was left with the knowledge that I had been a young fool to give my virginity to such a man."

I was glad that Michelle had come clean with me, as I had been aware that something had been bothering her, and I decided that it was time for a spot of confession of my own. "Is that all? I said, "I thought that you were going to tell me something really dreadful. I'm sure that making mistakes similar to yours is all part of growing up and I most certainly am not free of them, so I think this might be an appropriate time for me to make my little speech and tell you all about them."

After my little speech, she smiled. "Is that all, so isn't it time now for us to finish these drinks and – "

"Not yet, darling, you see there is something which I have been trying to summon up the courage to say to you, and now I am going to risk it…I'll just finish my drink to give me – not Dutch courage, but some good Scotch stuff! It is very simple, Michelle, and I hope you'll forgive my not getting down on my knees when I say this…I love you with all my heart, darling, will you marry me?"

At first she didn't answer, just drew me closer and kissed me…then said, "Charles, my very dear, I'm the same, as I also love you with all my heart, and right now I am the happiest girl in the world."

I couldn't help laughing. "Does that mean that I am accepted as your future husband?"

"I think so," she laughed, "but just ask me tomorrow morning before we get up. I'll know a lot more about you by then!"

It was as dawn broke that I wakened, to find that I still held Michelle in my arms. The room was warm, and the bedclothes had been cast aside and, in the dim light, with the cascade of her dark hair falling across the white of her breasts, I thought that I had never seen anything as lovely in my life. I bent down and teased one of her nipples with my tongue and, as her eyes opened, she gently stroked my face before whispering, "I love you my darling, that was a wonderful night…and now I really know what making love means. It was incredible, each time was better than the last…but…do you think you could possibly manage it, maybe even only once more, before we get up?"

"And if I do manage it," I said seriously, "can I assume that my proposal of marriage has been finally accepted?"

Until then we had spoken nothing but French that night, as she had insisted that it was the language of love. But now she suddenly changed to crude English when she laughed. "Too bloody right! You were accepted the very first time we made love, and I have never felt as happy in my whole life as I did then…so now, how about just getting on with it!"

Until that morning, Michelle had been true to her upbringing, and for breakfast, sticking to coffee and a croissant – or toast if all else failed – but when we were ordering I saw her looking at the menu while I ordered my usual: orange juice, black coffee, porridge and cream, and bacon and eggs…with rolls and toast. She then astonished me when she smiled at the waiter and said, "Just the same for me, please!"

She saw my surprise, but then whispered to me – and I hope that the people at the adjoining table didn't hear her – "after all that healthy exercise I think that a full Scottish breakfast is necessary…and to hell with my waistline!" I also hoped that nobody was within earshot when she finished the very last crumb of the toast, having demolished everything else on the table, and said, "Well that has repaired some of the damage and now if we have a nice, restful day, maybe I'll be ready for the rigours of the night!"

After breakfast we walked again towards the West Sands – the setting for the film *Chariots of Fire* – and our route took us, by way of Granny Smith's Wynd, across the 18th and 1st fairways, and we did so after two men had driven off from the 1st tee. We stopped to watch them playing their second shots and, as I thought it might interest Michelle, I said, "See, they are now playing to the green over a very famous waterway called the Swilcan Burn; their drives are a bit short, and they will be playing maybe 5 or 6 irons." If I had stopped there all would have been well, but I went on to boast a little. "I can usually get on with a 9 iron!"

To my surprise, she was suddenly standing with her arms akimbo, just as when I first came to her house and she glared at me. "I have just realised that I was premature this morning when I accepted your proposal of marriage…but it is entirely your fault as you have been guilty of making your proposal to me under false pretences, as it is only now you tell me that you play golf, and you have never even mentioned that before!"

"So what?" I smiled. "Why is that a problem?"

"Why? Because I have heard of golf widows, and no way do I intend to be one! So, tell me, are you a member of a golf club?"

I wasn't sure if all this was half fun or whole in earnest, so I took a chance of it being the former. "I'm a member of two golf clubs…but for goodness sake, walk on now as there are some others on the 1st tee waiting to drive!"

When we reached the safety of the beach road, she turned and kissed my cheek.

"There, darling, I hope I worried you! But, I have a nasty suspicion that I'll need to take up this ridiculous game so as to be upsides with you."

That seemed a good idea to me, and I went on to explain that while I had joined the Glasgow Golf Club, as my father had been a member there, I had recently, under pressure from my Great-Aunt Agnes, joined The Kilmacolm Golf Club, as she was a past Lady Captain of it, and I went on to say, "I'm sure she will be able to get you in quickly, and there is a very good professional, Iain Nicholson, who can give you lessons." One again she was standing with her arms akimbo. "You bloody ex-darling again! I am astonished that even now, at this early stage in our relationship, you would seem to be too busy to teach me yourself…this really has been a very revealing morning!"

But she then laughed. "Don't worry for now, as I didn't really mean these expressions of displeasure, however, I felt that I should remind you – just for your own good – that you must always be nice and considerate in your dealings with me, as I really do have a temper which is always on a short fuse!" And on that happy note I am sure she shocked a few staid St Andreans by welding herself to me and giving me a fierce kiss – which I reciprocated. It was a magical few days – and of course nights – and we spent the time getting to know each other, with my showing her some more of St Andrews, and also something of the countryside.

One day I took her across the Tay Bridge to Dundee, and then into the great soft fruit area beyond, and I said to her, "I can tell you one thing, Michelle, this is the place to come to in July if you want to assault anybody else. Just look around, because as far as the eye can see, all these fields are of raspberries!"

"Very funny," she said, "but don't push your luck too far; I've been very careful to show you that I've got a temper, so just look out!"

***

CHAPTER EIGHT

It was with considerable regret that Michelle and I packed our bags on the Thursday morning to make our way back to Paisley and, just as we were about to leave our room, she took my hand and murmured, "Do you know, darling, I feel like getting one of these blue plaques fixed to the wall at the head of that lovely bed, saying: CHARLES AND MICHELLE SLEPT HERE AND WERE VERY, VERY HAPPY!"

As I took her in my arms and whispered my agreement I knew that I had been fortunate beyond all my imagining in finding such a wonderful girl as my mate. But we hadn't much time for sentiment as when I had called Granny the previous evening, she had told me that Peter had confirmed that he and my boss, William, would be at our house for lunch, and that they would come early so that we could have a talk before the meal. So she warned me that we should get back by about half past eleven, or earlier if we could. What was exciting, however, was that she also told me that he had found the evidence he had hoped to get, and would give us all the details when he saw us. This had certainly given us something new to talk about on the journey home, as we couldn't work out what methods he could have used, and we were very curious. Anyway, we got back in plenty of time, and when we got into the house, I was amused to see that both Granny and Julie seemed to be taking a very hard look at us. Michelle too had noticed this, and she said to Julie, "Why all the close attention we are getting?…we've only been away for four days."

Then she turned to me with a laugh. "These two obviously want a blow-by-blow account of what we have been up to, so we'd better tell them our news…and I'm sure that both of our grandmothers will think that it is good news…you see, Charles and I have decided that we want to get married!"

The response was rather surprising, and not at all what I expected, as Julie turned to Granny and said, "I knew it… that's ten pence you owe me!"

I couldn't help laughing, and turned to Michelle. "Do you realise, darling, that these two old dears have been betting on our love life…isn't it disgusting!"

"Not at all," my granny said, "we have just been showing a healthy interest in what is going on, and from the stars in Michelle's eyes, everything must be well in that quarter. But what we have been talking about is just how long it was going to take for the two of you to make things respectable, and in this I must confess, Charles, that you have let me down. I felt sure that I could rely on your Scottish upbringing to make you wait even just a few more days before springing the question, and your impetuosity has cost me ten hard earned pence." But then she too laughed and turned to Michelle holding out her arms. "I am of course only teasing, my dear, so come and give me a kiss, as I'm absolutely delighted at your news. I told Charles about my feelings towards you before you went off, and I am very happy for both of you…and certainly he is a very lucky young man."

I was similarly complimented by Julie, and then Granny said, "This should be a time for champagne, but with this meeting we are about to have with Peter and William we'd better put it off for now…go and get your things unpacked so that we are ready for them when they arrive."

In fact they came together just a few minutes later, and we had pre-lunch drinks before we ate, and it wasn't until after one o'clock that Granny took us all through into the dining room…past the still-to-be-repaired door…where once again we sat formally round the table and got straight down to business. It was Peter who spoke first. "This, I feel, is a case of it's not what you know, but who you know – as it occurred to me when we were talking the other night that, what the thriller writers call our cousins, might be able to help. Now it so happens that I have friends in America, at Langley, who are connected with indexing the photographic coverage of the world which is given by the spy satellites, which now look down on just about every square yard of the earth's surface. Fortunately, one of them owed me a favour, which I called up, as I wondered if by any chance there might be a record of the Bayonne area going back for a number of years, and we struck lucky. Here, just look at these photographs." He opened an oversized brief case and produced a sheaf of big glossy photographs, each about two feet by eighteen inches in size, and passed them round to us one by one. "See," he said, "here is the first one, taken in August 1978, and you will see that most of the woods are still there…"

I found myself looking at a crystal-clear aerial picture showing the area from the southern tip of the Etang de Laguibe, as far as the outskirts of Bayonne, and he called our attention to an arrow on the print. "See, it is pointing to the wood there, and the large stone which can be seen near the road must be it."

Other photographs in the early 1980s showed little change, but one or two in the following years showed the woods being cleared and one in 1989 had happened to catch a kind of JCB machine which was working, obviously excavating the stone, and then another picture a few months later showed no signs of it, but tracks of the machine could still be seen heading through what had been the woods, and up to a large house under construction, where it could be seen that the stone had been installed as part of a water garden feature.

"We were very lucky," he said, "as we might have worried why the stone was removed, but these pictures explain everything. Odd, isn't it, that of all the stones in the area they had to pick ours for their garden! However, these survey photos aren't just pretty pictures as they can also give map references with which we can place anything on them within maybe a yard or so. So if you go there, you can go with a radio navigation aid – these are now no bigger than a quite small transistor – and if you feed in the map reference, it will take you to the exact spot where that stone used to be."

I was about to break in, but he held up his hand. "Just a moment now, you will appreciate that in getting these pictures, and in showing them to you, I have broken all sorts of rules and regulations, and..." He stopped for a moment and smiled, "...despite all this EC business, what makes it worse is that Julie and Michelle are foreign nationals. So, can I please have assurances from all of you that you will keep this to yourselves?"

We all did so, and then I said, "Peter, you are a miracle worker. I had imagined that I would have to spend ages finding the exact position of that stone, and now you tell me that I can just walk straight to where it used to be...and then I just need to walk thirty paces to the south, and then DIG! Incidentally, I can take half of your load off your mind, as Michelle has recently done me the honour of saying that she will marry me, so she will soon be as British as Granny here...although I am afraid that she still insists that she is

French!" My suggestion seemed an obvious idea to me, but Michelle looked over at me and shook her head. "Don't you ever think, my dear Charles, that you have now been elected to run my life for me – take your friend with you if you must, but I am coming too…"

But she didn't get any further, as Peter very firmly raised his hand. "Just a minute, Michelle, I don't think that either you or Charles are taking this matter seriously enough. You already have evidence of just how ruthless these Union Corse people are and, if you will forgive me, it is no situation for amateurs to make the decisions. I confess that my preference is just to get some of my own people to do the job, but I suspect that Charles will insist on going – and maybe he should as it was his grandfather who buried the stuff – but if he does he will go with one of my people"

That statement brought home to us – what we had tended to forget – that we had to be careful, and Michelle looked up at me. "Darling, I wasn't thinking straight, and for me, your safety is the only thing that matters. So, if you want to pass the job to the experts I shall quite realise why you are doing so…all I want is for whole affair to be over soon, and that we all live to tell the tale."

We talked some more, but at last it was agreed that I would go, and that Peter would provide a 'minder' for me. When it came to making detailed plans, he gave us his orders, and that is what they were when he said, "I confess that I expected we would come to this arrangement, and I suggest that we move as soon as possible. I think the best way for you, Charles, to get to Bayonne is to go there through Spain, so I suggest that you leave here on Tuesday and then catch a Brittany Ferries boat from Plymouth to Santander. There is a crossing on Wednesday, leaving at noon, which gets to Spain at lunchtime on Thursday, just a week today. Now I suggest that the best time to do the job is very early in the morning, so you and my chap will need to lie up somewhere for the night and be ready to get off, and over the frontier, very early on the Friday – it will be light by five o'clock so you should be able to get to the Bayonne area and do the job without any people being up and around to see you. Just as a precaution, I'll give you one of our cars for the journey – the Union Corse know the number of your Mondeo – and after you've done the job you can drive, as fast as you can, into Spain and up to the Embassy in Madrid, leave the car there and catch a plane for London. I'll get your boat tickets for Spain now, and somebody from the Embassy will give you plane tickets for the return journey."

He then paused before going on. "Now, as regards your departure I'll make arrangements so that it is not seen by any watching eyes that may be around – I'll explain all this later." As I listened to all these smooth arrangements – such as lending me a car which would be abandoned in Madrid – something didn't seem quite right to me. Certainly, Peter, this mystery man, was being very helpful, but…damn it!… he was being far too helpful. Why should he be putting so many official resources at our disposal? So I looked over at him. "You are being most helpful, Peter, but I confess that I am becoming unhappy as to the extent of all that you are doing for us. Don't you think that you also owe it to us to explain why?"

I confess that I was pleased to see him look embarrassed, as it proved that I was right in my suspicions, and it was a few moments before he replied. "You are too smart, Charles, as I hoped that nobody would ask that question. But, since you have asked it, I have no option but to try to answer it. Before I do so, however, I wonder if you will allow me to explain again some things to Julie and to Michelle…it is about certain concerns which we have regarding this M. Fouquet, and what we should like to do about him."

He turned and spoke directly to Julie. "You have already told me that, apart from your personal reasons, you do not like M. Fouquet's politics, and I have a suggestion to make which you and Michelle may not at once agree with, but to which I hope you will at least give due consideration. You see, you both know that he is no friend either of yours, or of the France you love, or indeed of Britain, and this makes me wonder if, just maybe, you will understand…and eventually agree with…a proposal which I am about to put to all of you. You see, your villain, M. Fouquet – the erstwhile Pierre – is well known in official quarters here in Britain as an enemy of ours – and maybe that hatred goes right back to 1952 when Charles' grandfather killed his German lover. Now, his present position, where he holds the government of France in his hands, is all very worrying. We are also concerned now about problems which may arise at certain conferences, which will take place soon, and the possibility of being able to disgrace him is most interesting to us. Having said that, however, we hope that we can persuade all of you here to agree that we deal with the procedure regarding what we do about him on an agreed basis. Like you, we would be delighted to see him out of office, but the timing, as and when we can achieve that, could be vital for British interests."

I suddenly noticed a certain ambiguity in what he had said…he had previously mentioned disgracing Fouquet, but now his line seemed to be getting him out of office and doing so within a timescale, and when I raised that with him, he laughed, saying, "I can see that you aren't going to let me away with anything…and yes, there is an important difference in the two options. The four of you here, two Burtons and two Lebruns, want vengeance on an evil man, which you see as disgracing him by exposing his ancient sin, and also his association with the Union Corse, which has led up to the death of M. Xavier Lebrun and all the rest of it. Now, it is possible that this course might, in certain circumstances, be convenient to Britain, but on the other hand it might suit our ends better if he were quite simply to be blackmailed towards taking his party into a more favourable attitude towards us and, having done so for a while, to then resign from public life. You would not get your public disgrace, but still you would have got him forced out of office which must mean a lot to him."

He paused and shook his head, as if to clear his thoughts, then he went on. "I am not sure at this stage what will be considered the best official option, as it will all depend on the circumstances when the time arises, but I hope for now that I can persuade you just to think of cooperating with us... with no commitment at this stage. What I would like to agree with all of you this afternoon is that we proceed immediately with the recovery of the jewels and, hopefully, the golden bowl, and then, after that, I would arrange for you to come with me for a private meeting with the Foreign Secretary who, I can tell you, is already most interested in the affair. He has asked me to say that he will not insist on your accepting our views in advance, but he hopes that, after the event, you will at least allow him to talk with you and then give his suggestions your consideration. You see, we shall then be in a rather odd situation...or at least we shall be if we have the bowl. The position then will be that, for our part, we shall know that we have the power to disgrace M. Fouquet at the time of our choosing, but is essential that we keep our action secret, in recovering the buried treasure. You see, as regards our ability to identify him I may tell you that Fouquet had a meal in a restaurant in Paris last Tuesday night, and one of our people was able to purloin a glass which he had used, so we now have a clear set of his fingerprints...it was disgraceful, wasn't it! Anyway, now, till he finds out that we have the bowl and we tell him that we have his prints, he will remain in blissful ignorance of events, but we shall then be in the position to choose the most appropriate moment to make our move."

It seemed incredible to me to hear him talking casually about these arrangements and our meeting the Foreign Secretary, but I noticed that William did not appear to be surprised, so obviously he knew more about Peter than the rest of us. But before I could speak, Granny looked over at him and shook her head. "Mr Armstrong – this is now too serious a matter for me to call you Peter – you talk in riddles, how on earth can you speak to us in this way? For what is probably the second most important politician in the country to get involved in our affair seems nonsense, as does the fact that he would seem to be dealing with this personally, since you mentioned a private meeting. Why would he be involved, and not one of his officials? Until this afternoon I have imagined that you were just a very helpful civil servant who happened to be based in Glasgow, but you must be a most important one to talk to us as you have done. As for me, either you come clean as to your position in this country – or – I want nothing more to do with your arrangements. If I am going for a swim I want at least to know how deep the water is!"

Peter looked at William and said ruefully, "You did warn me that I might have problems this afternoon, so..." He turned back to Granny. "Let me answer the easier of your two questions first. The reason the Foreign Secretary is dealing with the matter personally is because of this possible blackmailing of an important member of the French government. Now this is a very delicate matter and twenty years ago – even maybe ten years ago – ministers could trust their civil servants but now, while the mandarins – the 'Sir Humphries' of fiction – are mostly loyal to their masters, where juniors and secretaries are concerned, this is now not always the case. I don't, for example, need to tell you how many leaks get reported in the tabloid press. The problem arises in this case because, if we were to treat it on a normal basis, there would be meetings with ministers and their civil service aids, with secretaries to record everything which was said, all of which would be recorded and a mass of photocopies taken by just those juniors which I have mentioned. So what I and my Minister fear is just one of them, deciding that he – or she – might forget loyalties and expose what they think is a plot by a wicked government – probably one not of his or her personal persuasion – and get a nice wad of tax-free money for doing so. That, we cannot risk…"

"In this affair," he went on, "we are talking of disgracing, or maybe blackmailing, a minister in the government of a friendly power, and the scandal would be colossal if the story were to become public. However, I am fortunate enough to have direct access to ministers, and in cases like this we deal with the matters on a need to know basis…and in this case that means only a very small team of mine along with just the Prime Minister and the Foreign Secretary."

He paused for a moment, and then gave a rather wry smile. "You will appreciate that these arrangements have many advantages for ministers, one of them being that the government can categorically deny any involvement should things go wrong. So, Charles, you will appreciate that, for you, this could be somewhat of a disadvantage as, if there were problems while you are in France, we could not be seen to help you, or indeed to admit that we knew what you were up to…and I would ask you to bear this in mind before finally agreeing to go on with the recovery of the jewels and the bowl."

That was a bit of a shaker, and I'm not sure what my reply would have been, had Granny not seen a mail van drive up and, within a few minutes, the doorbell rang. I excused myself, and found that it was a special delivery letter addressed to me and, when I opened it, I found just a single sheet of paper with the message:

WE ARE NOT CONVINCED THAT YOU ARE TAKING OUR
WARNING SERIOUSLY. REMEMBER THERE COULD BE
UNFORTUNATE CONSEQUENCES IF YOU ARE FOOLISH
ENOUGH TO CONTINUE

For a few minutes none of us wished to break the silence, but at last I did. "You know, none of this makes sense…they have twice warned us not to continue, but they haven't said what we are supposed to do to convince them that we have so agreed…it is so stupid."

I could see that Peter was also puzzled, and as he began to speak it was hesitantly, but then he was suddenly stopped by Michelle. "I think all you clever gentlemen are missing the point…you see, I still think they are just encouraging us to continue! What they hope is that we will get so irritated that we decide to press on at once, just to finish the affair!"

Before she could go on, Peter suddenly laughed. "Michelle, you should make us all ashamed of ourselves! I think I would have come round to your conclusion – eventually – but you have crystallized my thoughts, some of which as you know I've had before. So yes, these rather general warnings have been puzzling, and my reading now of the situation is that the initial response, in Marseilles and in Avignon, which led to the death of your Great-Uncle Xavier and to the attack on you and Charles, was mounted hastily by the Union Corse. But now wiser councils prevail in the opposition. They must realise that a murderous attack on any of you here would raise a full-scale investigation, and I wouldn't put it past them to realise that you are in touch with some kind of authority. So what must their thoughts be? They know that you and Charles must be interested in digging up that old cache of jewels – and of the golden bowl – and they may also suspect that you have more information than they have regarding its location. Now, so long as things stay as they are, it remains a kind of unexploded bomb under the career of M. Vincent Fouquet, and he can hardly relish this remaining as a long-term worry. So, like Michelle, I now agree that he and his associates must have decided, in a way, to lance the boil, and they are taking the chance of needling you into proceeding at once in trying to dig the things up. Now if we are right in that assumption, they must already have made arrangements to keep the area under close observation so that they can watch while you try to find the treasure…remember that they do not know what we do regarding its location. It is this, I feel sure, that makes them try to hurry us up. So they must, as I have said, do whatever they can to get us to act at once. It follows, of course, they must also have very good plans so that, in the event of your succeeding, they will be able to recover the bowl from you. Remember that the Union has its base in Marseilles, so there are lots of foot soldiers in that area, ready to do their stuff and act against you. It is therefore imperative that we do nothing to alert them into knowing what we are up to, so secrecy is vital, and when you go…if you go…it must be a quick surgical strike: in – get the stuff – and then off!" He stopped there, and looked over at me. "You will realise, Charles, that this may be an argument for doing nothing at this stage, but I don't like the idea of doing so. If you were to decide to sit on your hands for the time being, I wonder very much what their reaction will be…my concern is that they might then decide to risk murdering you and Michelle, who are – let's face it – the people most likely to bother them. On this subject, you will realise that while we are still keeping a security watch on this house, and on the four of you here, we cannot continue to do so forever."

It didn't take us long to see the strength of his argument, and we all agreed that to take action now was the only realistic option. But then he turned to me again. "You will have realised, Charles, that all this might seem to make the enterprise even more hazardous, but it may surprise you that I do not think it really has done. You see, I think firstly that if we are correct in thinking that their policy is that of inciting you to go and recover the buried treasure, it is because they do not wish to risk the investigation which would arise if any of you were to be killed. Secondly, I also feel that they must think that they will be able to get that bowl back from you – soon after you have dug it up – and that they will be able to do so without injuring you, and so without causing any scandal. Now if there were no serious personal injuries involved in the affair it would be difficult to raise much interest – or a full scale enquiry – about a theft of an old bowl in southern France. In any case, if they did get the bowl, Fouquet and his mates would be able to claim complete ignorance of the affair, or knowledge of any of you. However, none of this will arise if your enterprise goes without any hitches…and it is up to me to ensure that it will…and to see that you can be back here in Britain – mission accomplished – within a few hours of digging up the treasures. You see, once they know that the bowl is in safekeeping, there is nothing else worthwhile they can do against the four of you. Despite all this, however, I would like agreement, before we proceed, from the most important person here, the owner of the treasures."

He stopped there, and turned to Julie. "If you will forgive my saying so, Mme Lebrun – and this also is too serious a time for me to call you Julie – there are now very few people in France who want old scandals about the dark days of the German occupation to be brought to light, and so we cannot rely on any official assistance in connection with our activities, more especially as they could lead to a crisis in the French government. So tell me, as a loyal citizen of France and in view of everything which has been said this afternoon, do you think that we should still go on with an attempt to disgrace a member of the French government, and do so at once?"

Julie didn't answer for a moment, then she shook her head. "Peter, you are very persuasive in your arguments about what action we should take, but you still haven't told us just what your personal position is. You must hold some important position, and I feel that it is our right to know what it is, before we make any decision about our future course of action."

He held up his hands in mock surrender. "Well, I have trusted all of you with a lot of secret information already this afternoon, so here is some more. You will, I am sure, have heard of MI5 and MI6, the two arms of our intelligence service, which deal with home and foreign matters. Now there have in the past been various scandals and mistakes, so a few years ago a small unit was set up which those in the know call Department 56, and for my sins I am its head. It is responsible for keeping a watchful eye on both these departments dealing with intelligence matters and – on rare occasions where secrecy is imperative – to take action on its own. It is important to keep Department 56 clear of the intrigues which are endemic in London official circles, so although I have an office in London my main base is in Glasgow."

He stopped there before saying very seriously, "I would particularly ask the four of you to keep this information to yourselves, and I do so despite the fact that it is known to quite a few people in government circles. Why I make this request is because – so far – the media have been kind enough not to expose our existence, but if they found information about us coming from you – civilians, including some foreign nationals – they would be sure to ask the question…what are they up to…and bang would go any chance of keeping our actions secret in this affair. So, Julie, I have come clean with you, will you agree to keep everything secret…what is your answer? Do we go on?"

I knew at once what her answer would be.

"Yes."

It was also the same answer from Granny and Michelle, so our discussion with him then turned to our plans. "It will take me maybe two days," he said, "to make all the arrangements, particularly in connection with getting one of my people who can be made to look sufficiently like Charles to fool any watchers – because so far as people here can see he must certainly not be seen as going to France! In view of our suspicions we must in the short term take every step possible to fool them into thinking that we are doing nothing for the present, and a delay of a few days will not look suspicious to them. We can't do anything immediately, this is Thursday, and I'll be back tomorrow, probably in the evening, with details of what I suggest we should do. If you will bear with me I'll call in the morning to confirm when I can come."

He paused for a moment, then went on. "You know, it is really rather funny, we have been making all these plans about digging up this golden bowl and none of us has asked what it is like. I wonder, Julie, if you can remember seeing it with the other valuables in your father's collection?"

"I've been thinking about that," she said, "and I do have a faint but clear memory of a small gold bowl, probably about the size of a finger bowl, coming from the break-up of the furniture and effects of a wealthy chateau. I'm sure I remember seeing it, and thinking how wonderful it must have been to be rich enough to be able to have bowls like this on your dining table."

"That is most interesting," he said, "and I wonder if you can remember whether there was any inscription, or a coat of arms, engraved on it?"

"No, I'm sure it was not inscribed, as I remember thinking how smooth and brightly polished the gold was."

He gave a nod. "That is very interesting, and I hope that we'll be able to see it for ourselves very soon."

With that, the meeting broke up, except for William having a word with me regarding my own plans. "There have been no questions raised in the office regarding your absence, a few days off after your father's death was quite normal, and your recent fortnight, which ends on Monday, has been assumed to be just a normal holiday...you were certainly due it, as you didn't take your full entitlement last year. What I suggest is that you now let me tell the others about your engagement, and I'm sure there will be a lot of gossip about how quickly you and Michelle have fallen in love and made up your minds to get married. I think you will then have to mention in passing something about her grandfather helping your grandfather to escape from France in 1942, and that it is only now, after more than fifty years, that your two families have met. You can come in tomorrow, just to introduce Michelle to your colleagues, and on Monday, when we should know when Peter intends you to go off on your quest. I can then invent some job for you to attend to, away from the office, in order to explain your absence. Peter's man, who is to pretend to be you, can go off to the place where you are supposed to be working...and you can nip off to France. Peter and I will tie this up between us."

I looked at him and smiled. "I can see, William, that you are enjoying this little affair...do you miss your old days in the Intelligence Service?"

"Of course I do," he said, "the days when one is young always remain special, and memory has a kindly habit of forgetting the bad bits, while keeping the good ones bright and clear. I can tell you, Charles, that when you are my age you too will look back on this adventure of yours in just the same way, and it is your good fortune that you will be able to do so with Michelle. Anyway, you should both come to the office tomorrow morning, and I shall greet you as if I hadn't met her, or seen you, since you went off to France. I'm sure that there will be so much interest about your coming back with a lovely French fiancée that there will be no time for other enquiries...tell you what, why don't you make it at about twelve thirty, and you can join us for lunch which will let your colleagues get a good look at her."

Just as they were leaving, Peter said to Granny, "As you may have seen, I am a great believer in action now, and I wonder if I may use your phone to call my secretary and get her to book the tickets for the Brittany Ferries crossing to Spain next Wednesday just to make sure the boat isn't full?"

That didn't take long and he smiled as he said, "Well, that's okay, and I reckon this has been an afternoon well spent. I'll call in the morning regarding the other arrangements.

When William and Peter left, Granny said to us, "Thank goodness to be on our own at last, and I want nothing said about the affair for the rest of today. We have a very happy situation to celebrate, by way of the linking of the Burtons and the Lebruns, and it has been, and really will be, a wonderful bonus for both families. I suppose that you two, Michelle and Charles, think that your getting married provides that link...well, it will be one but we two golden oldies, Julie and I, have decided while you two were off in St Andrews, that there should be another one."

Michelle and I looked at each other in surprise, we had been so wrapped up in our own affairs that we hadn't been thinking about anybody else, and anyway, what other link could there be? Granny stopped, and then looked over at Julie, saying, "Just look at these two, they think that their affairs are the only ones that matter, so you'd better tell them how wrong they can be!"

It was then to Michelle that Julie spoke. "My dear Michelle, it has been the privilege of my life to have seen you growing up, and being able to live with you and your mother after your father's death when you were only a tiny baby. As I am sure you know, you have become very dear to me, and perhaps even more so in recent years after your mother also died. But I am a realist, and I know that things must change, as you must find your mate and settle into your own nest with him. What makes it so wonderful for me is that I have found Marie here, in exactly the same situation as I am, as she too knows that Charles will leave her as well. While the two of you were away in St Andrews the two of us got talking and, even these few days have been long enough for us to decide that we'll be able to make a happy joint life together. That is as far as we have got so far, we don't yet know if we shall keep two houses, and just stay a few months in each...or move into just the one...we'll see. But I'd better warn you that you are now going to find two grandmothers working as a team, and being a considerable nuisance – but maybe a help sometimes – once your children come along!"

We didn't try to make any firm arrangements that day; apart from Granny and Julie not having decided where they were going to live, Michelle and I hadn't even thought about whether or not we would always stay in Scotland. But it was very satisfactory to find that our respective grandmothers were so happy about our decision...just as we were happy about theirs. Later in the afternoon, when Michelle and I went up to sort out our unpacking, we found another sign that our grandmothers thoroughly approved of what we were doing, as her things had been spirited from the spare room into mine. When we came down, Granny smiled, and said to us, "It is an illusion of the young that their elders and betters have never been young themselves, and I'll lay a hundred to one that the two of you had a double room in St Andrews, and so Julie and I decided that there was no point in keeping you apart here. You are going to spend your lives together, so why not start now?"

She stopped there and laughed, then said to Michelle, "I am glad, my dear, to see that young girls can still blush even in these modern times, but don't be embarrassed, young true love is a wonderful thing, and I'm sure we are right, aren't we, that you want to move in with Charles?"

Michelle looked thoughtfully at me, and gave me just a tiny smile, before saying, "I suppose so, but I would not for a moment like him to consider that he is essential to my happiness! Just remember, intended-husband-to-be, that we have still not tied the knot, so you'll need to be on your best behaviour until then!"

"Mind you," she said, turning to Granny, "he isn't a bad lad, and I think I could do worse."

***

CHAPTER NINE

Next day, on Friday, Michelle and I duly got to the office in time for lunch, and the news of my engagement had obviously preceded me. I had expected having to deal with a lot of good-natured ribbing about my sudden romance with a girl whom I had only just met in France but, as they saw her beside me, I could see that my friends realised just why I had been so uncharacteristically impetuous. We had lunch with William and some of my friends and afterwards he took us on our own back to his office, where he explained that Peter had phoned to say that he had made all the arrangements and that the two of them would come round to our house that evening, and they would bring with them the young man who was to take my place from Monday till we got back from France.

He was also able to tell us that he had managed to make arrangements with a cousin of his who had a wool spinning mill near Peebles, and that my substitute could spend each day in the office there, supposedly as me, while I was absent. Our firm did such legal work as the company needed, but the cover story was that my supposed visit there was ostensibly to be doing some private legal business for him. So he could drive straight from our house to Peebles in the morning, and go back there in the evening…the others in my office had been told that I was going to spend the rest of the week working there, so no awkward questions should arise.

He duly came round to the house at eight o'clock that evening, bringing with him a young man, introduced to us just as Hugh, who was to take my place. He was not unlike me as regards build and height, but there the resemblance ended…for one thing he was dark, and my hair was sandy… and I wondered how on earth he could fool anybody. Peter, however, saw my doubts. "You are wondering how Hugh here can be made to look like you, well, just let him have a good look at you, and you will be surprised what changes he can make."

Well, he had a quite large case with him, and just asked if he could sit across the room from me while the rest of us talked, and to see what he could do. It was rather creepy to see him sitting over there with a mirror in his hand, busying himself with facial pads and various other gadgets, and also looking through a selection of wigs, one of which was uncannily like my own hair. As for the very simple arrangements that were explained to me…I was to drive to the office on Monday morning, parking my car, as usual, in the nearby multi-story garage. I would then spend a short time in the office before walking back to the garage. By this time, my companion for the trip would be there with the car for our journey, plus Hugh who would change trousers and jacket with me – he would already be wearing a similar shirt and tie. It would then just be a simple switch, Hugh would drive off in my car and pretend to do his research down in Peebles till I got back, and my companion – whom I was told would be called Gordon – and I would head off for France. It all seemed very easy.

After we had talked for a while we were suddenly interrupted by Hugh, as he said to me, "How do I look now?"

What I saw was very surprising…he didn't look exactly like me, but nevertheless the resemblance was quite remarkable, and from any distance at all it would have been totally convincing.

I was full of congratulations, but Peter just said to him, "Good, I was sure you could do it, that will do very well…I'll be in touch with you tomorrow to tie up final arrangements with you." But when I saw him to the door, I felt I should tell him how impressed I was. However, he just smiled, saying, "We never expect any congratulations from Mr Armstrong… but believe me we'll get hell if we don't do well! But he is a wonderful boss to have, and you are in good hands. Anyway, best of luck in your enterprise."

By then, Granny had come up, and she said to him, "I understand, Hugh, that you will be staying with us for the few days when Charles is away, we'll try to make you as comfortable as we can, and if there is anything you want, do please let me know. I understand that while you will be going away each day, you will not go out in the evening, just in case you meet any of Charles' friends, but you are most welcome to join us if you so wish. However, there is a TV set in your room, also a video recorder, and if you are stuck we have quite a stock of tapes." Anyway, he seemed a pleasant lad, and I was sure that he would cause no problems. On a lighter note, before Peter left, he asked if by any chance we would all be free to come to dinner with Sue and him on the following evening, and we were very happy to accept.

My good luck with the weather continued, and next morning I persuaded them all to come on a 'mystery tour', as I wanted to show them something of Scotland in our immediate area. So by ten o'clock we were off, and first I drove to Greenock and then on through Gourock to the quay for the West Highland Ferries. We were again lucky, this time with the timing, and got almost straight onto a boat for the quarter of an hour or so it took to cross over the Firth of Clyde to Hunter's Quay, near Dunoon. As soon as we were on board Granny whispered to me, "I can guess now where we're going to, and you've chosen well!" Across at the other side we drove up the side of the Holy Loch, and I pointed out to them the anchorage, which for decades was the American base for Polaris submarines, but now remained as just a memory of the Cold War days. Soon afterwards I turned off to the right to go up the shore of Loch Long and, less than thirty miles from Glasgow, we were suddenly on a narrow single track road with passing places to be used when we met cars.

I could see that Julie and Michelle were astonished by this quick transformation, so I said to them, "Don't think that this is usual in Scotland, as this little corner of the country we are in now is by way of being an almost undiscovered gem. But it isn't so undiscovered as not to have a wayside inn, which will give us a good pub lunch."

In fact, the Ardentinny Hotel did us proud with a selection of dishes, many of which were based on fish straight from the Loch, and I had the good sense to ignore the New World wines and settled for a very drinkable Chablis. We ate our meal at one of the outside tables where we could look down at all the yachts and pleasure craft as they made their way along the sparkling waters of the Loch, and I could see that Michelle was beginning to think that there might, after all, be a lot to be said for Scotland. After lunch she and I walked down to the Loch side and engaged in what must be the most popular waterside sport in the world – trying to skim flat stones and seeing how many jumps we could get. After a while, she looked round to see that we were unobserved and put her arms round me, saying, "darling, I am going to love living with you in Scotland, it is a magical land."

I kissed her, but felt that a little honesty would not be inappropriate. "I must confess, darling, that you are seeing the best of it as the winters here are pretty long and cold and by mid-winter it is dark by four o'clock."

She laughed and said, "Well, for us I can't see that is much of a problem…it will give us a splendid excuse to go to bed together and early to keep warm, and that can't be bad!"

When we left Ardentinny we drove over to Loch Eck and then to Loch Fyne before turning east to Loch Lomond and heading for home down the famous Bonnie Bonnie Banks. I could see that Granny was pleased that our trip had gone so well, especially when Julie said, "I couldn't have believed that we could find all that wonderful unspoiled countryside so very near Glasgow…it has been a glorious day." And soon I could hear them talking about the possibility of the two of them spending the summers here, and maybe Julie selling the Avignon house, and buying one on the coast, near Nice. I looked over to Michelle who had been reading a paper, but now, like me, was looking at our grandmothers, and she gave a thumbs-up to me to show how much she approved of them.

I also had a feeling that dinner with the Armstrongs that night might also impress Julie, as I knew from the address I had been given that their house was in a showpiece area of Glasgow, and I reckoned that it would be worth seeing. We went through the Clyde Tunnel, and up from there by Byres Road to join the Great Western Road at the entrance to the Botanical Gardens. It is a most impressive road, lined on both sides as it is with elegant houses in a succession of terraces. In one of them, just a little way down was the Armstrong's, with a four-pillared portico leading up to a very grand entrance door. And it was equally impressive when we were shown into the entrance hall, which was floored with white marble, and I could see a wide flight of stairs leading to the first floor, and then continuing in a further sweep to an upper floor; the impression was of being in an atrium with a ceiling some thirty feet overhead. We had been greeted by a pleasant, middle-aged lady, but as soon as we were inside, Peter and Sue came out, and they introduced her to us, as our dear friend Janet. We learned soon afterwards that she had come as a nanny for their two daughters and had just stayed on to become one of the family.

One thing about living in the west of Scotland is that society still tends to be stratified, so small talk is usually easy as it is rare not to find some mutual friends or at least acquaintances, and that proved to be the case here. It didn't take long to find that their elder daughter, Sheila, was married to a Glasgow lawyer, Andrew Donald, whose name I knew. They then mentioned their younger daughter, Liz, and I suddenly remembered about her writing articles in the *Sunday Post*, including a quite famous story which she had filed about the break up of a big drug cartel. "Yes," said Sue, "there was quite a bit of excitement about that affair, which was shortly before their joint marriages – Liz married an Australian lad, and they are now getting a house into shape which they have acquired in Portugal."

But, as she had been speaking, the name Liz Armstrong suddenly rang a loud bell for me, and I said, "Is your daughter THE Liz Armstrong?"

Sue laughed. "I take it, Charles, that you play golf? Yes? Then you are right, she is the current Ladies' Golf Champion for Scotland."

But as she said that some further bells began to ring, and I said to her, "Don't be so modest, you haven't mentioned that you played Curtis Cup golf, and if I'm not wrong I also think that Peter here played in the Walker Cup." They laughingly admitted their prowess and, as we began to talk golf, it was Sue who noticed that Julie and Michelle didn't know what the hell we were talking about.

"This is very rude of us," she said, "to talk about golf, which is not a very popular game in France, I take it that neither of you play?"

They smilingly admitted their ignorance of the game, but Sue then looked questioningly at Michelle. "Look, my dear, as you are coming to live in Scotland – or at least going to marry a Scot – so I wonder if you would like to learn something about the game? I have nothing much on next week, so as Charles is going to France for a few days, would you like to come to my village club in Kilmacolm, say on Monday morning? I could arrange for you to have a lesson from our professional, Iain Nicholson, and after that we could go out and try a few holes together…now about it?"

I think she was surprised when both Michelle and I laughed, and it was an enthusiastic Michelle who spoke. "I can tell you, Sue, that you are a good angel. It was only after I agreed to marry Charles that I learned about the danger of becoming a golf widow, which would appear to be a hazard if one were so foolish as to marry a golfing Scot. So, perhaps I can get my own back by making him a golfing widower… how about that, Charles, my darling!"

"That, my sweet, I can take a chance on, but I can tell you that you are bloody lucky to be offered the chance of help from Sue. Just look at her two daughters. As you now know, Liz is our Scottish champion, and I'll be surprised if her sister, Sheila, doesn't get that same honour soon…so they were well trained. And I can tell you that I shall be delighted if you like the game and, if you do, I reckon we'll be able to get you in very quickly as a member at Kilmacolm. Mind you, Michelle, there is a hazard about any of our family going to Kilmacolm that maybe you don't know about. You see, there is a dragon lady in the village who lives very near the club, in the shape of my Great-Aunt Agnes, and although she is now bedridden, she is not without influence in the club, as she is one of the oldest past Lady captains. All this will certainly help your candidature, but never think you'll be able to go to Kilmacolm without calling in to see her."

But Granny broke in. "Don't let Charles paint an unattractive picture of her. She may be old but she is still great fun, and she will certainly very much enjoy meeting you – anyway, as you are now joining the family you will in any case have to see her soon."

She then turned to Sue. "Look, as for Monday let's arrange a time, you can go straight to the club and I'll take Julie and Michelle to meet Agnes, and after that she can easily walk up to the club to meet you. Julie and I can then spend the time with Agnes till you and Michelle finish your game."

Michelle suddenly leapt to her feet, saying, "This is wonderful!" and ran over to Sue and kissed her on the cheek. "I can't tell you how delighted I am to have come to Scotland and met all you nice people. I was quite happy about Charles, but I did wonder how his friends would take to me…but now that's all right!" Sue took her hands. "You are a very sweet girl, Michelle, and Charles is a lucky young man anyway. Come along now, and I'll look out some clubs for you to use on Monday."

It was a delightful evening, and they were generous to Julie as, although English was mostly used, they also changed to French whenever they saw that she was in difficulties. I could see also that they were intrigued by the double linking of the Burtons and the Lebruns now that Granny and Julie were talking of setting up house together. As we were leaving, Peter took me aside for a moment, and said, "I won't see you before you go off, but the very best of luck…"

But he couldn't go on, as the phone rang. Janet went to answer it, but came back to tell Peter that it was my boss Mr Henderson to speak to him. It wasn't long before he came back, saying, "That was William to tell me that M. Phillipe Duchene had been on the phone to him to find out how we were getting on, and he asked him to pass on his good wishes to you. He's been told about your going to France and asked us to tell you that if you are in any trouble, be sure to contact him."

***

We had a very lazy day on Sunday. I got a *Telegraph*, a *Times*, and the *Sunday Post*; as regards the last one I told Michelle that it was the most popular Sunday paper in Scotland, and would be a good introduction for her to the local vernacular. "If you can read it," I said to her, "you can not only speak English, but at least understand Scots too!"

But we did manage to deal with one important bit of business in the shape of our wedding as, so far as Michelle and I were concerned, the sooner it took place the better. Understandably, Michelle wanted it to be in Avignon where her friends were, and we roughed out a plan that I would take my summer holiday rather later than usual, in mid to late September, and if we arranged it then Granny and I could drive out without having to face the worst of the summer traffic, and similarly Michelle and I would miss the summer crowds on our honeymoon. She told me that she would think over places while I was away, and that I should do the same. However, I would never in a million years have guessed where, in the event, she would suggest where we should go.

Come next day I almost felt like a soldier about to go 'over the top', and certainly I'd had a very sentimental farewell from Michelle…but maybe sentimental isn't quite the correct word. I had wakened before her and in the dawn light I thought that she was the most beautiful sight in the whole world. She had a half smile on her lovely face and her raven hair made a jet black frame for it. Just as if she sensed my looking at her, I saw her eyes open, and the half smile became a full one. Without a word being said I found our arms wrapped around each other and soon, as I entered her, she gave a little sigh, saying, "That's better, just lie still for a while, darling, and let's be quietly happy together…I'm going to miss you so very much in the next few days…Please hurry back, and to hell with the jewels and the bowl, you are all that matters to me." When at last our climaxes came she was a little tigress and, when after an eternity of joy, and my easing myself away, she kissed me fiercely, saying, "What an exhausting business it is, sleeping with you, so maybe it's as well that you'll be away for a few days. But just be very careful that you don't get entangled with a French girl – if I smell another woman on you when you get back there will be hell to pay!"

***

The switch in the multi-storey car park went off without a hitch, but I was rather tense as I watched 'Hugh' drive off in my Mondeo, and I had a good look at 'Gordon' who was to be my colleague for the days of our trip. I was glad to see that he looked a tough young man – he confessed later to having been in the SAS – but he was no fool as his French was perfect, completely colloquial, and he admitted to speaking Spanish and Italian as well. Peter had done well for me as regards the car, as well as for my companion, as it was an almost new Rover V6. We had a good run south and turned off the M6 at Birmingham and then down the M5 till we turned off at Junction 13. At this point, we drove a few miles beyond Stroud till we came to a quite impressive pair of entrance gates, then up a drive which led to a singularly ugly kind of manor house, built of yellow bricks and having most inappropriate circular structures which could only be for imitation turnpike staircases.

Gordon laughed at me. "It's awful, isn't it? But the MOD isn't concerned with aesthetics, and no doubt they got the place cheap. It's used as a training centre, principally for language skills and disguises, but there is also another section which trains people to be really nasty if the necessity should arise. Everybody here has already learned one thing…never ask questions…so you won't be bothered with any. And we are going to spend two nights here, and we'll need all that time to rehearse our parts…and I can tell you that you ain't going to be pleased with yours. Let's go in now, and I'd better warn you that your ordeal will begin tomorrow morning with their make-up expert. I believe that you are going to be dark haired and somewhat unwashed and unshaven. It was a pity that you had to shave this morning, so that you could appear at the office all neat and tidy, but I'm sure you will be told not to shave tomorrow morning…but that's enough for now!"

I have been asked not to say much about that establishment but, after a good night's sleep, I then had to face the make-up experts, who were real perfectionists and, after their treatment I could hardly recognise myself. They had been told not to do anything which wasn't easy to reverse, so they hadn't tried to dye my hair, and instead had given me a (very) 'short back and sides' haircut so that a black wig could cover my own hair. When I say black I think that dark and unwashed and greasy would be a better description. Then, as for clothes, I had a very old pair of jeans, well worn trainers for shoes, and a black polo-necked sweater with short sleeves, which would expose my carefully applied imitation tattoos. As instructed, I had not shaved, and they washed a special dye over my face, which would turn my stubble black, but didn't affect my skin. If I had been a policeman I would have had me arrested, just on suspicion, anyway I was given a bottle of the dye to use each morning.

Poor Gordon had been made up quite differently. His wig was of long, very untidy blond hair, and his clothes were somewhat 'arty'. He was wearing a pair of very baggy trousers, with big patch pockets, and a kind of smock, also with even bigger pockets, of a type which I had only seen in pictures of painters in times gone by. I couldn't help laughing when I saw him, and said, "Before I left Michelle she warned me against getting involved with French girls, but I don't think that a gay young Brit had occurred to her! Come to that, have you done much painting recently?"

I was somewhat embarrassed as just before we went in to lunch together one of the make-up artists came over and said to us, "I would suggest that you two should hold hands sometimes, as you'd better get used to acting your parts. Please don't look embarrassed when you hold hands."

Gordon grinned, and said, "That's okay, sweetie, but just remember that you will need to hold my hand quite often just to make things look right...but as for painting, all I have done recently is on the walls of my mortgaged-up-to-the-hilt house.

Come next morning the car which I knew had been ordered for us was waiting for us but I was surprised to see that it was a very clapped out Peugeot 406 with French plates, which looked as though it had seen hard days, and many of them. I couldn't help laughing, and said, "Surely they could have done better for us than that?"

He also laughed. "But you see, all the mechanics of this car are almost new, and it is somewhat of a 'Q' vehicle. It has been tweaked, and there aren't many vehicles that can live with us. So please look happy, and let's get on our way!"

We had no time to spare when we got to Plymouth as our ferry left at noon and we got onto the boat in time for lunch.

Dinner that night was at eight o'clock and if I was embarrassed at lunchtime, it was much worse that evening in the dining saloon, and there were many disapproving glances in our direction...especially when Gordon stretched over the table to hold my hand. And that wasn't all, as after dinner we were in a seated area and again we got an unwelcome indication that our disguises were far too convincing. As we were drinking coffee, two lorry drivers gave jeering wolf whistles as they passed our table, but Gordon just laughed, saying, "I'll need to congratulate the make-up man, he would seem to have done a good job!"

"But tell me," I said, not at all happy about things, "why are we both made up to look so damn conspicuous? I would have thought that our plan would have been to keep a low profile?"

"That, my dear Charles," he said, "is because being conspicuous just now, is the flavour of the month in our outfit. You've probably heard about regiments and squadrons with inbuilt traditions, but that does not apply in our case. Every now and then we get new experts, with their own ideas, and the present one thinks that the best way to hide is to make yourself so obvious that nobody pays any attention to you... let's hope that he is right!"

So I can't say that I enjoyed my time on the boat. Off the boat at noon on Thursday Gordon explained that he wanted us, more or less, to hide ourselves for the day, so we drove up the road to Vitoria Gasteiz before turning east to Alsasua, then turned north to Tolosa before stopping at a small wayside hotel which, he had been told, was used to people arriving and departing at odd hours, and was handy for the frontier. That was important as, on the Friday morning, our departure was at 4am. Soon we were driving along empty roads, out of Spain and into France. It was less than forty miles to Bayonne, and still there was hardly any traffic, so we easily got to the little road that I knew so well, both from my earlier visit and from the photographs, and arrived before six o'clock, just at first light. Finding the stone was also ridiculously easy. Gordon just fed the coordinates into a little hand-held navigation set, and we were able to stop at the edge of what had once been a wood. As we knew from the satellite photographs, the trees had been cut down some twenty years previously, but nature had done its job and now there were quite large scrubby bushes, and a few small trees. Without our magic box we could never have known where to dig, but now Gordon just walked about a hundred yards into this confused landscape, then looked at the navigation set, and said, "Here is where the stone was, you can see that the ground is slightly different from the rest."

It all seemed so easy, there wasn't a soul around, and I mentally congratulated Peter on his arrangements. "Now," he went on, "it was your old grandfather who buried the treasure, so how about you doing your stuff right now and deciding where we should dig?" I had been told that I was similar in build to him, so I took out a compass and took a careful thirty paces to the south of the position where the stone had been, then said, "Let's dig up this gorse bush here, I reckon the treasure is under it!"

Gordon went back to car, and returned with a spade and a trowel and a big zip-up bag. I carefully eased the spade into the soft ground and, with Gordon's help, we soon made short work of the bush. After that, I had only probed quite a small area of ground, till I suddenly felt some resistance, and knelt down to test the position with my trowel. Suddenly I could see signs of leather, and I was soon able to expose an ancient suitcase, and it was a tribute to the quality of the leather that when we lifted it out of the hole and gave it a wipe over, it seemed not too much the worse for its long internment.

Gordon looked over at me, and smiled. "Well, my boy, this is it, you'd better be the one to open it!"

It didn't take too long to clean the muck off the locks, and they even opened with no more than just a little help, as I eased the catches. Then it was with a feeling almost of reverence that I opened the lid, and we saw a collection of quite small cloth bags, and also something rather larger wrapped up in some rough cloth. I carefully unwrapped the cloth and to my delight saw a small golden bowl, still bright, despite all these years, and we looked at each other in a spirit of mutual congratulations. But just then we heard the sound of a car, and Gordon said, "Have a look, Charles, and see if it is anything to worry about." I handed him the bowl, carefully re-wrapping it before I did so, and ducking down under the screen of the bushes I made my way back towards the road. But then, to my dismay, I saw that a big Renault had stopped behind our car, and that three large men were getting out. There was also an Alsatian dog that took just one leap out of the car and came straight at me. I hadn't a chance. One moment the dog was at my throat, but the next minute it had been called off, and one of the men was looking at me with a smile of satisfaction.

"Well now," he said, "we meet again! Mind you, if I hadn't been told that you were coming here this morning I don't think I would have recognised you."

I looked up, and saw that it was the second man who had attacked Michelle and me in Avignon. Suddenly a knife appeared in his hand, and I also saw that the other two young men were now standing beside the car, and one of them had a had a gun in his hand. Then just as the first man made as if to cut my face with his knife, he stopped and laughed at my fear, saying, "You are bloody lucky, my friend. Despite everything, I have been told not to hurt you in any way, so just be a good boy and take us to where you and you friend are digging!"

But, as he said this, there was a shout from one of the others. "Over here!"

It was all so easy for them. I was herded back to the site, and saw Gordon with the open case beside him, and my heart sank when I saw that the golden bowl was still there in full view, although it was still covered with the old wrapping. The man who had not got a weapon went over and picked up the bowl tenderly, and carefully unwrapped it, before giving a thumbs-up to his friends, and saying to us, with an almost friendly smile, "It may surprise you to know that we are not thieves, and all we are interested in is this bowl, and I can also tell you that even this will be returned to you in due course. You are quite free now to take the rest of this stuff back to Scotland with you, but we do have a message for you, which is…and he fished a sheet of paper from his pocket and read, 'Just forget all your suspicions. You now have no proof whatsoever, so just be very grateful that we are allowing you to go. You can take the rest of the stuff, but not the bowl, although this will be returned eventually.'"

But this civility was obviously not at all to the liking of the man with the knife, as he came over to me and waved the weapon in my face, saying, "You've been bloody lucky so far, Charlie boy, but if you'll take my advice you won't push it any further. Just go back to that nice girl of yours before anything nasty happens to either of you. Anyway, look at the bright side, there is now no need for you to go around in this ridiculous disguise, so you can pop off to some hotel in Bayonne, throw away that rather dirty wig, get yourself cleaned up and shaved, and have a nice breakfast with maybe a glass of cognac to celebrate getting all this valuable treasure."

What could we do? Two of them were armed, not to mention the fierce dog, and we could only look on in helpless rage as the man with the gun fired just a single shot which punctured one of our rear tyres, saying, "That will save you making fools of yourselves by trying to follow us." And, with derisive waves they drove off.

As I stood there I felt as if the bottom had fallen out of my world, I had been so sure that nothing could go wrong…how could it with all the expert help I had been given? But now everything was lost, and I couldn't escape the thought that I had betrayed what was almost a sacred trust, not only due to Granny, but also to Julie and Michelle…and, maybe worst of all, to my grandfather who left us this clue to treachery and murder and which had now been stolen by agents of the very man whom he had wanted to expose.

***

CHAPTER TEN

I then looked over at Gordon, and was astonished to see that he didn't look at all upset. He held up a hand to stop me speaking, saying, "Don't ask anything, just help me get this damn tyre changed. We've got to get away as quickly as possible!" I made to ask him what all the rush as about, but he stopped me again. "Just trust me, Charles. The game isn't over yet, but we must hurry." As he said that I remembered that the man from Avignon had told me that we had been expected.

"I can't believe your attitude," I burst out. "The Union Corse has been privy to our movements all along. What the hell else can we now do but to go home with our tails between our legs?"

"Charles, please trust me, all is not yet lost, so please save your breath...but we'll talk about this later and, as it seems a racing certainty that the natives in this country aren't friendly, please HURRY UP!" I mulled over the suggestion that all was not yet lost, as we hurried on with the wheel change, but I could make no sense of it. When we were nearly finished with the job, I saw Gordon go to the back of the car and carefully repack the old suitcase, before putting it into the big zip-up bag, which I had seen him with, and stow it away in the boot. Then as soon as the wheel was on he jumped into the driving seat and said, as we raced off, "Keep an eye open behind just to check that we aren't being followed."

Well, I did see a car, a long way behind us, which might – although probably might not – have been the Renault, but no normal car could have kept up with the breakneck speed of our car as we tore through minor roads, and then onto the Autoroute leading to Toulouse. Then he pulled into the side, and asked me to drive, saying, "Drive like hell, Charles. It is now time for me to make some telephone calls before we get to Toulouse. Handy gadgets these," he smiled. He got out his phone. "I am just going to wake up a colleague there, long before his usual getting up time." He got through immediately, and I heard him ask for a Mr Anderson, and say, "Hello, John, we are on the way home now, so will you meet us at the British Airways check-in desk…good…we'll see you at about eleven. After that I'd like you to get our car under cover as soon as possible."

When he had finished the call he looked over at me. "Sorry, old son, but I've still got to keep you in the dark, and I'm still going to do so till we get back to dear old GB… please trust me. Anyway, I have one more call to make, this one to your friend Peter Armstrong."

That was too much for me. "A friend? Not bloody likely! This whole operation has been a total disgrace! He's running an outfit which can't keep secrets…the only thing I shall enjoy today is when I tell him just what I think of him! Him and his so-called secret outfit!" Gordon gave me a somewhat apologetic smile, and then got busy on the phone. We were then on a rather busy stretch of road so I couldn't concentrate on what he was saying, but I could hear that he was talking to Peter and was surprised how very short the conversation was, and he certainly did not say anything about my feelings. That too didn't improve my temper, and I just thought that he must be afraid to mention it, in case it damaged his promotion prospects. After that, he didn't tell me anything, except to say that Peter would meet us at an office they had near Heathrow. However, I was just so fed up and unhappy about everything, especially about the loss of the bowl, that I decided I just had to go along with him – and get the whole disastrous affair over as soon as possible. I continued driving far too fast, so we got to Toulouse in plenty of time for the rendezvous. Gordon then surprised me yet again by knowing the best route to the airport, and when we got there he directed me to an area in one of the car parks.

"First thing," he said, "is to get out of these damn clothes and, come to that, I'll be glad to see you looking clean shaven for a change. I don't like you in this designer stubble. We'll change as soon as we get into the Terminal Building and our man can take all these disgusting clothes and gadgets back to the car. From now on we are, so to speak, travelling in our own skins otherwise we would not be welcome in Club Class!" We had, each of us, only a small overnight bag, sufficient in my case for toilet things plus a pair of slacks, a shirt and tie, a jersey, and a pair of somewhat more respectable shoes. So we were not heavily laden as we made our way into the Terminal Building, with me carrying both our bags, and Gordon with the zip-up case containing the suitcase with the treasure…although not the golden bowl.

We were met at the check-in desk, and Gordon told the man to wait till we had changed. We did just that and less than half an hour later we were both clean – and clean shaven – and free of our stupid clothes. I then heard Gordon say as he gave the bundle of our things to him, "I suggest that you wait for a day or two before leaving for England with the car, people may still be looking for it so, as I said, get it out of sight now and it might be best to go for one of the cross channel sea crossings rather than the Eurotunnel."

We then went to get our boarding cards, and I was surprised to see that our tickets had already been booked and that the problem of taking such a large bag as 'hand luggage' had been solved by an extra seat having been reserved for it. It was when we got ourselves settled in the Club Class lounge that I said to him, "Look, Gordon, surely it is time for you to come clean? Here we are in the south of France and I find that the seats on the plane have already been booked...and why are you taking such good care of a collection of jewellery which is damn all to do with the government? You are being too helpful, and that makes me suspicious."

"Look, Charles," he said, "I think that it is bloody silly keeping you in the dark like this, but I am acting under orders. Just be patient for a little while longer. We'll be back in England this afternoon, and all will be made clear to you then...that's a promise."

What could I say to that, but just shrug my shoulders, but then I went on, "Tell me, there is another thing: what on earth made them dress you like an old-style painter with these silly trousers and that smock with the enormous pockets? It looked bloody silly, I can tell you."

I was surprised when again he didn't answer the question directly, just saying, "My dear Charles, in my outfit we are trained just to do what we are told, especially if one is a common foot soldier like me!"

And that ended the conversation. Fortunately, we didn't have long to wait before our flight was called, so I hadn't long to brood over the ease with which the bowl had been stolen from us, and after the way that Gordon had brushed my questions aside I didn't like to suggest that we should have been given a little firepower of our own to defend it. It seemed all wrong that we had put up no sort of fight whatsoever, and I felt somewhat disappointed about what I had thought was an efficient Secret Service outfit. I had thought better of Peter Armstrong. When we came to board the aircraft and then take-off, at least British Airways did their very best to cheer me up as, once we were up to cruising height, it became quite difficult to resist the many tempting offers of liquor. However, I managed to do so – occasionally! – and was still reasonably sober, maybe because of an excellent lunch, which no doubt helped to absorb some of it, but still unhappy when we got to Heathrow. Gordon told me to wait till all the other passengers had disembarked before moving, but when we got off, at the end of the gangway at the entrance to the Terminal Building, we were met by a man whom obviously Gordon already knew. The man led us into the Customs and Immigration area where he nodded to one of the officials, who then unlocked a door which took us into a rather dingy passage, down some stairs, then through another door which opened into a narrow cul-de-sac road between two big buildings. There was a car parked there – despite a plethora of *No Parking* signs – and Gordon said to the driver, "Well done, Hector, let's be off!"

We only went a short distance along the M25 before the driver turned onto the M4 and about a quarter of an hour later we were driven into a quite large estate. In this instance, we had to go through a security check before getting through the entrance gates and then up a long drive till we came to a very substantial house. When we stopped at the front door – very grand with an imposing flight of steps leading up to it – Gordon said, "Bring your bag with you. There will be other transport when you want to get away this afternoon." He then led me up the steps, and I heard him ask a rather tough-looking army sergeant, "Is the Colonel here?" The answer was in the affirmative, and we then went up a flight of the stairs.

The sergeant knocked at the door of a room on the first floor gallery. I instantly recognised the voice which said,

"Come!" It was indeed Peter Armstrong, who was getting up from his desk, and coming over towards me. "Come in, Charles," he said, and held out his hand in greeting. "I think you and Gordon deserve a drink to celebrate the success of your mission!"

"Success?" exclaimed, "The whole affair has been a complete disaster! Didn't anybody tell you that we were jumped on just as we were digging up the old case and, while they let us keep the Lebrun family jewels, they took the bowl from us?"

To my surprise, he just smiled and said, "Let's have a drink anyway, I think whisky and soda is called for. Would you do the honours, Gordon?"

Obviously, he had been in this office before, as he knew which cupboard to go to and in double quick time I found a glass in my hand. It did nothing whatsoever for my bad temper, which had not been helped by Peter's casual remarks. It was after he had taken an appreciative sip of his drink, that he turned to me. "I can see that Gordon has done as he was told, and has kept you in the dark, so just let me take you back to the beginning of our involvement in this affair. I was, as you know, intrigued when William Henderson spoke to me about the odd adventures you and Michelle had been having, then the link to the Union Corse, and your story about a man who had got rid of his Pierre Dupont identity in strange circumstances. I was then even more surprised when I read your grandfather's papers, and later when it emerged that your villain, the young Pierre who had been forced by your grandfather to leave his fingerprints on that gold bowl, was now none other than our bete noire, M. Vincent Fouquet. I can tell you that very next day I spoke to the Foreign Secretary and was then at once instructed by him to do everything possible to assist you in your search."

"Instead of which," I broke in, "you sent us like lambs to the slaughter, and now we have no chance of bringing Pierre – alias Vincent Fouquet – to justice!"

"Not so fast," he smiled, "just wait till I finish. I can tell you that my first idea was to send you to France with a considerable number of minders so that you would have been sure to get the things safely away, after you had dug them up. But I was concerned about what would happen then...certainly if you had brought us the bowl we could have taken action at once against Fouquet, but what would the Union Corse have done then? For the present, they appeared to be most interested in keeping you safe. My worry was that they might take the easy option of killing you or Michelle, or maybe both of you as, without your testimony, we would not have been in a strong position. So, what could we do about that?"

He paused for a moment before going on. "What led me to an alternative plan was my belief that Fouquet, whom we had then to consider as being the mastermind behind the affair, while very anxious to get the bowl back, did not want any scandal such as would arise if any newsworthy incident arose while they tried to get it back. In other words, you would be perfectly safe if you were to dig up the treasures but only if they managed to recover the bowl from you without bloodshed. My next problem was to ensure that you and Michelle agreed to my plan to dig up the treasure, and I encouraged you to believe our advice to do just that...on this question you may remember that Michelle came out with this same idea...which was a great help! Just remember that right from the first night, my priority was the safety of you and Michelle, especially after that message was pinned to the dining room door. I wonder now if you remember that my man there took me aside and spoke to me confidentially, just after he checked the house? Well, he then told me that a bug had been put into the downstairs telephone." He stopped and smiled at me before saying, "And that was a bit of good news!"

It seemed to me that we were entering a world of nonsense, but he was continuing nevertheless. "Anyway, I then decided that you and Michelle would be perfectly safe, so long as the baddies believed that you were going to proceed with finding and then digging up the bowl…and at the same time we could reassure them about this, by them hearing phone calls on your house phone, which indicated that you were doing just that. You may remember that I phoned my secretary from your house asking her to reserve your passage to Santander and I even gave her details of the car you would be in – that Peugeot 406 you used. So as an extra precaution I even put one of my people onto that same ferry boat, and arranged that he could stay on the car deck…it was then good news when he saw a man put a bug under the rear wing of your car, so we knew they would be sure to find you when you arrived to dig up the treasure! I also of course briefed Gordon not to put up any resistance if you and he were confronted with armed men after you finished your digging operation, and I took the decision to keep you in the dark, lest you inadvertently gave away the fact that he was working under instructions by not putting up any resistance."

I couldn't believe what I was hearing, and burst out, "Do you mean to tell me that you deliberately made it easy for them to steal the bowl…I just can't believe it! You have betrayed the trust which my family and Michelle's family placed with you…how could you be so horrible to us?"

He didn't answer, just turned to Gordon, saying, "Open the case, please." I saw Gordon open the bag, and get out the old case, then open it and produce something that was well wrapped up. He then carefully undid the wrapping, while obviously taking precautions not to touch whatever was inside. Eventually he folded back the last of the coverings, and to my astonishment, I saw that it was a small golden bowl. I went over to have a close look, and Peter shouted, "Don't touch it, Charles, that is the original bowl, complete I hope with the old fingerprints!" He beamed at me. "We aren't quite as silly as you thought we were, so how about having a little more whisky while I tell you the rest of the story."

I had a sense of fierce joy, that everything was so very much all right, but I was still cross at having been kept in the dark…also, of course, I couldn't see how the hell it had all been managed…how could the bowl be here when I had seen it dug up, and then taken away, by the three men who had attacked us in the morning? "I can tell you," he smiled, "that we really were always on your side and as I have often said, our first priority was always your safety, and that of Michelle. Anyway, the next thing which gave me an idea, was the fact that I had learned from your grandfather's papers…the one to the Air Ministry, and the other which had remained hidden in his desk till you found it…that he had identified the bowl as being English, as it was hallmarked from London. I may say that I mentioned this the other day to your grandmother, and she confirmed that gold and silver articles were a hobby of his. I then noted, from the papers, that your grandfather had also mentioned the fact to Pierre Dupont that the bowl had a London hallmark, and you will also remember that I asked Mme Lebrun if she remembered what the bowl was like…and she told me that it was small, like a fingerbowl. Having found all this, I discussed matters again with the Foreign Secretary, and he agreed that a change in our plans was called for. What I then did was to get one of my people to scour London – and, if necessary, all Britain – for a golden fingerbowl with a London hallmark, with a date 1939 or earlier, and he was able to find one. I know that you were surprised by the way which we dressed

Gordon, like a trendy artist, but these large pockets enabled him to carry the false bowl without anything showing. So, when the two of you dug up the real one, Gordon was expecting trouble, and I believe that he asked you to get back to the road to see what was up, so it was then easy for him to get the false bowl from one of his big pockets, and quickly re-wrap it in the old wrapping for the Union Corse boys to find it. He could then, in just a few moments, wrap this original bowl here, to protect the vital fingerprints, and put it into one of his big pockets."

He stopped and beamed at me, saying, "It worked out very well, didn't it? Now we have the bowl, and we can choose our moment to act against Fouquet. At the same time, both you and Michelle are in the clear because, as for now, the opposition believe that they have the real bowl." I could see why Peter was so pleased with himself, but I also remembered that we had a promise from the Foreign Secretary no less, that whatever was going to be done with the evidence on the bowl, we would have to agree to it, so I reminded him of the promise, and asked what they were going to do about it. "Oh, that's all taken care of," he said, "We have an appointment to see him tomorrow morning at twelve o'clock. But we can't phone Michelle or your grandmother to tell them the news, because the phone there still has that bug. So I'll call Sue who is in Glasgow and she will go round and tell them that you are safely home and that everything went according to plan…but she will also tell them not to broadcast that news on the phone! She will also tell them that one of my people will come round this afternoon to remove the bug. You can explain all about this when you see them, and I suggest that we get you on to the first available plane to Glasgow. You'd better take this old case with the jewels so that you can give them to Mme Lebrun, just as she should have got them nearly sixty years ago! I may say that I'd rather not see them as they are, I am sure, very valuable and there could be all sorts of problems regarding estate duty, or whatever it is called in France – but if I never see them that is something I don't need to worry about!"

"As for now," he went on, "you can show them the jewels, but we'll keep the bowl here for the present! I think also that I'll tell Sue to keep the news from them, that we have the golden bowl as we'd better keep quiet about that for now. Anyway, you'll enjoy telling them all about it! I'll also book seats for the two grandmothers, and you and Michelle, on an early shuttle to Heathrow tomorrow morning."

It certainly was a clever plan that Peter had put into effect, and felt I could almost forgive him for keeping me in the dark, but I also realised that it had all been done with a view to keeping Michelle and me safe, so I mentally shrugged my shoulders, and said, "A few minutes ago I was inclined never to speak to you again, but I suppose – to paraphrase a saying – that everything was done for the best in the best of all possible ways...so I'll forgive you...just!"

"I'm sorry," he smiled, "to have kept you in the dark, but you can see what my problem was, and I'm extremely glad that everything worked out so well...anyway, I'll call Sue right now." And that was all, except for him to say that he would look forward to seeing us in the morning, and that we would be brought to his London office from Heathrow, so that we all go together to the Foreign Office.

Gordon, who had remained silent throughout our discussion, then said, "You can put the old case into the bag I used, and I know that Peter is going give you a chit, which will persuade British Airways to let you take it as hand luggage."

***

Michelle met me at Glasgow Airport, and I felt that as though I hadn't seen her for an age, and yet it was only on Monday morning when I had left and now it was only four days later, on Friday afternoon. But it was heaven to hold her in my arms again and to know that all our problems were over. I surprised her, however, by not telling her all the details of my adventure, just saying, "Bear with me, darling, I'd like to tell the story to the three of you all together. It is a long one, and anyway this bag contains the case that my grandfather buried, with the treasures which belonged to your great-grandfather, so you'll want to see them as soon as possible."

Well, she accepted that, but not very enthusiastically; she was, as I knew, a believer in action now, and she said, rather sadly, "I know that it is bad news, as when Sue was here this afternoon to tell us that you were safe, she said that she wouldn't tell us about the bowl – except that it had been stolen from you – but what the hell, you are here safely, and that's all that matters."

However, when we got home I was given no time before I was told to tell the three of them the story, but just before I began, Julie said, "It is like a miracle for me to see that old case again. It is one which I often used as a girl. I'm so excited at the prospect of opening it, to see what is in it, but first of all get on with your story about the bowl and your adventures, as I'm sure you must have had some, considering all this secrecy."

So, it was with the old case still closed that I told my story and just to tease them, I told them just as it had happened to me. So at first they were puzzled about my story about the failure of my mission and the loss of the bowl, but then surprised and delighted to hear that in fact it wasn't lost and how well things had worked out. It was Granny who spoke first. "I suppose, as Sue warned me, that this is why a young man cane here about an hour ago to remove a bug – whatever that is – and it's nice to know that the house is back to normal. But I feel like crying when I think of Henry, my dear husband, burying these treasures and the bowl all these long years ago, and now you, Charles, can give them back to Julie…your grandfather would be very proud of you. And it is amazing that it has turned out to be so very important…when he buried this case, he was just thinking about exposing a minor crook, but now it has become a major element in Franco-British relations. But, as I've said, having read his papers, I am sure that all he wanted at the time was to expose that unfortunate queer – I suppose we must now call him 'gay' – Pierre Dupont."

"Don't call him a queer," I laughed, "or you'll get us in trouble with the Political Correctness Mafia."

But then Julie broke in. "We can discuss all this later, but as for now, how about Michelle and me getting to open the case to see what there is in it?"

She leaned forward, and released the catches which sprung open, just as they had done when I had dug up the case, and we saw the collection of anonymous bundles, with no indication as to what they contained. Granny had the sense to say, "Wait a minute, Julie, I'll get some trays to spread all the things out." And she came back with a few, which she gave to Julie. For a few moments she was irresolute, but then she turned to Michelle, saying, "I think it should be you, dear, to be the first to find what treasures your great-grandfather possessed. After all, but for you and Charles, we would never have got this far." I watched Michelle as she took one of the trays from the pile, and opened the first of the bundles, and poured out a dazzling cascade of diamonds onto one of the trays. We all gasped with amazement at how many and how big they were. Then came another with a shower of emeralds, and a flood of blood-red rubies, followed by other bags of assorted jewels.

The last bundle was rather larger than the others, and it contained jewellery, rather than jewels, and it was no less impressive than the rest. It showed all the signs of having been put together in a hurry, maybe in 1940 when the Germans were over-running France, but it was a sensational collection of fine contemporary pieces. I saw Julie pick up a diamond necklace, and put it around Michelle's neck, and I heard the click of the clasp as it closed, none the worse for having been buried for all these years. She was wearing just a skirt and a plain jersey, but with this dazzling band round her neck, she looked like a princess.

It was such an incredible collection that for a while none of us spoke; we just looked and touched and marvelled. It was Granny who made the first sensible remark when she said, "I shudder to think what this lot is worth, and fortunately I do have a safe in the house, and the sooner this lot is under lock and key the happier I shall be."

"And I'll tell you another thing," she went on, "I know, Julie, that you will want to take all this lot back to France, but you shouldn't do so till it is properly insured. Now I am friendly with a jeweller in Glasgow so, if you agree, I'll see if I can get him to come here and at least give us some figures which an insurance company will accept."

I left the three ladies pouring over the treasures while I went upstairs to have a bath and change my clothes, and when I came down I found that everything had been tidied away and it was time for some pre-dinner drinks. Granny was the first to speak after we were comfortably settled, and she told me that she and Julie had decided that they wouldn't come to London, and that only Michelle and I should go with Peter to see the Foreign Secretary, and she turned to Julie, saying, "You explain, dear."

"The reason," said Julie, "is that this is really a British matter, although in a way you may be interfering with the government of France. Please don't get me wrong, I agree with all you are doing, but I still think it will be better if I stay out of it." It seemed a sensible point of view, but now I had the problem of how to cancel their air tickets, so I called Sue, who promised to fix things, and to tell Peter of the change of plans.

Then it was Michelle's turn, and she said to me, "Now, Charles, we have heard all about your adventure, but aren't you interested in hearing about mine?"

I hastily racked my brain to try to remember what she could have been doing to involve an adventure and, fortunately, I came up with the right answer, and said, "Sorry, darling, I should have asked you…how did your golf go?"

"Well, now, do you want the good news, or the bad news, first?"

"Settle for the good…"

"Right…now as you know, Sue took me to Kilmacolm on Monday morning, where I first of all met your Great-Aunt Agnes – and I can say that we got on well together. Then I walked up to the golf course, where I met Sue and had a lesson from the professional, Iain Nicholson, and after that she took me out to the practice ground to let me bash some balls around. There was then still some time before lunch so I was allowed to play a few holes for real…and that was enough for the first day. I can tell you that Sue was astonished how immediately keen I had become, and she took me back yesterday morning for a full 18 holes. What finally hooked me," she went on, "was that although Sue is a super player, better, I am sure, than I shall ever be, I nevertheless managed to win a hole from her! It was the 17th, which, as you will know well, is a short, downhill hole, and I put my tee shot less than half a metre from the hole, then managed to sink the putt for a two."

"Clever girl," I said, "but what is the bad news?"

"Well, as you can guess, I was so delighted with myself that when we finished the game I went straight into Iain Nicholson's shop and bought myself a full set of equipment – clubs, bag, shoes, a golf jersey, balls…the lot! I think I'd have kept on buying more and more if Sue hadn't stopped me."

"But I'm delighted, darling, both at your prowess and for your new-found keenness for the game, so where is the bad news?"

"Perhaps," she smiled, "I'd better give you a kiss before I mention it…you see, I didn't have enough money with me, so I charged it all to your account with him. But, darling, I see that your glass is empty, maybe if I get you a drink, will you then forgive me?"

It was after dinner when we had a final discussion about what line Michelle and I should take when we saw the Foreign Secretary in the morning, and we ended up of a like mind… that we didn't mind some delay in exposing Fouquet, but we couldn't agree to a very long one. Once that was agreed, my thoughts turned straight to how quickly I could decently get Michelle off to bed with me, and fortunately I had a perfectly genuine excuse as I had been up since four o'clock in the morning, and we were having to make an early start, to get the shuttle at 8.15, which would get us into London at 9.35, in time for our meeting. When I suggested that we should make it an early night, I saw Michelle give me a tiny nod, and she said, "I'm tired too, all this excitement is exhausting, isn't it?"

But, as we got up to go, I saw a very knowing look pass between Granny and Julie, and I realised that the two old girls knew exactly why we were in such a hurry…after all, they too had once been young. When we got upstairs and into our room, we hardly said a word as we got ourselves washed in my en-suite bathroom and ready for bed. But when we had slipped into bed, it was as if a dam had burst when she embraced me fiercely, saying, "Charles, my own wonderful husband-to-be, I have been so worried while you've been away, and it is super that things have worked out so well. After we've done our business with Peter and the Foreign Secretary, let's give ourselves a night out in London…damn it, let's go to a posh hotel! We can certainly afford it now that you've got our family treasures back! Let's make it the Ritz, I've always wanted to stay there. There's just a hint of naughtiness in the name which, I must confess, I find rather attractive!" She then paused for a moment, then whispered in my ear, "But to hell with conversation, just love me…"

All too soon it was time to get up and make an early start for Glasgow Airport, and we went in my car, which could be parked there till we got back the next day. I suppose that it was a good flight, but I'm afraid that I hardly remember anything about it, except for a few moments near the end. Soon after we were airborne I had nodded off, and didn't awake till Michelle nudged me to put on my seat belt as we were then on the approach to Heathrow. Having done that she whispered to me, "I do hope, darling, that I didn't keep you awake too long last night…if so I'll promise not to do so again. You must be sure to tell me anytime when you want rid of me, and to get off to sleep!"

"That is very kind of you," I said seriously, "but I shall try very hard not to disappoint you and…ouch!" She had pinched me. Then we laughed and she gave me a kiss, much to the amusement of the elderly man in the seat next to mine.

We had been speaking in French, and he murmured quietly to me, also in French, "You are a lucky young man, I can see from her ring that you are affianced, and it is good to see two such nice young people being in love."

Michelle had heard what he said, and she leaned over and patted his hand, saying, "That is sweet of you to say so, and I can tell you that I am quite satisfied with him, but tell me, how come you speak such good French?"

"That's easy," he said, "like me, your man here is doubly lucky – I should know, because I too was fortunate enough to marry a French lady – and we've already ticked up over forty years together." Almost as he said that, there was a bump as our wheels hit the runway, and he smiled at us, and went on in English, "There we are, back to earth again, so we can get back to being normal Brits, and ignoring each other, but I have very much enjoyed our little chat."

I had been told that we would be met by an official driver who would carry a board with my name, but first we had to go to collect our bags…or what was more important, Michelle's bag…as she had insisted in bringing some fancy clothes, for that night on the town I had promised her. But just as we got to the carousel in the Baggage Reclaim – and before the bags had arrived – there was a public address announcement: "Will Mr Charles Burton, recently arrived from Glasgow, please come to the British Airways Enquiry Desk."

"I wonder what that can be," I said, "perhaps Peter has changed our plans, I'd better go and see what it is. You stay here and collect our bags, I'll come back after I've got the message."

When I got to the desk, the girl I spoke to said, "Hello, Mr Burton, I'm glad you got our call, as your friend…"

She stopped and looked around. "Wonder where he can be, he was here a minute ago, and it seemed very urgent."

But nobody appeared, and after a few minutes I suddenly became nervous and, to the surprise of the girl, raced off back to the baggage area. By this time the bags from our flight had arrived, and most of them had been collected, but our two were circulating, now on their own, in the nearly deserted area. I anxiously enquired of the staff people there if any of them had seen Michelle, but naturally to have noticed one person among all the others was too much to hope for. But then one girl called me back, saying, "You know, I did see a young woman standing by the carousel when two men came up to her and she went off with one of them, leaving the other man to collect whatever bags she was waiting for. What surprised me was that as soon as the other two went away, he also departed, and without collecting any luggage – and it must be these two bags over there."

***

CHAPTER ELEVEN

I just didn't know what to do and in the nightmare of my thoughts I went over and picked up our two bags as they moved past me on the carousel. But then I noticed that an envelope, addressed to me, had been stuck to mine. In the envelope was a piece of paper:

It would be very unwise to contact the police. Anyway, Michelle will be perfectly safe if you are sensible. Tell Peter Armstrong that we shall be in touch and you can also mention that he has been careless as 'M' cannot be correct.

I couldn't understand the second part of the message, but decided that all I could do to begin with was to act on the first bit. So, despite the horror of the situation, I didn't call the police, but instead went in search of the man who had been detailed to meet us. He was in the arrivals hall, carrying a board with my name. He looked puzzled when I came up to him. "I thought I had missed you, sir. Where is the young lady?"

It didn't take me long to explain the disaster and I realised at once that he wasn't just a driver as, after a few pertinent questions, he fetched a mobile from his pocket. "I'll get on to Mr Armstrong and find out what his instructions are."

But then he changed his mind and handed me the phone, saying that it would be better if I spoke to him. Peter was horrified when I told him what had happened, and when I read him the message he told me not to get involved with the police, at least not at this stage, but to come and see him at once in his London office. He explained that he was talking on his car phone as he was being driven to London from the house in which I had met him yesterday and that he would be in his office around the same time as I got there. It seemed awful to me to leave the airport without getting anything set in motion to find Michelle, but I could see that it would be a hopeless quest unless we got some clues, and Peter and his organisation did seem to be my only hope. Anyway, my contact drove me from Heathrow into London at considerable speed, eventually into Park Lane and then into an upmarket residential area where we turned into a tiny driveway, which led to a small but elegant house. Our arrival must have been noticed; the front door opened as soon as we were out of the car, and we were greeted by a formally-dressed soldier, a sergeant, who ushered us into the entrance hall where another functionary was waiting, this time an army officer, and I was led to a lift by my soldier guide who called it by inserting a card into a box on the wall. We went up to the second floor where Peter was waiting to greet me, and he took me into a rather formal but luxuriously furnished office.

He gestured to me to sit down and I could see that he was both worried and embarrassed. "I can't tell you, Charles," he said, "how badly I feel about this development. I did think that we had kept you and Michelle out of the firing line, and I think that I have found out the stupid mistake that has led to this situation. I have just asked one of my people, whose fault it must surely be, to come and see me." Almost as he said this, there was a knock on the door and a young, formally dressed man came in. "You wanted me, sir?"

"Yes, James. I am told that you have recently got yourself to be engaged to be married and that you were involved in a busy social round last weekend. Is that the case?"

"You can say that again!" he smiled. "My in-laws-to-be, Sir Thomas and Lady McLean, insisted on making my engagement a big affair." All this friendly chit-chat seemed nonsense to me: what possible relevance did it have to Michelle? But then Peter said, "I hope that the job I gave you last Friday morning to find a pre-war golden bowl before Tuesday evening didn't make you late for the party?"

"No, sir, but I did have a hell of a job to find the bowl. I started the search as soon as I got your instructions and I was getting rather worried by the late afternoon of Saturday, as I was having no luck at all. I began wondering if I was going to miss the part and be very unpopular! But then I found a perfect one in a small shop in Hammersmith. I hope, sir, that it did the job." He stopped there, then added with a self-satisfied smile, "So that kept me in the clear with my in-laws."

"Yes," said Peter. "It was a nice object, but can you remember the date of the Assay mark?"

For a moment the young man looked worried. "Yes, I can. It carried the code letter M for 1947, certainly not pre-war as you requested, but it was otherwise so perfect." In a flash, everything was clear. This bastard had given us a bowl that was marked with a date some five years after the original bowl had been buried, and Fouquet or his friends had seen this, so it was no wonder that the whole deception had blown up in our faces. I had been sitting on a chair beside Peter's desk, and now I jumped up and seized the idiot by the lapels of his immaculate suit, saying, "You stupid idiot, you were so keen to get to a bloody party that, to save time, you disobeyed your instructions. I'm going to…!"

But Peter was on his feet, and pushed me back from the astonished and rather apprehensive man. "Charles," I know what this cretin deserves, but believe me he will regret that mistake for the rest of his life." He then turned to the unfortunate James. "When you joined this organisation it was made clear to you that you had to obey orders or, if there were problems, that you must explain your difficulties before doing anything which differed in any way from those instructions. You were told last Friday morning to get a pre-war golden bowl. You failed to do so and, worse, you produced an incorrect one – with an Assay mark which showed it as past-war – without telling anybody. In our line of business we must have integrity, and you have shown that you do not understand the word, so get back to your office now and clear your desk…you are finished as regards a career in the Security or Intelligence services. The best thing you can do is resign from the civil service. If you don't, I'm sure that a clerk's job could be found for you in a remote and troubled corner of central Africa. Not the sort of life that your fiancée has been looking forward to. Now, bugger off and tell my secretary within the next quarter of an hour whether you intend to resign."

"But, sir," he muttered, "surely a little mistake like this isn't that important. The man who sold me the bowl said that only experts ever looked at silver or gold marks."

"No doubt he did," said Peter quietly, "but you had clear instructions, and nevertheless you made a terrible mistake, so get the hell out of my office before my young friend here beats you up." If the matter hadn't been so serious, I could almost have felt sorry for the other man who now looked as if he was going to burst into tears. He took a somewhat apprehensive look at me, then turned and almost ran from the office.

"Just a moment, Charles," said Peter, "I must go and issue some instructions that will blight that young idiot's career. No way could I ever trust him again, of course…not that saying this is any consolation to you. It is damnable. We had everything sewn up nicely, and then that idiot blows the whole thing sky high. Mind you, I also blame myself for not getting the date stamp on the bowl checked, but it never occurred to me that he could be so stupid."

He was only away for a few minutes, and came back and put a hand on my shoulder. "Well, that's done. But what are we going to do about Michelle? I think you'll agree that to begin with we should not involve the police. As we know, Fouquet is paranoid about avoiding publicity, and that is the better of the two cards that we have – the other one, of course, is the fact that we still have the correct bowl. In their letter they warn against contacting the cops and they also say that they will get in touch with me. Although it may seem unenterprising, I suggest that we do nothing till we hear from them…I'm sure they won't keep us waiting long."

Almost as he finished, his phone rang, and I listened eagerly to hear what he said, but it was obviously only his wife, Sue, and I heard him say, "Yes, they do have Michelle, so if they call, give them the emergency number, which you know. If they do call, ring 1471 and let me know if you are lucky enough to get the originating number. Maybe, if they're French, they won't know to dial 141 first."

When he had finished, a few moments later, he jumped up, called for his secretary, and I heard him arranging for a trace to be put on what he called Secure Line Two, and also for them to be recorded. The he turned to me. "The opposition don't have any of my official numbers, Charles, but they may have got Sue's number from when their bug was in your house. If so, then they will phone her. She will then give them a number here so, I hope, they will call very soon."

He was right, but it wasn't a phone call but a fax, which arrived about ten minutes later. It was short and very much to the point:

Dear Mr Armstrong

I hope that you dismissed the stupid man who bought that bowl. It really was a very silly mistake.

I also suggest that you are more sensible in future, and we shall happily end this unfortunate conflict as soon as you exchange the real bowl for the fake one.

You will be glad to know that Michelle is well and quite recovered from her ordeal. She is, however, very keen to see Charles again as soon as she can.

However, to find her might be difficult as she is now far away from here, so tell him to be at Gatwick airport with his passport in time to catch the British Airways flight to Marseille at 6.40 am tomorrow.

He should bring an overnight bag, and also the one that Michelle omitted to collect this morning. She misses her toilet things.

We shall arrange a room for him in the Gatwick Moathouse and will soon reunite the young lovers, unless, of course, he makes things awkward by bringing any of your friends or anybody else. If so, the deal will be off, which would be sad for all concerned.

But if all is well, he will be reunited with Michelle as soon as we are reunited with the original bowl.

We were quiet after we read the fax, but then Peter said, "Look on the bright side, Charles, she would seem to be safe and, as we can't now refuse to give them the bowl, the whole operation is off, as far as we're concerned. All we'll do is keep a watching eye over you."

But that didn't please me at all. "But look, Peter," I said, "all our troubles have followed from cooperating with you, so wouldn't it now be safer for me to go off, as they insist, quite on my own? It would seem that you were right when you said Fouquet and his chums are being very careful not to harm us, so I should be quite safe if I just go along to wherever they have Michelle, and make the exchange."

Peter was unhappy. "I don't know about that, Charles, as I feel that going off without cover is unwise. Certainly the recovery of the bowl is all-important to them, but I am concerned that they might think to organise a convenient accident. With their organisation, I feel sure they could be clever enough to kill either or both of you without a breath of suspicion against them. Now, the first thing I am going to do is ask Sue to go round and see your grandmother and Julie. They, of course, still know nothing of this business, and we can't keep it from them forever. Anyway, I think it best if Sue breaks the news to them and perhaps also stays the night. I'll arrange for calls to my house to be diverted to your home number."

That seemed to make sense to me and it didn't take him long to arrange matters. He then left his desk and called me over to sit on one of the armchairs that flanked the fireplace. "Let's be quiet for a while," he said, "and see if we can't come up with any good ideas." But as far as I was concerned the only good idea I had was to do exactly what they had told me to do. I was damned if I was going to do anything whatsoever that might put Michelle into more danger. About ten minutes later, Peter suddenly said, "That's it! How about this for an idea? It isn't perfect but at least it has the merit that the opposition won't know anything about our real plans, and they may think that we don't have any!"

"You've lost me," I said. "How do you intend to try and deceive them? And remember that I won't do anything which could lead to reprisals against Michelle." He sounded almost embarrassed when he said, "Of course, I know that, but you will remember that we have discussed the question of who has been leaking information. Now, I wonder if you remember that fax which you sent to M. Duchene from that hotel in Avignon. I have always wondered if the girl who sent it realised that it contained somewhat sensitive information. She might have thought that it could win her some pocket money. Now, and this is only a hunch, but I do wonder if the Union Corse got it and, if they did, did they know who he is and also his address and phone number. I was concerned about this, so I had some checks made. It turns out that he has a married daughter who lives in Marseilles – right in the Union Corse heartland. I reckoned that he could be subject to blackmail."

His phone rang, and I realised that my boss William Henderson was on the phone. I couldn't make any sense out of the side of the conversation which I heard, but at the end he explained to me that M. Duchene had called him with a rather odd message, saying that he was now suffering from TB and was one behind as regards diseases.

Peter smiled at me before saying, "That was worrying, wasn't it?"

I could make nothing of us and said so. He just shook his head, saying, "I can tell you that Mr Henderson was very pleased at having understood the message – just think, one ahead of TB is UC, so he was telling me that he was in the hands of the Union Corse, so we can mislead them by giving false information to M. Duchene!"

"Wait a minute! I'm not going to put Michelle in any more danger, and giving them false information is far too dangerous."

"Don't worry about that…certainly we are going to give them nothing but the strict truth, which should not give them any concern and will satisfy them that we are in their power." Worried as he was, he had to laugh at my puzzlement, and explained that he wanted me to ring M. Duchene to explain about the failure of my mission – to give him a full account of the affair – and that I was off in the morning to take the bowl to them in order to secure the release of Michelle. "That's all, and you'll be saying nothing but the truth. So what harm can there be in that? It should reassure them that we are playing ball."

"Now," he went on, "I seem to remember that Duchene mentioned that he does a lot of work from home, so it might be an idea to give him a call right now. It will greatly be to our advantage if he talks. In any case, the opposition will then know that you are really going to do just as they said, with you travelling with no back-up."

We were lucky as in just a few minutes I was connected and, although he

sounded pleased to hear my voice, his was oddly strained. "Hello, Charles, I was about to ring and see if there was any news about your mission…what happened, were you successful?"

I told him the story in detail, as I thought that the more information I gave him, the better my chance that he would believe me. At last I came to tell him about our arrival at Heathrow in the morning, with Michelle being abducted and, as I spoke, I became quite certain that everything I told him was not news to him, so he must be in their hands. I then finished with a long explanation of how I decided to do exactly what the opposition wanted. He expressed his full agreement. "You are very wise, Charles. Obviously these people just want the one thing – to get the bowl from you – and if you do that, it should be the end of the affair. You will then have your lovely fiancée back and also, of course, you have already recovered her family treasures, and the matter of the bowl is far less important."

I replied that I was in full agreement with his views and then told him, just in case Michelle was being held in Paris, that it was good to have him as a friend nearby, should I want any help. He then said, "My dear Charles, I shall be at home for the next few days, so do please call me if there is anything I can do. May I wish you every success, and I do hope that you are soon reunited with Michelle."

Peter had been listening to our conversation and I was interested to find that he too had felt that Duchene was under some sort of strain, and had known about the affair, and that the abduction of Michelle wasn't news to him. "I am delighted about that," he said, "as I'm quite sure that your story is now being relayed to the opposition…certainly I hope so."

He then called his secretary on his internal phone, about flights from Gatwick in the morning. She was back in a few minutes, and when he looked at the information, he suddenly smiled, saying, "That's it! Look, Charles, the morning flight to Marseilles is at 6.40 and it's a direct one. I'll lay long odds that this is the one you'll be on. I am so sure of it that I'm going to get two of my best people to head off to Marseilles this afternoon, and they will be at the airport when your flight gets in. Is that okay with you?"

"Yes, it is," I said.

But before I could expand on that, he went on, "The only thing I am going to ask you to do is swallow a tiny gadget tomorrow morning, before you go off. It's a miniature homing beacon, only the size of a small pastille, easy to swallow. I can assure you that our men will have no need to follow you closely. They should be able to track you quite easily at a safe distance as our gadget has a range of a few miles, and for me it is a racing certainty that you will be taken to wherever they are holding Michelle. My bet is that your destination will be Fouquet's estate which we know is only some twenty kilometres north of Marseilles."

"But wait a minute," I said. "Surely you aren't thinking of storming the castle and rescuing the prince and princess? That could easily end in both of us being killed."

But I needn't have worried as Peter said, "Of course I realise that, and if they play ball with you by way of releasing you both, then you have my word that my men will not interfere in any way, unless we have good reason to do so. It is in case of things going wrong that I am making these arrangements, and if they do you have only to call for help and our men will come running."

"But how the hell do I call for help?"

"The homing gadget is a clever little beast, and you will have in your pocket a small ring of keys, including one which looks like a car key of the type that operates locks remotely. It even has a Ford logo on it, as they may remember that your car is a Mondeo. Nothing will happen if the door-locking button on it is pressed once or twice. But should you want our help, all you need do is press the button three times in quick succession, and the beacon will then emit an SOS signal. You will see that this leaves matters entirely in your hands, and you will be completely on your own, unless you want help. But as for what we do after you and Michelle are clear and away, I have some plans, which I'd better keep to myself."

As for me, I could only hope that the opposition did what they had promised and allow me to get away with Michelle, without any rough stuff, as nothing whatsoever counted compared with her safety. As for what Peter did after we were both free – that was his problem, not mine. He allowed me quite a while to make up my mind, but then said, "Is that okay with you?"

"Yes it is, but I hope I can trust you when you say that you will have no other men with me…I must have your assurance on that."

"Yes you have, but you must realise that I must have agents in the area if I am going to have any chance of recovering the bowl after you have handed it over. But they will keep well away from you." He stopped there and looked over at me. "Now, since we are agreed about that, I must make some arrangements about the bowl. Since you brought it to me yesterday, it has been under lock and key. But now I am going to give it to some of our experts, just to see what prints there are on it which have survived since 1942. You'll remember that one of my people bribed a waiter to give him a glass that had been used by M. Fouquet, so we have a record of his prints."

"But wait a minute, "I said, "if he hears any signs of your still being involved, won't it blow sky high the whole arrangement of getting Michelle back?"

"Not a bit of it. You see, he must know that we are not going to miss the opportunity of doing this, and he must also reckon that, without the actual bowl with the prints on it, we will be in a very weak position to do anything about it. Trying to make a scandal about such an old affair, and based on fingerprints from a bowl which we no longer have will get us nowhere. So, there is no doubt that actual possession of the bowl is important. Anyway, let's have a look at it now…"

He went over to a wall safe, then carefully brought out the small bowl, unwrapped it carefully without touching the surface, and laid it down on a side table. It did seem so small to have caused all this mayhem, and Peter smiled at me. "Doesn't look very much, does it? But let's have a look to see what date mark it has…"

He got out a magnifying glass and smiled at me. "You can see, Charles, that having to use this is an early sign of old age, as you will be able to see the marks quite clearly without any assistance…look, there is the Leopard's Head signifying that it was assayed in London, and I can tell you that the records of all the dates and other marks go back as far as 1544 in the time of Henry VIII. See there that script letter 'o' which…", and here he consulted a small book, "…is the date letter for 1909, in the last year of Edward VII's reign, then a crown and the figure '18' showing that it is 18 carat gold. The other letters show the makers, but you would need a bigger reference book to identify them."

"So," he went on, "it was made just before the 1914-18 war, in the golden years of Edwardian society, and I wonder what great house ordered a set of golden fingerbowls? Now, even that tiny bit of information will be interesting – should we get the bowl back – to try and find out where any of the other bowls have ended up. Anyway, I'll arrange now for it to be examined and a record kept of all the fingerprints they can find."

By then it was lunchtime and he suggested that we eat in his office, and then he would have me driven down to a country house near Windsor that specialised in electronic matters. "They will supply you with the device that you have to swallow. I'll ensure that you are not seen, so I suggest that you 'surface' – if I can put it that way – when you check into one of the airport hotels at Gatwick. You'll get there in the late afternoon, and we'll be careful to ensure that you are left quite on your own."

I was becoming somewhat reassured, but then I had to face the problem of reassuring Granny and Julie. By this time I knew that Sue must have got to our house, and would have told them the sad news, and I dreaded having to speak to Granny when she phoned, as call she certainly would. In fact it was Sue who came on the phone and said to me, "I don't need to tell you that both Marie and Julie are devastated by the awful development, so do try your best to calm their fears…"

The telephone conversations with both Granny and Julie were awful as they were distraught. It was doubly hard for them because at least I was about to do something, but they had just to sit and wait. All I could do was try to be as cheerful as I could and to assure them that I was going to do exactly what the opposition wanted, so as not to put Michelle in any more danger. I felt an awful heel as I did so, but what else was there for me to do? When I hung up the phone, Peter said to me, "If ever there was a case for a white lie, this is the time and place. Don't let it worry you, as swallowing a small radio beacon isn't much. Come on now, let's have a drink before lunch, and afterwards I'll have you driven down."

After our meal, one of his assistants came in and they talked quietly for a few minutes, and then he said to me, "While we have been eating, my experts have been recording very carefully what fingerprints were on the bowl. You'll be glad to know that some of them tally with the samples we recently got from Fouquet. So, at least it is now confirmed…he is indeed Pierre Dupont. I don't know what use, if any, we'll ever make of them, but at least we have them. Now, here is the bowl, carefully wrapped up in this cardboard box…for God's sake, look after it!"

"Now," he want on, "as I have said, I wouldn't want the opposition to know where you are off to this afternoon. So I'm going to take you down to our basement garage and, in case they are watching, you will be hidden under a rug at the back of a car when you leave. You will, of course, have your overnight bag and also Michelle's, and when you are finished with our people, the driver will take you back into London and drop you near Victoria station. You can then arrive, all innocent, at Gatwick by train. You can then take a courtesy bus to your hotel, and once you are there, you will be alone. Don't look out for anybody and only if things go wrong when you are in France should you press the key button three times."

It is a fact that men usually find it hard to express emotion, but I felt quite choked when Peter took my hand, saying, "All the best, Charles, I feel so responsible for having got you and Michelle into this awful situation!" He then embraced me for a moment, before saying, "Take care. I wish I could do more for you…good luck!"

***

When I got to Windsor I was taken to a kind of space age laboratory, rather like the one in the 007 books which provided James Bond with all his gadgets, and a young technician showed me the homing beacon which was to be my lifeline. It was about the size of a quite small sweet, or a tiny sausage, with a smooth plastic covering, which gave no clues as to what was inside it. He showed it off to me very proudly, saying that it had a range of nearly five miles, and would have a life of some forty-eight hours after it was switched on…but, he warned me, only an hour or so once it was switched to the SOS mode. "You'll have to swallow it tomorrow morning," he said, "try to get your bowels moving and have your breakfast early enough so that you leave at least an hour between ending your meal and swallowing the gadget. That should be easy as I don't want you to swallow it till you are through the pre-boarding scanners, and are airborne. To fool them I am going to put it into this little box which will make it invisible to them." The box was nothing to look at – just about the size of a matchbox, and he smiled as he gave it to me. "Doesn't look much, does it? But it too is very clever – so you will be a walking electronic miracle!"

"And how do I switch the beacon on?" I asked.

"It turns itself on whenever its temperature gets to more than ninety degrees fahrenheit, and it will do so within a very few minutes after you swallow it. Obviously, you will then have to try to keep your bowels from moving so long as you want the beacon to operate." I was just about to leave, when he called me back.

"As a taxpayer I am sure that you would like to save the Exchequer money if possible so, when this business is over, it would be very kind if you could retrieve it, and return it to us. Micro circuits like this don't come cheap … this one cost over two thousand pounds, plus another couple of hundred for the box, although you'll have to dispose of that after you swallow the beacon.

When we went out to the car I was surprised to see that my bag and Michelle's had been moved to another one, this time an ancient, and very shabby Ford Escort. As I looked rather doubtfully at it, my technician smiled at me. "Just another precaution, in case the opposition saw the previous one, but it isn't really as bad as it looks, and the driver is quite competent!"

It was late afternoon when my driver dropped me near Victoria station. I then caught a fast train to Gatwick and, thanks to a courtesy bus, I was delivered to the Moathouse at Hurley before six o'clock.

It was absurd as, despite the ordinary-looking people in the hotel, I still wondered if unfriendly eyes were watching me. I felt that an early night was the best plan, so by ten o'clock I was in bed and looking at the TV news to pass the time. But then my phone rang and when I picked it up a voice said, "Good evening, Mr Burton, we are glad to see that you would appear to be obeying our instructions. Just remember, we are watching you, and we would remind you that you must travel alone…if we have any reason to suspect that you are disobeying our instructions, it will be most unfortunate for your charming girlfriend...just remember that. Don't look for us in the morning, we'll find you. Just be near the check-in desks in the morning at a quarter past five and wait till we contact you."

There was a click, and that was all. It was an eerie feeling to think that my every move seemed to be known about, but what I couldn't understand was why they were bothering? Was it just to keep me off balance? However, all I could do was shrug my shoulders as there was no point in worrying... it couldn't help me. I had no option but to do exactly what they had told me to do, and I could only cross my fingers and hope that they really meant what they said; that once they got the bowl, they would release Michelle and let us get back to Britain, and back to our normal lives. But it was easier said than done, and impossible to stop worrying about, especially as I couldn't see the need for the complicated arrangements. If it really was true that all they wanted was the bowl, why not demand it from me here and now, in the hotel? It was on the table beside my bed, neatly parcelled up in the box that Peter had found for it. Surely to give it back now would be a lot easier than getting me to France, and maybe to Fouquet's country house near Marseilles.

But I couldn't help the unpleasant thought surfacing that the only reason for wanting to get me there, might be to ensure that I was completely in their power, and of course they already had Michelle. But, on the other hand, they were aware that the authorities here knew of my actions, so was it reasonable to suppose that they would risk harming Michelle or me?

And what devilry were they up to now?

It wasn't a happy thought with which to lull me to sleep, and it was a long time before at last I nodded off.

***

CHAPTER TWELVE

It was my bad luck that having tossed and turned for most of the night, I was in a deep sleep when my wake-up call come at a quarter to four. I had arranged such an early call because of the advice I'd been given to have a solid breakfast maybe two hours before swallowing the radio beacon. I had a simple but adequate breakfast in my room. Time seemed to crawl by after that as I tried to find anything interesting in the morning papers, and it was only when I was about to put them down that I did see something of interest. It was in the foreign news pages of *The Telegraph* and I noticed an article about the French government, and the fact that there were problems with one of the coalition partners, Le Parti de Socialisme et d'Amical, who were pressing for closer links with Germany. They quoted some extracts from a speech by their leader, M. Vincent Fouquet, which was most critical of the attitude of Britain at a recent EU conference. In his speech, just before the conference ended, he had insisted that the real friends of France lay with their comrades across the Rhine, and that the name La Perfide Albion had, over the years, been well earned. I hadn't time to read more as I had to remember to get ready for my appointment at the airport. In fact there really wasn't much need to hurry, but I still went downstairs, giving myself plenty of time to get my bill paid and arrange for the hotel courtesy bus to deliver me to the terminal building in plenty of time before the deadline. I felt oddly conspicuous as I stood there with my hand luggage, my small bag to take with me on the plane (which contained my overnight things and the bowl) and Michelle's larger bag with all her things, and which I would check in at the terminal.

At the airport, I hesitated at the check-in area. Almost immediately, a young man came up to me, saying, "Good morning, Mr Burton, here is a ticket to Marseilles on the six-forty flight. Get yourself organised and remember that we are watching you to make sure that you're not being…how shall I say…escorted, by some of Mr Armstrong's men." He was now smartly dressed in a business suit, but I recognised him as one of the three men who had surprised us two days before when we were digging up the treasures. He was the one who had fired the shot to puncture one of our tyres. He saw a flicker of recognition in my eyes, and said, "Yes, we are old friends, aren't we? But don't try to be clever this time. Just do as you are told if you value your girl's health. Anyway, I'll see you again when we get to Marseilles." He didn't wait for any reply from me, just thrust the ticket into my hand and walked quickly away.

Checking in was not uneventful. It wasn't the fancy box in my pocket that set off the alarm, but the bag with the bowl. When I opened my case and showed the bowl to the official, he looked surprised but said nothing.

The other passengers on the flight looked so ordinary that it seemed impossible that any of them, apart from the man I had seen, were part of the opposition team. Everybody seemed to be either wrapped up with the morning newspapers or else making obscure calculations, no doubt about the latest exchange rates for pounds against euros. I refused the offer of a second breakfast on the flight. A little while before we got to Marseilles, I repaired to the toilet and swallowed the beacon, crossing my fingers that it would work.

It was when we got there, and after I had retrieved Michelle's bag from the carousel, completed customs and immigration, and had walked into the arrivals hall, when the next surprise came...in the shape of another of the men who had been in the team who came on us after we had dug up the treasure – and the bowl. He was the man who, at the end, had made the rather polite little speech, and once more he greeted me in a quite friendly fashion. "Well, Charles, I'm sorry we have to meet again in these unfortunate circumstances, and as we are going to spend some time together, I had better introduce myself. My name is Albert Durand, and I must confess that I don't quite understand why the events of sixty years ago should have become so important now. But I am acting under orders, so please let's have no heroics...I have to say it, but remember that we have the girl, so just come quietly with me to the car, and try to look as if we really are friends."

What could I do but go with him? We walked out to where the car was parked, in an area festooned with 'No Waiting' signs. I was not too pleased to see that the car driver was the same chap who had been in the two-man team which had tried to kill Michelle and me back in Avignon, and who had also been the front man in the team who took the bowl from Gordon and me after we had dug it up. His greeting to me was far from friendly, just, "Which bag is the bowl in?" And when I told him, he said "Good, we'll be sure to keep it safe this time. You were stupid to try and cheat the boss with that fake bowl, so don't try anything this time." He then turned to Albert. "Right, he's all yours now," and with a nod to him he walked off.

I was surprised that Albert didn't start the car at once, and I wondered what, if anything, Peter's team were doing. But then we did start and after a while passed a large, empty, stationary bus which at once pulled out behind us and followed very closely. A few minutes later, when we were about to clear the airport area, I heard a cacophony of car horns behind us and looked back to see that the bus had stopped, slowing across the road so that nothing could follow us. "Just a small precaution," Albert said. "You see, the boss didn't feel like trusting you, just in case you were foolish enough to have friends here, and that little lot will stop any attempt to follow you."

I hoped that I looked unconcerned, as I said, "I don't know why you are taking all these precautions, as my instructions were to come alone, and that is what I have done."

"That's good, because even if you did have people here, they wouldn't have been able to track you. That bus is going to have a complete breakdown for the next five minutes at least...so now we can relax and enjoy the journey. Isn't it a beautiful day!"

I tried to work things out as we drove along, and it occurred to me that there would seem to be only quite a small operating team against me. I decided to put identity tags against them...the two who had attacked Michelle and me were the three who had taken the fake bowl from us, one of which was A1. The other two I could call B1 and B2. B1 I had seen at Gatwick when I got the ticket from him, before he followed me here, and B2, the polite man, I now knew to be Albert Durand. Although this was conjecture, it did give me a tiny bit of satisfaction to work out something about the opposition. What also gave me a crumb of comfort was the fact that, if I was right about the small number of the opposition, then it was odd for such a large organisation as the Union Corse to use so few people, and I wondered whether the whole affair could be more of a private vendetta on behalf of Fouquet and the man, Maurice Durand, who had given a false identification of a corpse back in 1945.

But I had then to think about other matters, as I was also trying to remember the road map of the area around Marseilles, which I had seen in Peter's office, so I knew where Fouquet's estate was. But we were not far from the outskirts of the city when we turned off the main road and stopped in a lay-by. He opened a small case. Inside was a laptop PC. "I am sorry, Charles," he said. "I'm afraid that I have also been instructed to see whether you have any electronic items with you which might help your friends to locate you. I have been told not to trust you in any way. Despite that, may I first ask you if you do have electronic items that might help your friends to keep track of you?"

This was the last question I wanted, and before I could answer, he laughed, saying, "Let me give you a word of advice, Charles. Never play poker for large stakes! Your expression has told me clearly that you do have something with you…so, to save time, why not tell me what you have?" But then he went on, almost straight away. "But, don't worry, I'm not going to embarrass you by forcing an answer, as I have a good idea what you have and also where it is."

He then switched on his PC, then got out what looked like a large electric torch which he pointed at my midriff, saying, "Look at the screen here." For a few moments all I could see was a straight line, but then he pushed a button on the PC marked *Search*. A pulsating blip appeared on the screen. He gave a small nod of satisfaction, then pushed another button, this one marked *Overload*, and the blip suddenly flickered before disappearing.

"Sorry about that, Charles. The massive overload that I subjected it to has rendered it useless. But now, I'm afraid,

I'm also going to have to check both your bag, and Michelle's as well."

He first unzipped and checked them, then admired the golden bowl. Then he smiled and said, "That's good, they are both clear. As you know, I am not entirely happy about this business, but I am glad to see this bowl, which should end things. As for now, you are clean...and I propose to tell my great-uncle that you were clean in the first place...there is no point in complicating matters further."

I didn't know what to say, so just murmured okay as he started the car again. But I had noted his remark that he was working on his great-uncle's instructions, and as he had told me that his name was Albert Durand, his great-uncle had to be the M. Maurice Durand, who had wrongly identified Pierre's body in 1946, and who was now an important man in the Union Corse.

Back on the road again I was sure he was trying to confuse us as to where we were going as we went from main roads to minor ones, then back to main ones again, and I wondered if my friends in Peter's team, even if they had seen me at the airport, would now have any idea where I was being taken. Now, with no beacon to help them, I felt sure that they must have lost all track of where I was. It was only about twenty miles after clearing the city boundary when the car turned down a side road, and then stopped outside a pair of imposing entrance gates. It was at once obvious that the gates were more than just ornamental, as two armed guards came out of a gate house and had a good look at the car, before opening the gates to let us in.

The drive was at least 400 yards long and it led through an area of immaculate parkland where I could see a herd of red deer grazing peacefully. My heart sank as I looked at all this open area, and the livestock, and I wondered what possible chance my friends had of getting to the house, if they ever found me, without being apprehended. But then we were arriving at the house, which looked like a picture postcard of a French chateau…it was all so immaculate and beautiful, and so unlikely a base for a crooked politician or a criminal organisation.

The car drew up with a crunch from its tyres as it ran over the smoothly-raked gravel and the door was opened by a suave, quite elderly man – a butler, I reckoned. Albert was all smiles, as he ushered me in and said, "Charles, my great-uncle has asked me to welcome you to his home. His name is Maurice Durand. He has told me to say that you will be tired after your journey and he suggests that you now meet him and that I arrange for your charming fiancée to join you. I hope that is her overnight bag that you have with you. She has been feeling a little lost without it."

I just didn't know how to deal with this pretence of normality, but I felt I had to try and progress matters, saying, "I'm afraid, Albert, that I only know you from the time of our brief meeting near Bayonne, and I suggest that we don't mess around in play acting. All I want is to get Michelle back with me, and all you and your great-uncle want is to get the original bowl, so let's make the exchange and finish the deal. Once that is done, you have my word that I won't take the matter any further…you have already made it clear that you have a very long arm and, I can assure you, I want nothing more than to end things."

"Well said, Charles," he replied, "but I am afraid that this business of yours is really nothing to do with me and, of course, it has given me no pleasure to have forced you to come here today. But my great-uncle is most interested to meet you, so please come with me, and you can make your suggestions to him." He turned to the butler and told him to take Michelle's overnight bag to her, explaining that Michelle would soon be down and, in the meantime, that I should come with him with my bag, which contained the bowl. I was led into a large hall, floored in marble, with a flowing staircase leading to the upper floors, and then into an enormous salon with open French windows leading to a shady patio, where I could see a very old man dressed in a formal suit in the fashion of half-a-century ago, even down to a watchchain stretched across his waistband, bearing a large gold medallion. He looked at me with no sign of welcome. There was a long silence before he said, "M. Burton, you have recently caused an old friend of mine a great deal of worry. When he heard about your enquiries, he asked me, as an *obligement*, if I would make sure that your investigations led to nothing. But you have been extremely lucky, and it is only in the past twenty-four hours that we have been able to spike your guns. I understand that the real bowl is in this bag here, and my old friend will be very glad to get it. Unfortunately, however, he is very busy these days…you will know his important position in the government…and won't manage to get here for perhaps an hour. You will need to be patient until he arrives, as he insists that the handover is made to him in person. But you won't be lonely, as you will have the pleasure of having the companionship of your fiancée, Michelle…my great-nephew, Albert, who brought you here, will soon bring her down."

I tried, as I had done previously, to suggest that we might just hand over the bowl now, so that Michelle and I could leave at once, but he just waved the idea away. "No, M. Burton, my old friend M. Fouquet is very keen to see both of you in person, and I feel sure that you will agree to indulge an old man, as there will only be trivial inconvenience to the pair of you." It was nicely put, and I could see that arguing would be a waste of time. However, everything was being handled very politely, and I felt reassured that maybe we didn't have too much to worry about. But just then I heard the sound of footsteps and my worries came straight back at me when I saw Michelle being led into the room. She looked as if she was convalescing after a serious illness; her face was white, and there was an unsteadiness in her step which distressed me. I ran over and embraced her. I could feel that she was trembling; apart from being distressed, I suddenly became very angry. I turned to the old man.

"M. Durand, I had thought that the people in your organisation, especially ones as important as you, would be men of honour. I find it incredible that you could ill treat a young girl, my fiancée, like this. Are you not ashamed?"

For a moment he did look embarrassed, but that passed and he shook his head. "M. Burton, everything we did, everything that we had to do, was for the best. It was, of course, necessary to convey her from London in order that a travesty of justice did not take place, which we knew was being orchestrated by the two of you and your friends. What we did was to ensure that she made the journey in such a way as to cause her the minimum of inconvenience or of worry, so we administered a quick-acting drug when my men intercepted her at Heathrow. She was brought here by ambulance. It seemed better if she were somewhat sedated during her long run, first through the Channel Tunnel, and then here by road. Anyway, she got here late last night and she is still suffering from the after-affects of the drug. But I can assure you that, within a few hours, she will be entirely her old self again."

Michelle suddenly seemed to come alive. She turned to Durand and said, "You have a hell of a nerve, to talk as if it were your God-given right to abduct me and to bring me to this house of yours. How can you act as a puppet of M. Fouquet, when he was a party to killing my great-grandfather, and you, on his behalf, have already endeavoured to conceal his guilt by arranging the murder of my great-uncle, Xavier Lebrun."

To my surprise, I noticed Durand's eyes open wide with astonishment, and he said angrily, "But you talk nonsense, my child! I don't know what story you have been told but my old friend Vincent Fouquet had nothing to do with your great-grandfather's death. He was killed by the grandfather of M. Burton here, with the assistance of a Frenchman, M. Emile Jeanfils. Having done so, they arranged to bury a fortune in jewels which they had stolen, and to try and frame Vincent with the crime by getting him to handle a golden bowl. All my actions, right back to 1945, when we gave a wrong identification of a body, have been to ensure that the evil scheme of M. Burton's grandfather did not work. When, after the war, we found that he was dead, the problem seemed to be over but now, thanks to you and young M. Burton, it has come alive again. It would be a travesty of justice if the name of an innocent man were to be blackened after so many years. He is, of course, completely innocent, but mud sticks. That is why I have acted as I have done, and I certainly intend to ensure that you and your family, and M. Burton, never get the chance to bear false witness against him."

"Is that what M. Fouquet has told you, and what you believe?" she asked quietly. "If so, you have believed a lie for some sixty years. Hasn't it worried you just why we have been so interested in the golden bowl? We did, after all, recover the treasure trove of jewels, against which the value of a single golden bowl is trivial. However, I now understand that Fouquet is coming here and I look forward to taxing him with the crime...I know that he didn't pull the trigger that killed my great-grandfather...that was done by his lover, Major Hassell...but he was an enthusiastic partner in the enterprise."

M. Durand was suddenly angrier than ever. "How dare you say that Major Hassell was Vincent's lover! There never was, or could have been, anything between them! I have known him for sixty years! Your suggestion is disgusting and, if you value your life, you will never mention it again. I can also tell you that your incredible attitude gives me another problem about what to do with you and M. Burton."

A lot had become obvious to me…Fouquet must have told the same story to Durand back in 1942, the same story that the Germans had told Julie, and which she and Michelle had also believed until I showed up. I wondered if this was the key we were looking for and whether I could persuade M. Durand to let us go. So I said, "Might I suggest that this matter is just one more reason why we should just exchange the bowl here and that I now return for Michelle's freedom, as there is no point, and a lot of danger, in digging up the history of old times. You have your beliefs, and we have ours, including…I can tell you…documentary evidence. So why not forget the whole thing, just as we'll do if we do a deal now."

For a moment I thought he would agree, but then he frowned. "No, certainly not. I believe Vincent implicitly, and I owe it to him to cast your lies back in your teeth. By talking as you have done, your position, and that of Michelle, is now much more serious. I had not realised until now that you were both so misled, and have come to believe this stupid story about the guilt of my friend. Not to mention the absurdity that he could have had an intimate association with a German! That is all quite ridiculous! He now, of course, advocates friendship with Germany, but he is, and always has been, a patriotic Frenchman. To suggest he was a wartime traitor is nonsense!"

He suddenly stopped and seemed to have trouble breathing, putting his hand to his chest as if to contain a pain, but in a few moments he composed himself, turning to Albert and saying, "Take them away. They distress me. I don't want to see any more of them until Vincent gets here." Albert Durand seized my arm, and was about to escort me and Michelle out of the room, when I suddenly had an idea, based on the fact that people always like the opportunity to show off how clever they've been.

Look," I said, "I wonder if you would be kind enough to satisfy my curiosity?"

"Curiosity?" He frowned. "What the hell do you mean?"

"What I'm interested in is how you've managed, so very cleverly, to keep track of what Michelle and I have been up to...for example, having someone in Bayonne even before I got there. Damn it, you even knew the day and time when I was going to go down that little road near Bayonne and dig up the jewels."

As I talked he began to look more relaxed, and smiled before saying, "Yes, as you say, we have been quite efficient. I pride myself on the arrangements I made. The first alarm bell was, of course, the little article in *The Herald* which came to the attention of M. Fouquet's office. I, of course, knew of the false trail which had been laid by your grandfather, when he forced Vincent to handle the gold bowl, and so it seemed a simple precaution to frustrate you in your search...by getting rid of items which might be of interest to you in the Records Office of the Bayonne Mairie. Unfortunately, this wasn't enough to prevent you finding the address of Mme Julie Lebrun, the old jeweller's daughter, and when you left Bayonne it seemed a simple assumption that you would then try to get in touch with her and with Michelle, her granddaughter. I still didn't think that Vincent had anything much to worry about, so it was rather a shock when Dr Xavier Lebrun made enquiries of the gendarmerie in Marseilles.

"It then so happened, by one of those unfortunate coincidences, that I had to go into hospital that very morning for some tests, and I heard about his enquiries. All I could do was to tell my number two to do whatever he felt was appropriate. I confess that his actions were inappropriate, but when I took control again, I stopped a lot of that nonsense. Anyway, I was able to make use of a valuable new source. I wonder if you remember sending a fax to M. Duchene from the hotel in Avignon? Well, the operator was a clever girl and reckoned that a copy of it might be worth a few francs. So that gave us a lot of useful information, and he has been very useful, and in our pocket since then. So, go now with Albert, and let's have a truce. I'll ask him to get you glasses of wine. You won't have long to wait now. Vincent will be here soon."

I kept very quiet while Albert led us out of the room and I allowed myself to be taken with Michelle up the elegant flight of stairs and then into a pleasant double-bedded room with an en-suite bathroom. When we were on our own we just looked at each other in silence for a few moments, but then I found her in my arms, with tears streaming down her face. All I could do was hold her close, and I felt so guilty about getting her into this situation…if only I had never started on the quest, none of this would have happened. But, when I stumbled out this confession, suddenly the old Michelle surfaced. She said, "Never say that, darling. Don't you realise that if you hadn't done so we would never have met?"

"That thought, I can also tell you, has cheered me up, so let's look forward to getting down to business at the meeting, and hope that our truth will be believed instead of all the lies."

***

CHAPTER THIRTEEN

It wasn't long before Albert came back and looked seriously at us. "Look, we've only got about half an hour before Fouquet gets here, and I'd like it if we could have a talk. You see, I'm aware that you two must think of me as one of the bad guys. No wonder, I am a member of the Union Corse and you will only have heard one side of the story. But I was surprised this morning when Michelle told us a very different story – "

"But tell me," I broke in, "Just what were you told?"

"He told us the old story about my wicked grandfather and what followed, about young Pierre Dupont having seen the awful events through a window and about his having been forced to handle the golden bowl. He stopped and looked at us. "So that's the story, and it's one that everyone has believed for all these years…until you started your investigations. So that is the story which I was told, and which I have believed since I was a boy…can you convince me that it is untrue?"

"I'm sure we can," I told him, "and fortunately Michelle has some papers with her to show you which tells a very different story. I think you'll find them interesting reading."

She smiled as she opened the small zip-up bag she had with her, saying, "I too am sure you will. "It has been a strange affair," she went on, "because, as you know, Charles' grandfather was killed in the RAF soon after he got back to England and, before that, his companion, M. Jeanfils was run over by a bus. So, at that time, the only record which was left of his adventures was in this first paper, a copy of his statement to the Air Ministry back in 1942…anyway, here it is."

Albert frowned as he scanned the paper, and then looked up at her. "Is that all the records he left?"

"No!" I said. I went on to tell him of the papers that had been stored in the secret compartment of his desk, and then I also gave these to him.

He read them carefully, then went back to the first paper, and re-read it before saying, "It's a puzzle, isn't it? You two have read, and I'm sure believe, these papers. But everyone seems to have heard a completely different story. Only one of them, of course, can be true…but which?"

I broke in to say, "Just ask yourself, Albert, what possible reason would my grandfather have had to make that original report to the Air Ministry, if he and M. Jeanfils had in fact planned to steal the jewels? By telling the authorities why he had buried the treasures, he made it impossible for him ever to lay claim to them. And remember how keen we have been to bring your friend Fouquet to book…when I read those papers I became interested in trying to see if justice could be done. Michelle, when I got in touch with her and showed her the papers, had even more reason to become involved. The murder of her great-grandfather had been properly explained for the first time."

He sat quietly for a few minutes, then said, "I'm afraid that I can only agree with you, but this will raise all sorts of problems. You would see this morning how upset my great-uncle was at the very suggestion that M. Fouquet, or Pierre as he was then, could have had any sort of relationship with the German, Major Hassell. You may also remember that he had to go into hospital for tests on the very day when Dr Lebrun made his enquiries in Marseilles. Those tests showed that he has major heart problems. He should, in fact, have had immediate surgery, but he wanted this affair settled before he did so. Instead, he's on pills, which I hope will see him through until he does have surgery.

"I can appreciate that you have no alternative but to confront Fouquet with these papers, but they may be a body blow to my great-uncle. It was only the mere suggestion of Pierre, in 1942, being other than an innocent young boy, which caused the minor attack when Michelle told her story. Please, therefore, be as gentle as you can."

Here we were being asked to feel sorry for the man who had orchestrated this bad business, and all of our problems, and although he hadn't personally ordered the murder of Dr Lebrun or the attack on Michelle and me, he certainly was responsible for our most unwelcome presence here. But Michelle had a softer heart than mine, and said, "I'll try to make things as easy for him as we can. I'm sure that Charles will say as little as possible about the...association...between Pierre and the German major."

Albert said, "Let me say, Charles, that it will help if you make things as easy for him as you can. I know that this must sound odd to you, after all the trouble he has caused you, but believe me he is the best friend you have in these parts, and you must hope that he stays in command. You already know that his chief assistant, a M. Georges de Forges, died when he was in hospital. Now, I know him well, and he would like nothing more than to avenge the death of the man you wounded in Avignon. He had to be killed to avoid an investigation. The dead man was, you see, a favourite of his, and it was a blow to his self-esteem that an amateur, like you, Charles, could come out best against two of his top men."

That was by way of being a most efficient conversation stopper, and soon afterwards one of the other men, the man who had met me at Gatwick, came in and said to Albert, "Come with me, and bring them with you. M. Durand is ready for them." He led us down the stairs, and back into the same room. I saw that it had been rearranged, as if we were applicants for a job. There was an arc of chairs, with old Durand in the middle, flanked by a man whom I recognised as Fouquet on his right, and a nasty-looking character on his left, the kind who makes it seem all too likely that we are indeed descended from monkeys. In front of them was a small table with the golden bowl set in the centre, and then two hard chairs, presumably intended for us to sit facing Fouquet and his companion. There were also two other hard chairs, set at a distance from ours. In one of them, Albert was sitting and, after we were put into ours, the other was filled by our escort, B1, the man from Gatwick. This was done in complete silence, but I was very conscious of the fact that there were no signs of friendship on the faces of our inquisitors. In particular, Fouquet looked as though he would like nothing more than to slit our throats.

It was old Durand who spoke first, and he surprised me by sounding quite pleasant. However, his words were less so. "I am sure that I do not need to introduce my old friend Vincent Fouquet to you but here, on my left, is my assistant M. de Forges. As I told you earlier, the two of you have caused a great deal of distress to Vincent, and now we have to decide how to deal with you. You realise, of course, M. Burton, that since we have the golden bowl, the wicked plan of your grandfather to incriminate Vincent is now a thing of the past. But I do wonder if it is possible to trust the pair of you not to spread calumnies, especially as you have no false evidence to support them."

He paused for a moment, then went on. "That, I may say, is what I intended to say before our talk earlier, but Michelle had sowed a seed of doubt in my mind, so now I have to ask if you can prove your allegations?" I saw Fouquet turn angrily to Durand. "Maurice, surely you cannot believe any of the tales they tell? Surely we're not going to stop trusting one another after so many years?"

"No doubt, Vincent, you are right. I certainly hope that you are. But we owe it to this young pair to hear what they say. So, M. Burton, tell us your story, but keep it short." This was the one Rubicon we had to cross…it was possible that, if we gave them some kind of assurance that we now believed Fouquet to be innocent, they would let us go. But I was doubtful, and I looked at Michelle who gave a tiny flick with a finger, pointing towards the bag where the papers were. I could only hope that the truth would be for the best. "M. Durand, as I told you, my grandfather left a very full account of the affair which led to the death of Mme Lebrun's great-grandfather. But what I didn't tell you was that we have copies of his deposition."

I was interrupted by M. Fouquet. "Don't waste our time, M. Burton, we have all seen your grandfather's report to the Air Ministry. Fact is, I have a copy of it here. I don't know why you've made such a fuss of it as it is a tissue of lies. He must simply have written it to hide his awful murder of a helpless old man and his theft of a fortune in jewels."

He then looked at me. "It is, of course, true that he did force me…I was just a boy at the time…into handling the bowl so that my fingerprints were on it, possibly with the idea of turning me, an innocent observer, into a handy scapegoat. However, justice has been done by the recovery of the bowl. I now want to ensure that we make you two pay for all the worry you have caused."

"But M. Fouquet," I went on, "or should I just call you Pierre? That is not all that my grandfather left. It was this, his other notes, that led me to make my own enquiries."

Fouquet's eyes had narrowed. "What other notes?"

Michelle opened her bag and handed me the papers, which I then handed to M. Durand, the papers that had lain undiscovered in my grandfather's desk. "You will see," I said, "that there is a French translation, as well as the original English, and it makes nonsense of all that M. Fouquet has said. It is also more detailed than the report to the Air Ministry and shows that Pierre was far more than just an observer…he was there with his lover, the German major."

Fouquet grabbed the paper, skimmed through them, then turned to Durand. "This is nonsense! A complete tissue of lies! Don't believe a word of it, Maurice!"

Durand, who had recovered himself, shook his head sadly. "Don't waste your breath, Vincent. When all this fuss about the golden bowl first arose I began to have concerns about it, and I have recently been asking myself questions that I should have asked many years ago. Earlier, Michelle raised my doubts again, and this paper settles the matter. I have treasured you over these long years. Now I know that you have been deceiving me from the very beginning. Because of that, there is nothing which I, or my organisation, now need to do. Equally, there is nothing that needs to be hidden…so these two young people are free to leave immediately. I am sure we can rely on them to be discreet. As for you, your party is now ready to get rid of you and I shall make it my business to ensure that it does. Don't waste your time, Vincent, in trying to make me change my mind…I don't want to see you again, so please get out of my house!"

As he said this, he suddenly began to gasp for breath, and I saw Albert rush forward to catch him as he swayed on his chair, and then fell forward towards the table, upsetting the bowl, which fell to the floor and rolled under a chair. It was Albert and I who managed to carry old Durand to a couch and to lie him down, but it was quite obvious that he was dead. We stood beside him for a moment, and then Albert leaned forward and tenderly closed his great-uncle's eyes. As I then turned around, I was surprised to see that Fouquet and M. de Forges seemed to be in high humour, and Fouquet laughed as he shouted at me, "That was a stroke of luck! Now there is nothing to stop me arranging, with my good friend M. de Forges, what should happen to you and your bitch of a woman!"

I didn't know what the hell to do. I felt helpless. All I could do was to go back and sit beside Michelle and take her hand. I saw Fouquet looking at us gleefully. "That is so sweet! So, hold her hand while you can. In the meantime, M. de Forges and I will work out the best way to kill you. Personally, I would like to strangle you right here and now, but that might cause problems. We'll have to arrange some suitable kind of unfortunate accident, and I might even come to your funerals and look sorrowful. That will be nice for you, won't it?" He looked around for a moment, then said to our escort, B1, the only name I knew for him, "Where has young Durand gone?"

He shook his head. "I don't know, sir. He went out into the hall, I think." Fouquet frowned. "For now, take these two back to their room, make sure they are securely locked in, and then find Durand and bring him to me. But first, go to the armoury and get yourself a gun. I want no slip ups in dealing with these two."

All we could do was sit there. I didn't know about Michelle, but I was terrified, especially when our escort came back with a large handgun. "That's good," said de Forges, "take them away now."

As he said this, Albert came back. "Where the hell have you been?" demanded de Forges.

Albert said quietly, "I've been following our normal procedures and have phoned Claude Marcellin to tell him the sad news. Naturally, he is very upset and will be here very soon to make the necessary arrangements." It seemed an innocuous statement, but it was obvious that both Fouquet and de Forges were furious. "What the hell did you do that for?" demanded de Forges. "The situation calls for immediate action and, as the late M. Durand's chief assistant, it is my duty to deal with the matter."

He stopped for a moment and then had a whispered conversation with Fouquet, whom I saw give a quick nod of assent, and then he turned back to Albert. "Maybe it is for the best, despite your precipitate action. I am sure that the Capu will confirm my appointment when he arrives. I presume is he coming by helicopter?"

Albert nodded, then said, perhaps burning his own boats, "I was not aware, M. de Forges, that you were expecting to take M. Durand's place. Are you sure? These appointments are always in the gift of the Capu, M. Marcellin, and he may have other ideas. After all, you made some stupid mistakes in this affair which have caused a lot of trouble."

Fouquet was shouting. He also now had a gun in his hand. "Be very careful, young man! It would be foolish of you to make an enemy either of me or M. de Forges! I've have had my suspicions of you for a while, and now you have no indulgent great-uncle to protect you. Just remember that!"

Fouquet turned to us. "No tricks, now. Just get up the stairs, and I'll be right behind you. I can tell you, M. Burton, that if you try anything, I won't shoot you. I'll shoot this pretty girlfriend of yours, which you might think would be rather a pity."

All we could do was obey instructions, and we found ourselves back in our room with the door securely locked. Once again, the only way to ease the pain was to hold each other tightly, and I felt her tears on my cheek, and maybe some of my own. But soon my irrepressible Michelle eased herself away, saying, "Do you know, the more people who are involved in this business, the better are our chances. On their own, I'm sure that Fouquet and de Forges are capable of any mischief. So, let's hope that this new man, Marcellin, will keep them in order. They referred to him as the Capu which, I seem to remember, means chief of chiefs. Let's hope that he has some sense."

***

CHAPTER FOURTEEN

We didn't have to wait more than about half an hour before hearing the beating of the helicopter's rotors, and we caught a glimpse of it through our window as it came in to land. All that occurred to me was what an important man this M. Marcellin must be, to have a helicopter as his beck and call, all tanked up and ready to go at a moment's notice. It was Albert who came for us a short time later. Before he had time to say anything, Michelle went over to him and kissed his cheek. "I am sorry about your great-uncle. He was no friend of ours, but I could see that he meant a lot to you."

"That's nice of you," he said. "But, as to his not being a friend of yours, I guess that in the last few moments before he died, he was just about to become one. But, come now, the others are waiting. It may surprise you to know, and this is good, that the invitation from M. Marcellin is to join him for drinks."

"Are we in the clear, Albert?" I asked.

"No, not a bit. But he is a great believer in doing things in as civilised a fashion as possible. But don't let that fool you, as Fouquet and de Forges are thirsting for your blood! But if you tell your story carefully and clearly, I reckon that you should be okay. Anyway, I have done what little I can to prepare the way for you. In the phonecall after my great-uncle's death, I had to tell M. Marcellin about your presence here. He is therefore interested in the matter."

"But tell me," I asked, "what is his position? I heard him referred to as the Capu...

He smiled. "Just think of the Union as being an army. If my great-uncle was a brigadier, Marcellin is the general."

There was no further time for conversation. Albert hustling us downstairs and into the room where we had been before. But all the signs of earlier activity had disappeared: the inquisitorial chairs and the table had been removed, and I now saw Fouquet and another man – who had to be the new arrival, M. Marcellin, sitting in comfortable chairs with a low table with drinks beside them, and with the golden bowl as a centrepiece. On the other side of the table, de Forges was sitting on the couch to which Albert and I had, not long before, carried the dead M. Durand. There were also three other seats. Michelle and I were ushered towards two of them. Albert took the third.

There was a moment or two of silence, but I could see that the new man was in charge. He looked oddly like Peter Armstrong – middle-aged, but still very fit. I couldn't help but think that he must have been in something like the French Foreign Legion. I also got another strange impression that he seemed to be hugging a secret to himself, like a small boy about to release his pet mouse into his sister's bedroom. When he spoke it was with the air of decision that comes with high command.

"Let me introduce myself. My name is Marcellin, and you two must be Mlle Lebrun and M. Burton. Come and sit down on these chairs beside me. We have much to talk about." The he turned to Albert. "See what these young people would like to drink, and then freshen up our glasses."

Despite the friendliness, he didn't look all that friendly, and Fouquet and de Forges seemed to be displeased at the way things were going. Nothing was said until Albert did his job: Michelle with a glass of white wine, and me with a whisky and water. Marcellin took a sip of his drink. "This affair, M. Burton, I have known about for some little time. As you know, the late M. Maurice Durand was an old associate of mine and, because of his seniority in our group, I raised no objection when he asked if he might use some of our facilities in a private capacity, particularly when he informed me that he was acting on behalf of M. Fouquet here, his old friend, who has at times been of service to us, and for many years has been a useful contact to have had in the Quai d'Orsay. I had no reason to believe that there could be any doubts regarding the rightness of their cause and, anyway, when it all began, it seemed so very simple. I was under the impression that all that was required was to ensure that this golden bowl did not get into the wrong hands."

"But," he went on, "mistakes were made, especially during the time when Maurice was in hospital, and de Forges was in charge. The killing of Dr Lebrun was a sad event for which I express my sincere regrets." I could see that de Forges was furious at this public censure, and I couldn't resist twisting the screw.

"I wonder, M. de Forges, if you know that you were wasting your time when you murdered Dr Lebrun. You see, he kept all his medical records in a duplicate book. When Michelle and I saw him, he gave us a duplicate copy of the page on the autopsy of the supposed Pierre Dupont. That showed that the body could not have been his. The corpse and Pierre Dupont were different heights and weights. The corpse had black hair, Pierre Dupont had fair hair." I turned to Fouquet. "You must have spent a fortune on hair dye over the years!"

I saw him flush angrily but, before he could speak, M. Marcellin held up his hand and said, “Leave it for now, Vincent, but tell me, M. Burton, where is this page which you say explains what happened back in 1942?”

Before I could answer, Fouquet shouted, “It is true that M. Burton brought a paper with him this morning! I can show it to you if you like, but it is only a copy of what old man Burton sent to the Air Ministry. It is of no interest.”

Michelle leapt to her feet and glared at him. “You are conveniently forgetting that the other paper which I gave you this morning, also written by Charles’ grandfather, tells a very different story.”

Fouquet looked up. “Okay, so where the hell is it?”

As he spoke, it occurred to me that they had destroyed it, and a glance at Fouquet’s face confirmed this. My heart sank. It was Michelle who put into words my feelings. “Have you bastards destroyed it?”

Marcellin laughed. “Well, now, that is a very direct question. He turned to Fouquet. “Do you know where this paper is?”

“No, but it’s junk anyway! A complete tissue of lies! In any case, we have all seen this single paper before, which we got from the Air Ministry.”

Marcellin turned back to me. “What do you say to that, M. Burton?”

That was an easy question for me. “It is obvious that M. Fouquet is a frightened man and will do anything to keep these papers hidden. But he won’t succeed. I presume that you have a fax machine here? I can get you a copy in a few minutes.”

Before he could answer, Albert broke in. “That won’t be necessary. You see I saw M. Fouquet tear up the papers and tell one of the servants to burn them. I intercepted him and stuck the pieces together…here they are, sir. Both Fouquet and de Forges were hugely annoyed, and from glances between them, blaming each other for not having made sure that the papers were really destroyed. Marcellin, I could see, was rather amused.

He said to me, "Well, it is a happy accident that your papers have survived, after all. But before I read them, please give me a brief explanation of the affair from your point of view."

I was becoming well-practiced at this, so it didn't take me long to explain all the circumstances and when I had finished he skimmed the papers, and then read them more carefully before saying, "Well now, these papers are most interesting, and I confess that I find them very persuasive. The story that I have previously been told indicated that M. Burton's grandfather intended to steal the treasures after the war. But how can that be the case when he told his Air Ministry about it?"

He looked at Fouquet. "What is your answer to that."

But it was de Forges who answered, and suddenly he seemed more sure of himself. He said angrily, "My friend Vincent doesn't need to answer the question. You see, I and others have become dissatisfied with your leadership. That means that I am taking over this unit of the Union. One of my first tasks will be to eliminate this pair here. Nobody can prove they ever came here and, while there may be suspicions, there will be no proof."

He stopped for a moment, then produced a handgun and fired one shot at M. Marcellin who fell to the floor. De Forges got up, obviously to make sure that his victim was dead. Then there was another explosion and he stopped as if frozen…the thing that I particularly remember was the expression on his face…he just looked astonished. Then there was a second shot and the light went out in his eyes and he fell. It was only then that I saw that the second shot had come from Albert. He fired another shot through de Forges' head, before turning to me. "I seem to remember that you have an old saying in Scotland, *to mak siccar*. Well, that is what I have just done. He was a shit and the world is well rid of him."

Everything had happened too quickly for me, and for Michelle. Suddenly she burst out: "Look, he's alive!"

"Too bloody true," gasped M. Marcellin and staggered to his feet. "I was wearing a rather fancy bullet-proof vest," he explained, "and I also arranged for Albert here to keep an eye on things. But while the vest stops the bullets getting through, I am going to have the mother and father of all bruises." He turned to Albert. Well done, son, you were right to warn me and you will be a very worthy successor to your great-uncle. The formal business of your appointment can take place tomorrow."

Then he turned to us. "I am sorry that you two have been unwitting catalysts by way of bringing this internal Union affair into the open, but I have suspected for a while that de Forges was planning to get rid of me. You see, there has been a conflict between a group which he led, who want to involve us deeper in the drugs trade, and the majority of us who see the damage that drugs are doing to our young people, and who just want to get out of the obscene trade. Anyway, I have known for a while that he might engineer something. I decided this morning to give him a chance to show his hand."

As he'd been speaking, two men had appeared, as if by magic, and the corpse was removed, the fallen chairs lifted, and Albert was busying himself with another round of drinks. Throughout this, Fouquet hadn't said a word, just remaining, crouched, in his chair as if he feared for his life. Looking at him, it occurred to me that, to him, this must almost have been a rerun of 1942. Now we had Durant, his long-term friend or lover or whatever, had died…then de Forges who had seemed oddly protective of him. Just as all those years ago, a young Pierre had seen his boyhood dreams shattered, here he was, an old man, looking at the ruins of his political career.

Marcellin had no time for pity, and just looked at him with contempt. "Sit up, Vincent, and pay attention! It is clear that you were foolish enough to be a party to this scheme. I've never thought much of your intelligence, but I had to make sure that you had been stupid enough to be part of this ridiculous project. In any case, it would have been a waste of time as that idiot de Forges would never have been confirmed in my job." He thought for a moment, then continued. "All things being equal, you should now be as dead as your accomplice…and maybe that sentence should have been carried out in 1942. But I think that it will now be sufficient punishment to strip you of your powers.

"Let's complete this whole thing now. So, the deal is, you get on the phone to your party. You tell them that you've not been well lately and have decided to retire with immediate effect. You'll say that you don't feel up to returning to Paris to make a public announcement. Instead, you'll make that public announcement here in Marseilles."

He paused. "If you don't agree, I shall arrange for the whole story to be on the front page of every newspaper tomorrow. I myself will keep quiet and I'm sure that I can persuade these two young people to be discreet. Also, of course, the British government will be happy to see the back of you."

He then turned to Albert. "Take him into one of the other rooms, listen to his calls, and see that he does exactly what I have instructed him to do." It was obvious that there was no fight left in Fouquet. Without Durant and de Forges, there were no friends left. "Believe me, I never thought that he would try to kill you! The whole thing is a nightmare!" He stopped. "Perhaps it will be a good time to retire."

It was a strange moment for Michelle and I as we watched him go, as here was a man who had been a party to the murder of her great-grandfather and who had also been keen to see us killed in order to hide his involvement in that old crime. But now, justice of a sort had been done. For a moment, we just looked at each other, but then she smiled.

Marcellin was also smiling. "Now, apart from celebrating our success, I have some things to do following the, shall I say, sad and sudden death of my friend George de Forges! Fortunately, I brought one of our doctors here to deal with the death of M. Durand and he can now arrange the necessary certificates for both cases. I don't think it would be a good idea to attribute both cases to heart attacks, so I think a car crash for de Forges, hastening here following the death of his old friend, would be a better explanation. My people will make it look convincing. Now, I have a telephone call to make."

He punched a long list of numbers into his mobile phone. "Yes, everything is over. De Forges is dead and Fouquet is at this moment wrapping up his political career. He will resign his post immediately, which will please you, and announce the fact at a press conference in Marseilles tomorrow." Then, to my astonishment, he went on, "Oh, yes, Charles and Michelle are none the worse. Would you like to speak to them?"

With a smile, he handed the phone to me. I could see him even more amused by the expression on my face when I realised who was at the other end – as Peter Armstrong was the last person I could have guessed. He shut off any enquiries from me as to how he and M. Marcellin came to be working together, saying, "Just wait until you get back here. In the meantime, I am sure that M. Marcellin will explain things from his point of view. All that matters now is that the whole affair is over and it has worked out extremely well."

He paused for a moment. "Tell Michelle that both of your grannies are well, and that we'll all meet up in London tonight. You'll have plenty of time to catch the British Airways flight which leaves Marseilles at nineteen hundred hours. Seats are booked on it in your names, which you can pick up from the check-in. A car will meet you at Gatwick and take you to the Savoy, where your grannies will also be staying the night. We'll have a late celebration in the River Room when you arrive."

Michelle had been sitting quietly. She now turned to M. Marcellin and broke in. "How on earth can you and Peter Armstrong be in this together? That, if you'll forgive me, sounds a most unlikely combination!"

He laughed. "I quite agree, my dear, and if you had asked me that question yesterday I would said that it would have been an impossible combination. However, late last evening I was surprised to get a call from him in London in which he spoke about a matter of joint interest. Maybe he'll be able to tell you later. Then Albert phoned this morning with news of M. Durand's death, which altered everything…and that was when I decided to come here. Look, let's defer any more talk until after lunch, and then I'll do my best to explain things after that." He smiled at us. "I know that you've both had a trying morning and, believe me, the best treatment for both of you is fine food and wine."

We started with a plate of smoked salmon, followed by fillet steaks and then strawberries and cream. I was astonished by the lavishness of the wines which accompanied each course, a Premiere Cru Chablis and a 1961 Mouton Rothschild.

"I'm glad you seemed to enjoy it," he smiled, "and I'm also glad to see that your French grandmother has brought you up so well and to know the good things in life." He turned to Michelle. "Keep up the work, my dear, and you may yet turn this Scotsman into quite a good imitation of a civilised Frenchman!"

Michelle looked over at me and blew me a kiss. "I can tell you, M. Marcellin, that I am quite happy with him as he is...and just remember that we've been recently having rather a lot of problems with Frenchmen. So I'm going to do my best to become a good imitation of a Scotswoman."

"Well said!" he laughed, "and on that happy note we had better take our coffees back to the other room so that I can tell you a little more about my involvement in this affair. Most of it, of course, you already know. Maybe I should have suspected something," he said, "but what saved the situation here this morning was that young Albert became worried when you, Charles, arrived and he found you were carrying a homing device inside you. He did, of course, deactivate it, but it was a sign that you and Michelle were not ordinary young people, but that you must have powerful forces on your side. But it was only later when you and Albert had talked that he became convinced that Fouquet was no angel. That's when he decided to do something. That's when he phoned me."

"Incidentally," he went on, "I must congratulate your friend Peter Armstrong on his ingenuity. The device that you swallowed was given to you in order that we should find it! I'm afraid that Albert was so pleased at finding it that he merely checked your other bags rather quickly. However, that didn't matter, because, as Peter had already told me, Michelle's bag also had a sophisticated device hidden inside the handle. When the bag is unzipped, the beacon wakes up." M. Marcellin was looking rather embarrassed. "He therefore would quickly find out where you were once the bag arrived here. Peter's message to me was therefore quite clear. You were coming to Marseilles today and would probably be taken to a house owned by Durand, and that he would raise hell with the French police and government if we were unsuccessful in getting both of you freed."

"What I don't understand," I broke in, "is that if you knew about what was happening, then why didn't you at least phone here this morning and tell them to stop everything?"

He looked at me sadly. "Charles, it is a fact of my life that I always have to keep an eye open behind me. As I said, this seemed like the perfect opportunity to bring things into the open with de Forges. However, I also decided that I couldn't risk doing anything immediately. I had a great deal of difficulty getting Peter to agree to letting things develop to a point where I could come to the chateau. The death of M. Durand provided that excuse.

He sat upright and stretched. "That's it, I have been frank with you. You know now that I have both risked your lives and saved them." He stopped, then laughed. "But one good thing has come out of this affair. For the first time, there has been cooperation between the British Secret Service and the Union Corse…Vive le EU!"

He stopped there and smiled. "Well, it's been an interesting time, but I now see that my normal life is catching up with me. It's almost time for me to leave. However, Michelle, there is one thing that Peter sent here which I would like to keep."

He nodded to Albert who handed him a parcel. He turned to Michelle. "I'd like to give you this as a present."

She undid the parcel to find within it an Armani bag that seemed to be made from the finest leather and a zip-fastener made from gold. Michelle, at first lost for words, eventually said, "Why on earth do you want to give me this?"

"Simple, my dear. I propose to exchange it for your old, rather shabby bag. I'd like, if I may, to copy Peter's rather clever beacon." Michelle said nothing, then shrugged, tipping her belongings from one bag to the other.

"Albert will look after you," he said. He then gave us an embarrassing smile. "I should also like to take this opportunity to wish you both a long and happy married life. If you get bored at any time, you can just think back to the exciting times you had when you were courting."

He came over and saluted Michelle with a kiss on both cheeks, then gave me a firm British handshake. We watched him and Albert walk to the helicopter. I saw Albert take his arm, and they had a quite lengthy conversation, at the end of which M. Marcellin put his arm around Albert, as if to wish him well. A few minutes later we saw his machine rise into the air but, as it did so, I saw him give us a wave before it turned south, and I also noticed that Albert hadn't moved, but was just standing where he had been before, and looking after the disappearing craft.

***

CHAPTER FIFTEEN

Michelle and I also stood in silence as we watched the helicopter disappear but then, suddenly, she was in my arms and I found her sobbing her heart out. I knew just how she felt as for the whole day we had been on a rollercoaster of emotions, ranging between terror and euphoria, while all the time we had both tried to hide our feelings. But now, all that was in the past and, despite a feeling of vast relief, it was hard for me not to mix my own tears with hers but then I took her in my arms and kissed her. "It's all over, darling," I said. "It is now just a nightmare, which has passed."

She eased back from me just a little, and managed a tiny smile. "I know, but suddenly I just couldn't be brave any longer." But then she straightened her back, and said firmly, "You're right…it is all over…"

She then glanced over my shoulder at a mirror, and I could see that suddenly she was well on the way to recovery when she said, "What a sight I look, for goodness sake…give me a hankie, I haven't got one with me." I found one, and after she had mopped her eyes, and given her nose a good blow, she was herself again, saying, "That's better…I wonder when Albert will be ready to take us to the airport?" We didn't get an immediate reply to that question as it was more than ten minutes before Albert came back, looking extremely cheerful, and he looked at Michelle, whose eyes were still red, and went over to her.

"I am terribly sorry that you've had such an awful time, but it's all over now, and you may be interested to know that I shall be eternally grateful that you and Charles were brought here!"

"Are you indeed," said Michelle, who was in no mood for friendly chit-chat. "Well, all I can tell you that the sooner we are away from this bloody place the happier I shall be!"

I could enthusiastically agree with that sentiment. "Too true!" I said, "Is there anything to stop us leaving right away? I presume that you have a car here, ready and waiting? Anyway," I went on, feeling far from friendly with the Union Corse, and all its members, "I see that you are looking cheerful, and I presume that M. Marcellin has now confirmed that you are getting that job you were after?"

"Quite the reverse!" he said to my surprise, and then went on, "Don't worry, we have plenty of time to get you to the airport, so before we do so, can I tell you why I am so glad that you have been here? Please sit down…both of you…it won't take long." Well, we did so, but without much enthusiasm, certainly I was not at all interested his affairs, but Michelle looked at me, and shrugged her shoulders before plumping herself down on the couch. So I sat beside her, holding her hand tightly, and hoping that she wouldn't remember that not so long ago the body of old Durand had lain where we now were. As for Albert, he went over to the chair that had been occupied by M. Marcellin, and looked rather doubtfully at it before sitting down. Obviously something serious had happened to him, and it was a few moments before he spoke – and when he did so it was very slowly and deliberately. "I am sure that the last two days have been very trying for the pair of you, and I am desperately sorry to have played quite a major part in your distress. But I am sure that you will be able to put this behind you, and then carry on as if it had never happened…but thanks to you I cannot!"

He stopped, but then smiled. "No, I cannot, as my life is now going to be quite different, and far better. You see, as you know, I was brought up by my great-uncle, and I have always considered myself lucky to have such a rewarding career in prospect in the Union. And don't think that it is all bad, as I can tell you that while we most certainly make a lot of money for ourselves, we also fund more charitable projects than many organisations give us credit for. However, it is only in the last few months that I have questioned what I want in this life, and that started when I met a very special girl from Nice at a Christmas party, and we very quickly fell in love. She thought, at first that I was just a final year university student with electronics as my main subject, and she never questioned the oddity that I had already completed a legal course…and that in fact is the profession which I have trained for…to look after the legal affairs of the Union…but she was horrified when she learned just what this career of mine was going to be. Anyway, I saw her last week, and she then told me that I had to choose between her and my membership of the Union, and she gave me just two weeks in which to make up my mind."

He looked at me, and smiled again. "You see, since then I have been puzzling over her ultimatum, but today I've had the privilege of seeing you two…young and happily in love…and I began to wonder whether my sweet Cecile was not right, and that there were indeed more important things in life than even the dazzling career the Union can offer. Then came the affair of today, and having to kill de Forges…well, I'm not sorry I did so…but it did pull me up short, when I heard M. Marcellin talking about having to look over his shoulder all the time, while I could look at the two of you, being happy just to look at each other…that settled it. You would see," he went on, "that I had a talk with M. Marcellin before he flew off, and I told him then that I wanted to quit, and he surprised me by saying that he had rather expected me to take that decision. So we parted on good terms, but I am afraid that you now see before you a young unemployed and, soon to be struggling, lawyer who will have a hard time establishing himself. But I won't be on my own, as I've just rung Cecile to tell her my news, and now – like you two – we also are engaged, and we hope to be married very soon!"

I still didn't feel too friendly towards him, but Michelle was different, and she jumped up and kissed him, saying, "Let's make bygones into bygones, so Charles and I wish you all the joy in the world, and your Cecile is a lucky young lady."

That seemed to please Albert, and he smiled at her. "That's sweet of you, do you think I might be able to persuade both of you to come to our wedding, which, as I have said, I am going to arrange as soon as possible?" To my surprise, Michelle looked pleased, and said, "Of course we shall, but only if you come to ours, which will be in Avignon sometime in the late summer."

He looked rather seriously at her before answering. "Certainly, Cecile, and I will be proud to come, but just check with Charles before you ask us to yours, as I think he is looking a little doubtful." What could I say then, but that they would be most welcome?

But Michelle smiled at me before saying, "Don't you worry, Albert, the wedding invitations will be sent out from my grandmother's house, so I shall be in charge of them… you'll get an invitation!"

It was when we were getting into Albert's car for the journey to the airport that it suddenly occurred to me that we had seen nothing of Fouquet since before lunch, and I asked him where he was. “Oh, he left hours ago, and one of our people…” But then he suddenly stopped, and laughed before going on. “What I mean is that one of the Union people – not mine any more – has been working with him this afternoon on a suitable speech for him to make at the airport. You may in fact hear it before your plane leaves as the press conference is being held there. It’s timed for about six o’clock, and that’s an hour before your take-off time. Anyway, you may wonder why we are being so careful about what he says, but that is because of an idea that M. Marcellin had, by way of repaying some of your distress. You’ll probably find that, apart from his attributing his retirement to ill health, he will also say a few things which will, I think, please your Peter Armstrong!”

We checked ourselves in, and were able to watch the TV coverage of the arrival from Paris of Fouquet’s deputy, and there was a sympathetic murmur from the people when Fouquet himself came on the scene. Then the coverage continued from a big room which had been arranged for the major press conference. When Fouquet spoke I could see why he had been such a successful politician. His address was masterly. He explained his sadness in having to give up his political life, because of a combination of uncertain health, and old age. But after mentioning some of the high spots of his career he then electrified the audience by saying, “And, my friends, I feel that this, in any case, is the right time for me to go. I have been very fortunate, and have greatly enjoyed my career, but it is unfortunate that elderly people often tend to cling to their old ideas…past, shall I say, their sell-by dates…and I’m afraid that I have sometimes been guilty of that in being so unfriendly towards Britain. Looking back over my life, I cannot remember when I formed these unfortunate opinions, and I say ‘unfortunate’ because I should have remembered, as I do now, that it is only because of

Britain fighting on – alone for a long time – against Hitler, that we French have the freedom which we enjoy today. It is of course true that we have had, and sometimes will continue to have, differences of opinion with them…but when these occur, let them be occasions for friendly arguments, and not divisions. One reason why I am so happy to hand over the leadership of the Party is that those who follow me will, I know, not make the same mistakes that I have made."

There was more along the same lines, and Michelle whispered to me, "That must be the apology which Albert mentioned."

As I watched him I realised that he was not just a good orator, but also a superb actor. I could guess how much he must have resented having to make these statements on the orders of the Union, but nobody could have thought so, it looked as though they came straight from his heart. Anyway, the press conference ended with a speech by the new Party leader, in which he paid a fulsome tribute to Fouquet, and hoped that he would have a long and happy retrial…all very touching, but Michelle said, "Makes you sick, doesn't it? Just think that it was only this morning that he was looking forward to having us killed."

We found that Peter had again done well by us, as we were upgraded to club class, and we knew that there would be more drinks after we were airborne, and I said to Michelle, "I reckon that when we get back to Paisley we should go on the wagon for a few days…and we have a celebration dinner to look forward to in the Savoy tonight."

However, I was then surprised to see a twinkle in her eyes, and she seemed to be fighting back a giggle, but nevertheless said very seriously, "I suppose that I can give you the benefit of the doubt, but I confess that I've begun wondering – very seriously – whether I dare marry a man whose memory is so bad. Still, I suppose that it is just possible that your present failing is due to too much alcohol!"

"What the hell are you talking about, darling, what have I done wrong?"

"Oh dear," she said, "it is worse than I thought, as it isn't what you have done, but what you haven't done…don't you remember even now!"

"Remember what?"

"Just think, darling," she said, "what have you been trying to do in recent weeks?"

"To expose Fouquet, of course…and we've done that."

"Yes, but how were you going to do it?" She suddenly dissolved into a fit of the giggles.

"Why, to dig up the golden bowl, which formed part of your family treasures …and…" Suddenly a light dawned, and I burst out laughing, before leaning over to kiss her. "Of course, we left the bloody thing sitting on the table in that house before we left."

"That's it, my sweet, but it may console you to know that in fact I only thought about the bowl a few minutes ago. Do you think that Albert and the others will send it on to us?"

But I didn't get to answer the question, as one of the flight attendants came and

handed me a very neat parcel, and said, "You must know some very important people to get this delivered just before take-off." We both looked at the parcel and it was easy to guess that somehow Marcellin had got the bowl to us. It seemed a fitting end to our adventure. We looked at each other and Michelle put our feelings into words.

"You know, I don't really care now, about anything to do with this affair – all that matters is that we are together, and both safe and sound, and all I want for the next few days is to have a very quiet time with no excitement."

"However, I said, "that won't start till tomorrow, as we still have that dinner to face tonight, and you can be sure that the grannies, as well as Peter, will want to know every tiny detail of our adventures. But that will be the end of it."

But it turned out to be too much to hope for as although the arrangements for us to be met at Gatwick worked quickly and smoothly, another problem did arise at once, as before we drove off the driver handed me an envelope, saying, "Mr Armstrong asked that you read this before we get to the hotel."

It was a short note, but I read it with dismay, and Michelle saw that something was amiss. "What's wrong, darling?"

"Just read this," I said, and handed her the note.

Dear Charles.

We are in trouble. That reporter friend of your's, Adam Brown of The Herald, has been nosing around, and he called at your house this afternoon before Marie and Julie left for London. It so happened that their taxi was at the door when he called and the taxi driver, who knew Adam, said that they were off to meet you and Michelle in London. Marie didn't give him any information when he tackled her as she got into the taxi but she let slip that she and Julie were meeting you this evening in the Savoy, and I'm afraid that now he is right here in the hotel. Newspapers of course have all sorts of ways of finding out information, and he has been a busy lad as he knows that you flew to Marseilles this morning and are coming back now with Michelle, on a flight also from Marseilles.

He has also found out that this is the second time you have been in France, since your first visit, and he is annoyed that you haven't got in touch with him – as in fact you had promised to do.

He seems a persistent young man, and my bet is that he will try to catch you and Michelle at the reception desk when you arrive. If he does, please make any excuses you like and don't talk to him till after you see me. I have a plan which I hope will solve all our problems, but you and Michelle will need to be briefed about what to say.

Michelle and I looked at each other in dismay, and I said, "Blast my Great Aunt Agnes! As you know, she told some of her friends about my original trip, and my chum Adam heard about it, and put that small article into *The Herald,* which started everything. Certainly, I did promise to tell him how I got on in France, but with all the complications it never occurred to me when we got here that I had to meet him. That, probably, was a mistake as no doubt he is now suspicious, and thinks that there must be a story in it. Anyway, let's hope that Peter has the matter under control, as if our story gets out we'll be notorious."

And with that small comfort we had to sit and worry during the journey. When we drove up to the hotel, Michelle whispered to me," This is very grand, I wonder who is paying the bill – it should be HM Government considering all we've done for them!"

But I couldn't answer the question as Adam wasn't just waiting at the reception desk, he was waiting at the entrance to catch us. He came up to me, saying, in not too friendly a fashion, "You are a difficult chap to get hold of. You popped off to France just to check up about your grandfather's escape from France back in 1942 and then, surprise, surprise, you came back in double quick time with this beautiful French lady, no wonder that you've been the talk of Paisley. But not only that, as I understand that since then you've recently been back to France twice more – come on, old man, you've got to tell me your story. But first of all, please introduce me to Michelle who, I understand, is now your fiancée."

I hated the prospect of having to deceive him, as we had been in the same class in school, and were really quite friendly, but I knew that I would have to do so, so I said, "Okay, Adam, I'll come quietly, but not just yet. We are both tired and in need of getting unpacked and having a bath, so give us half an hour and we'll meet you in the bar. We can't, unfortunately, spend too much time with you tonight since, as you know, both our grandmothers are here. We are going to be late enough for dinner in any case, so we'll have to keep it short, and then have a longer chat when we are back in Paisley. Anyway, for now, I'll allow you to have just one chaste kiss on Michelle's cheek, and you can ask her a few – a very few – questions when we meet."

He smiled and said some very complimentary things to Michelle, and gave her two kisses, just to be independent and then said, "Half an hour's time in the bar, but let me say that you are a lucky young chap to have found such a wonderful girl as Michelle..." He turned to her. "Anytime you get fed up with Charles, give me a ring and I'll come running. Talking about running, you two had better run off now and get yourselves organised, so don't be late."

At the reception desk we were given a note that Mr Armstrong wanted to speak to us before we did anything else – not that that did us much good – and that he wanted us to go up right away to the suite occupied by the grannies. It was not at all what we wanted to do, but we were good children and did what we were told, and arranged that our bags would go straight up to our own room. We found that Julie and Marie were sharing a quite luxurious suite, with two bedrooms, sharing a reception room, and each with a bathroom. There they were, and the grannies gave us a quite emotional reception, while Peter was much more business-like and as soon as was decent he got us sat down, saying, "You would see from my letter about the problem that has come up in the shape of that damn reporter."

I broke in to tell him that we had already met Adam, and that I had arranged to meet him in the bar in half an hour, and he frowned before going on. "Well, that doesn't give us much time, so you'll need to get word perfect at once in your story. Fortunately, we have no other appointments to keep because as soon as this question of interviewing you came up, I cancelled our dinner reservation in the River Room and we'll get dinner sent up to us here so that we can keep out of sight. No question of my involvement has arisen as yet so I must keep out of sight till he leaves. It is, of course, unlikely that he would know who I am, but one cannot be too careful, so let's sit down and talk of the problem. Back to today…as soon as I learned from M. Marcellin that you were both well, and that the affair was over, I arranged for both Marie and Julie to come to London. I thought that you all deserved to be together for a night of luxury at the expense of the taxpayers after all you have done for us. Unfortunately, however, just as they were leaving, your friend Adam came round to your house and Julie saw nothing wrong in telling him that she and Julie were off to the airport in a few minutes to meet the two of you and catch a flight to London.

"It was very awkward," Granny said, "it was only a few hours after Mr Armstrong had told us that both of you were safe, and Julie and I were still in a somewhat emotional state. But he was difficult to get rid of and, as our taxi arrived, I unfortunately let slip to him that we would be staying at the Savoy tonight. So it is my fault that he knows then that we will all be here."

Peter looked up, and smiled at Michelle and me. "Remind me not to get involved with you two again, as every time we make any progress in this affair, some other problem comes up, and you will need to talk to this damn reporter. It is a pity that this problem has arisen now that everything has finished so very well, the last thing we want is some investigative journalists digging up the fact that we endeavoured to compromise a French politician, as that could negate all the good work we have done in forcing Fouquet's resignation…also, I couldn't see M. Marcellin being at all pleased at the involvement of the Union Corse being exposed."

A problem like this was the last thing that Michelle and I wanted. We'd both had a trying three days, and here I was with her just wanting a bath, a drink, and a quiet family meal…but now? However, Peter continued. "That young Brown is persistent, and nowadays these damn newspapers can find out almost anything and as he seems to know all your movements we'll have to tell him something new."

As he said that, I had done some thinking, and said to him, "Surely it won't be too difficult, I don't think we can avoid telling him of Granddad's report to the Air Ministry, and I can add something of the rest of the story, and how I managed to find Julie and Michelle. We needn't go into anything about the attack on Michelle and me in Avignon , as he can't have heard of that."

I then turned to Michelle. "But I'm afraid, darling, that I'll have to tell him something to explain our sudden trip to Scotland, so I can tell him how quickly we fell in love, and that I had to bring you and Julie back to Scotland to meet Granny… and then…"

I stopped as I couldn't work out how best to explain the other two trips, without exposing the truth, but Peter smiled, saying, "Now we come to the hard bit, don't we, so how about this, and he numbered the items off on his fingers:

"One. None of you then knew where to dig to find the treasures, but you can say that Julie had been thinking and suggested an area of woodland as being a good area in which to search because it was on the road, and old Flying Officer Burton must have been in a hurry so it might have attracted him. I suggest saying that it was your first area to search, and that also you decided that you had to get hold of a metal detector. Fortunately, you also remembered a young civil servant, Gordon Robinson, whom you had met on holiday and who mentioned that divining was his hobby, and you wondered if he would lend you his gadget. So, Charles, the story is that you had his phone number and, when you called him, to see if you could borrow his equipment, it was to find that, by a happy chance, he was leaving the very next day to deliver a car to the British Consulate in Marseilles. He was excited to have a challenge such as this, and offered to take you along, and have a quick look, just to see what he could find. Also, by another happy chance, he had booked a P&O crossing from Portsmouth to Santander, and you could join him. Also, going to the site near Bayonne would not take him too far off his route to Marseilles.

"Two," he went on. "Your trip was successful, and you flew back with a fortune in jewels…we'll hope that Julie will allow you to show them all to him in Paisley tomorrow."

"But three," he frowned, "we now come to the hardest bit, concerning Michelle going off to France today with you, and both taking a flight to Marseilles, and now, here you are, back here later today with her..."

He stopped for a moment, and then looked at his watch, saying, "Damn it, it isn't long now till you've got to see the chap, so I'll hurry, and this is the best explanation I've come up with. What I want you to say is that Julie was surprised that there wasn't a golden bowl among the jewels, and that she became more and more certain that, being so attractive, it must have been buried with the other items and that you and your friend might have overlooked it, possibly because it was quite big and it would have been awkward to put into the case in which you found the jewels – so your trip today was to see if you could find the bowl. I have made a few other arrangements, first to get an entry inserted into the British Airways computer records to show that a Mlle Michelle Lebrun is shown as having flown to Marseilles with you this morning…there will of course be no record of her arrival in France, in an ambulance, the day before that, and there is also an entry in the Avis records to show that you, Charles, hired a car when you got to Marseilles this morning. Finally, the two of you got to Bayonne and found the missing gold bowl."

"That," he smiled, "was quite expensive – just to put these false records in – and we'll also have to pay a bill in due course to cover that mythical car hire! I'll give you a bag to put the bowl in, and you can let him have a quick look at it…which, shall I say, will bring an air of verisimilitude to an otherwise bald and unconvincing narrative."

"There!" and he turned to Michelle and Julie, and laughed. "There is a bit of colloquial English which you won't find in text books!"

He stopped again, and then said, "Well, I think I have covered everything, have you any questions before I go, and go I must as you will realise that he mustn't suspect that I am here, or even that you know me?"

But, as he had been talking…and going on, and on, and on…I had been getting more and more unhappy, so I took a deep breath, and said, "Sorry, Peter, but I can't do it that way. Just remember that I am going to be speaking to a reporter who must have had a lot of experience in seeing when people are speaking the truth…also when they are not…and here you are expecting me to tell him this long tissue of lies, and that without any rehearsals…no, it would be sure to fail. We've no time now to argue, so what I am going to do is to give him just three juicy baits – the first is my whirlwind romance with Michelle, she will be beside me when I see him and a love interest never fails – the second is Granddad's original report to the Air Ministry which indicated the possibility of buried treasure, which in fact we have found, and the third is to give him a sight of the golden bowl. I'll tell him that I can't go into all the details tonight, as it is a long story, but that he can have an 'exclusive' tomorrow if he comes to our house. Also, if he brings a photographer they will be able to get pictures of the treasures. With all that laid out before them tomorrow, they won't be too keen to try to pick holes in a very plausible story – and by then I'll be word perfect in it!"

"There is just one thing, however," I went on, "to do this Julie, and Michelle, will need to agree to this public exhibition of their treasures – and maybe they'd prefer to keep them as a secret?"

"Not a bit, Charles," Julie said, "fact is that I welcome it! I have decided, you see, that the best thing is to sell most of the stuff, just keeping the pieces which Michelle would like to have, and get rid of the rest by auction. A nice article in the paper will be a bonus, by way of a free advertisement, when it comes to the sale!"

Peter suddenly laughed, saying, "All's for the best in this best of all possible worlds! And this, I can tell you, Julie, is another example of colloquial English. And, as for you, Charles, I think you probably are right, so off you go right now to see this damn reporter and the best of luck."

I stood up to go, but Michelle shook her head, saying, "You men are always in such a hurry, and you, darling, will have to get used to not getting your own way all the time! You see, no way am I going down to a smart bar area in this luxury hotel to meet your friend, looking like a tramp as I do now…damn it, I haven't changed my clothes since this morning we were virtually under a sentence of death and I want rid of them – right now! It won't take me long, but I am going to have a bath and change into a frock before we go down, and although we may be late, you can always blame me for the delay…okay, partner?"

I thought in that moment that I was among the luckiest of men, and I gave her a kiss, and said, "Sure, I know when I'm beaten, come on, let's go off to our room and get changed."

However, despite her very definite statement, Michelle had changed her mind when we got to our room. "Look, darling, let's just have a quick wash, I'll change my frock, and we can go down to this damn friend of yours and get rid of him as soon as we can!"

"I couldn't agree more," I smiled, "but I've just got time to teach you a little bit of colloquial English…what you have in mind is what we call *a lick and a promise* – it's a good phrase, isn't it?"

Well, we did what the phrase said, and it wasn't long till I was knotting my tie, and I heard her say, "How's that?" And I looked round to see an immaculate Michelle in an elegant frock and without a hair out of place.

"In that short time, it's a miracle. How do I look?"

She gave me a careful inspection, then said, "You'll do very well…so well that you may give me a kiss, but don't squeeze me tightly, and I don't want this frock crushed!"

Then, as we left the room, she said, "Cross your fingers, darling, surely this really is the time to hope that our adventure is finally over…"

***

EPILOGUE

Michelle's wishes were granted, as that night did prove to be the end of our adventure because, just as I had hoped, Adam was delighted to have the offer of such juicy titbits as the story of Granddad's report to the Air Ministry, with the suggestion of buried treasure, which took me to France, and about my romance with Michelle. "That is good," he said, "a romantic love story is always popular!"

I then said to him, "Look, Adam, I have a lot more to tell you but right now, as I've told you already, Michelle and I are very tired, so why not come round to our house in Paisley tomorrow afternoon and I'll fill in the details. Also, if you bring a photographer with you I'll let him take pictures of the amazing treasure trove of jewels which we found, and I can also let you have a copy of Granddad's report, which started the whole thing off."

With these promises in his pocket he went off happily, but not before buying a congratulatory round of champagne. As we drank it, Michelle gave me a quick wink which said very clearly…so much for cutting down on our drinking!"

***

Next day, back in Paisley, I could then tell him of bringing Michelle, with Julie, her grandmother, to Scotland and the discussions we then had which led to the idea that she might be able to help as regards a place to dig. I could then tell of how I went back to France again and was able, with her instructions, to find and to dig up the jewels. After that I explained that, when I came back with the treasures, Julie realised that something was missing because there should have been a golden bowl – a favourite of her father – in addition to the jewels, and that led to the third and very recent trip when Michelle and I were able to dig it up as well. I didn't give him any time to think up more questions, by taking him and his photographer through to the dining room, where we had spread the treasures – and, of course, the golden bowl – on the table…and they looked fantastic…quite sufficient to shut him up.

But as I watched the photographer taking picture after picture I couldn't help remembering that when I had been telling my tissue of lies to Adam I had noticed a copy of *The Herald* lying on a side table and the headline was about the sudden resignation of M. Vincent Fouquet...the bete noir for the British in the French government...and I smiled to myself at the Pulitzer Prize winning scoop which he would have had, if only I had told him the truth.

Peter came round some time after Adam and his photographer had left, and was pleased to find that all had gone so well. "I can tell you," he said, "that my masters are very relieved at how things have worked out, both for you and for us. But you will understand that so far as the government is concerned, none of this happened! Even although Fouquet was all kinds of a villain, Britain cannot be seen to have dabbled in French politics. I should think that despite all you have done, the most you and Michelle can expect by way of thanks is to find that your names are now on the guest list for Royal garden parties in Scotland! But, before we leave talking about officialdom, just remember that you will have to give your expurgated story to that chap in the Air Ministry Historical Section whom you contacted and, of course, you'll have to tell him that you have no idea why that Parisian lawyer wanted a copy of the report…that should tidy up the official records!"

The story, which appeared in *The Herald* next day, made us local celebrities for a short time and the publicity did nothing but good when most of the jewels were sold at auction by Christie's, and Julie found herself with a windfall of nearly half a million pounds, even after many of the better things – including the golden bowl – were given to Michelle.

***

The next couple of months were a busy time for all of us…I had the easiest time of it, just doing my normal office work…but Granny, Julie and Michelle had much more important things to deal with. The first involved discussions which Michelle and I had concerning what we were going to do, and where we were going to live, and in the event we came to a happy compromise when she said, "Look, darling, as a completely bilingual lawyer you can easily work either in Scotland or in France – but as yet you haven't had a lot of experience. So for the meantime why don't you just carry on in your present practice and continue with your work here? We've got plenty of time to make up our minds before the kids get to schooldays!"

And then, just a few days later, things were made very easy for us when Marie and Julie firmed up their arrangements to live together. They decided to keep the Avignon house for some winter living, and arranged with Great Aunt Agnes for both of them to move in with her – on a permanent basis – for the rest of the year. It was a sensible arrangement as her house in Kilmacolm was absurdly big for a single lady, and she was delighted to have company – at least for part of the year. This move, of course, left the family home in Paisley free for Michelle and me, although it was far too big for a young couple. But Michelle just smiled at me, saying, "We'll need to work hard, my lad, to fill at least two of these spare rooms!"

But sensible as these arrangements were they involved a lot of building work…in Great Aunt Agnes' house to provide two separate suites for both of them, and in Avignon to provide one for Marie. As for Michelle and me – as regards our new and far too big house – Granny took what furniture she wanted, and left the rest of it for us. Fortunately, Michelle liked what was left, and she only added a few treasures from Avignon so as to give it her personal stamp.

***

For much of these months Michelle was in Avignon, and she and Julie spent a little time going down memory lane by visiting Bayonne and what was left of Urdes. It was Julie who got the idea of looking up the ninety-year-old gentleman who had come to her wedding…and who had told me her married name…and she delighted him by showing him the silver epergne, which he and his wife had given to her as a wedding present, back in 1939. They also, at my suggestion, contacted Maurice Lefarge...the assistant in what had been Martin's jewellery shop in Biarritz...to thank him for the first bit of information which set me off on the trail. They took him and his wife to dinner, and gave them the highly expurgated edition of my story, and told Maurice, of course, that they had no explanation of why the shop manager had tried to stop him talking to me. I didn't manage to get to Albert's wedding, as there were limits to the amount of holiday leave I could get, what with what I had already had – plus three weeks for a honeymoon still to come – I just couldn't get any more. But Michelle went, and they were invited to come to ours in Avignon on the first Saturday in September. It was a long journey for my friends to come to the ceremony but about twenty of them clubbed together and hired a bus so as to come to France in comfort and in the most economical way. I could see that both Julie and Michelle were glad that they had done so as it at least showed their local friends back in Scotland that Michelle would not be entirely friendless!

As promised, Albert and his wife also came, and they brought with them a square parcel, with the request that we shouldn't open it till after the ceremony, so it wasn't till we were changing out of our wedding finery and into travelling clothes that Michelle undid the string and opened the box. By this time I had guessed what it might be, and I wasn't disappointed, as she called out, saying, "Look! He's given us the fake golden bowl, and has an inscription put in it."

TO MY FRIENDS CHARLES AND MICHELLE
MAY THEY HAVE A LONG AND HAPPY MARRIAGE
Albert Dupont

As I read it, I heard her laugh, and she passed me a little note that had been enclosed, and which he had also written in English. It read:

You will see, Charles, that apart from changing my life for the better, you have also infected me with your Scottish parsimony. I am sure you will remember that this bowl came to us by courtesy of your friend Peter Armstrong, so although we give it to you and Michelle as a wedding present, with my love and that of Cecile, your kind government paid for it!

Just as we finished dressing there was a knock at the door, and our two grannies came in. They just wanted a quiet moment with us before we joined the throng downstairs and, after all the hugs and kisses, Michelle laughed, and said, "With my increasing fluency in English, let me say, *all's for the best in the best of all possible worlds* – we've been so very lucky."

As we were making our way out to the car I noticed Albert, and went over to him for a moment, and said, "You couldn't have chosen anything we'd rather have had, but although the bowl didn't cost you anything, I am concerned about what you had to pay for the paper and string which you used to wrap the parcel – look, here are fifty centimes which will repay you…and also why not come to Scotland sometime soon?… You can then stay with us and get some more education in parsimony?"

He solemnly took the coins, and we both burst out laughing before he turned to Cecile. "Let's do that, darling, we mustn't turn down an offer of free board and lodgings!"

"I hope you do come," I managed to say, seriously. I was then swept away with Michelle, over to where my poor Mondeo was almost invisible under a mass of streamers, and I shuddered to think what the inside – and our luggage – would be like. When at last we made our escape from the crowd of our friends, we pulled into a quiet street and tried our best to get rid of all the signs of our recent marriage, but we realised that it would need more than a lick and a promise to get the car clean again. But we did our best and set off to drive just sixteen miles to our hotel for the night. Michelle knew it of old, Le Vieux Castillon in Castillon du Gard, a lovely big hotel with a Michelin Star for cuisine. We had decided not to go any distance on that first day, because although our honeymoon hotel was some seven hundred miles away we felt it was better to leave it as a comfortable two days journey after our first night. It was thanks to Michelle that we were making such a long journey to our honeymoon retreat because soon after she and Julie had got back to France to make wedding arrangements, she had occasion to go to Paris, and decided that although we had already phoned and written to apologise to M. Duchene, she really must take the opportunity to go and do so in person for the inconvenience and, more than that, which he had suffered in the hands of the Union Corse. She could also congratulate him on his clever message to William Henderson when he said he was now one behind as he was suffering from TB, one less than UC – a clear indication that he was in the hands of the Union Corse. He had already forgiven us, and hoped that we had forgiven him, and was delighted to see Michelle again, and also interested to hear the details of the rest of our adventure from her own lips. It was when she was drinking the inevitable glass of wine with him that he mentioned that he was on the point of going off for another little holiday at Penina in Portugal.

"You'll remember," he had said to her, "that I had to cut short my earlier one when I had to come to Scotland in such a hurry, to see you."

That got them talking about the hotel there, and the golf courses, and he explained that he and his wife had first gone there in the mid sixties – not long after the complex had been built by Henry Cotton and his friend John Stilwell – and that they had at once fallen in love with the hotel. He had also waxed lyrical about not only the golf courses, but also about the enormous swimming pool, the biggest hotel pool in Europe. For good measure, he also gave her a brochure of the hotel – and explained that it was now called Le Meridien Penina. It had all seemed very attractive to her, and…surprisingly…she had suggested to me that we should think of going there for our honeymoon, so that I could then teach her more about golf.

"Apart from some other things!" she had laughed.

I did wonder at the time if it might be a recipe for divorce to go to a golf hotel so soon after marriage, but in the event no such disaster took place, and we both thoroughly enjoyed playing on the wonderful courses and swimming in the wonderful pool…apart from many – very many – other personal wonders.

But I wondered again one morning about whether we had been wise to come to Penina, as I woke about eight o'clock and looked at my lovely Michelle, still sleeping peacefully. But I was in no mood to indulge her, so I inched nearer and – as I often did – teased one of her nipples with my tongue. Her eyes opened, and she smiled that wonderful smile of hers, and wrapped her arms around me. But then she suddenly pushed me away, saying, "What's the time, darling?"

"Ten past eight."

"Oh, damn it," she said, "we'll need to get up right away for breakfast as our tee-off time is at nine o'clock."

I was far from pleased at this news, and said, "But why on earth did you book such an early time, damn it, we talked about having a lazy morning."

"Would you have preferred that?"

"Too right I would," I said rather angrily.

"That's good!" she smiled. "You see, I was only teasing you, I've arranged for nine holes at eleven o'clock, so you have plenty of time to do what you...I hope...were intending to do!"

She stopped for a moment, and crept closer again.

"And I won't lie back and think of France or Scotland – or whatever – I'll think instead of my very own wonderful husband."

***

We did not, in fact, manage to meet the eleven o'clock deadline for golf that morning.

***

About the Author

Gray Laidlaw is 88-years-old and lives in the Erskine Home, in the west of Scotland where, in very comfortable surroundings, he was able to complete this novel. He attended St Andrew's University and served in the RAF during World War II, primarily in the development of early radar. In 1944, Squadron Leader Laidlaw was posted to HQ RAF Fighter Command in charge of radar on all night fighters. It was also there, in 1943, that he met his wife Margaret who was a WRAF Section Officer. They were married in 1944 and had two children.

After the war, Gray enjoyed a successful business career in Glasgow, only taking up writing at the suggestion of his wife after he retired from the glass trade. "I've been very lucky to have had wonderful years at St Andrews University and in the RAF, and a long and happy marriage to my dear wife," says Gray. Past But Very Present is dedicated to his wife, who died in 1998.

ISBN 142511474-1

9 781425 114749